It s
was s
the sk
of a mountain—and half a mile away a man was
starting to walk toward him, a tiny figure also,
growing larger almost imperceptibly with each
step—walking a straight line through the dandelions and up the hill, not deviating from that
straight line—just walking up the side of a mountain to kill him. Ted had the sense that it didn't
matter whether he waited there or ran. If he ran,
they would come after—up the mountain and
down again, under the oceans, to the poles, to
the center of the earth. He wanted to shout,
"This doesn't make sense! There must be some
mistake!"

The Kreuzeck Coordinates

The Kreuzeck Coordinates

Philip Ross

TOR

A TOM DOHERTY ASSOCIATES BOOK

This is a work of fiction. All the characters and events portrayed in this book are fictional, and any resemblance to real people or incidents is purely coincidental.

THE KREUZECK COORDINATES

First printing: February 1985

A TOR Book

Published by Tom Doherty Associates
8-10 West 36 Street
New York, N.Y. 10018

ISBN: 0-812-58792-8
CAN. ED.: 0-812-58793-6

Printed in the United States of America

FRIDAY, JULY 15 12:00 HOURS—
OBER-FLATTACH

The crash came from behind Ted Barstow just as the little barmaid leaned over to set a stein of beer on his table. She had almost passed him, carrying a tray of glasses, then remembered one of the drinks was his. He snapped around. At the table beside the window a woman held her jowls up against her cheekbones between pudgy, gold-ringed, sparkling fingers.

"*Mein Gott, mein Gott, mein Gott!*" she gasped. Her husband, all gray, half-stood, furiously brushing splinters of glass from his vest with his napkin. Dignified rage, a schoolmaster erasing dirty words scrawled on the blackboard.

That's all Ted saw at first. Then he focused on the window—on the no-window: Only the part with the end of the lettering—*STSTUBE*—remained below the jagged break line. Across the steeet, people—frozen clichés of surprise—looked back at him. He stared at them stupidly; seeing but not seeing, not comprehending.

Cold and wet in his lap. He spun back. The stein was

overturned; beer flowed across the table. Ted raised his eyes and stared into the wide blue eyes of the young barmaid. Her eyes were incredibly blue: as blue as the sky halfway above the horizon on a clear, clear day. He knew it was ridiculous to think about the color of her eyes, but he looked at them for what seemed to be an eternity. Her face was on a level with his. She was on her knees by the table. Her frosty-morning, halfway-up-the-clear-blue-sky eyes almost matched the color of her dirndl bodice; and matching the roses embroidered on it, a thin line of red ran down from the hole above those eyes.

MONDAY, JULY 11 14:45 HOURS—
SALZBURG

Rudi Bischl took a small sip of beer. He wanted to drain half the stein—for the wetness, not for the alcohol—but because of the alcohol, he only sipped. The beer was his admission fee; he had to order something, and a soft drink would have made him appear even more adolescent than he did. Countering that appearance was one of his life's goals. He had worn his brown double-knit jacket with the padded shoulders, even though the weather was too warm for it, because of the bulk it gave his thin frame. He tried to remember to keep his chin down to minimize its narrowness and the length of his neck

Older people always told him what a blessing it was to look young, how he would come to appreciate it someday. They did not consider being taken for seventeen when you are twenty-three to be a serious problem. They didn't take anything about him seriously. That was a continual bitterness to him, because he himself was serious about everything.

He kept himself from looking down the length of the room. To be seen staring after the girl, watching for Herr Tobler to come, might make him seem too eager. He forced himself to lean into the corner of the booth as though relaxed and in control.

He studied his hand against the black-plastic table top. Along his slender fingers there were bright green highlights from the neon tube running above the line of booths that stretched down the black-mirrored wall, and blue streaks between his fingers from the zigzags over the dance area to his left. Rudi was appalled. The colors turned flesh tones ghastly. How could anyone think those colors suitable for a place where people would come to entice one another? What that light would do to the make-up tints the girls were wearing. . . . He pictured them. Now, on Monday mid-afternoon, there were only two other people in the room—men sitting in a booth close to the door; but Rudi pictured the room as full: women with blue-black lips and smudges like bruises on their cheekbones, their bodies jerking and writhing, watched out of shadowed eye sockets by green-haired, booth-kenneled spectators. He ought to come back and photograph it—do a series. It would be better than Lautrec.

The imaginary scene both attracted and repelled him. He had been brought up strictly; he had an almost prudish morality. Yet the drama, the pictorial possibilities of grotesqueness, drew him. Even *the* photographs: He had been sick with disgust, anger and shame; yet even those pictures snapped at moments of opportunity were composed, taking advantage of sidelighting from the little window.

He let his gaze rise from his hand and fix on the dark mirror to his right. A figure startled him by materializing there and staring down at him.

"Rudi Bischl. Huh. How're you making it?" The word used for "you" was *du*, the way German speakers address members of their families, close friends, children or dogs.

Despite himself Rudi wet his lips before answering. "Good, Hermann. All's good by me. And you?" He had to ask, had to be familiar too, even though he had always feared and hated Hermann Tobler.

Hermann bobbed his head up and down on his thick neck several times before answering. "Good. Yeah, good, Rudi. Very good." He swiveled his head slightly, not taking in the entire establishment but enough to refer to it as evidence. "Good," he said again.

"You've made big changes."

"Yeah. No money today in old men playing cards." Hermann paused for a moment to strengthen the implication that there was money in a disco bar. Light glinted from his imitation pearl buttons and gleamed satinly from the shirt rounding over his shoulders and the swell of his belly. Rudi wondered what color the shirt was in daylight. Here it looked to him like rotten eggplant. "Matti said you wanted to see me," Herman said now that the pleasantries were over.

"No. I . . . I wanted to talk with your uncle. I thought he still owned the place."

"Why?"

Rudi stared up. He told himself that it was a long time ago when Hermann could bully him and he was too small to fight back, when all he could do was to tell his mother, who told Hermann's mother so Hermann didn't beat him but taunted and shamed him instead. That was then, and now was now. Rudi made himself stare directly back and say, "Is Uncle August here?"

"Yeah."

"I'd like to talk to him."

"Okay." Hermann flipped his hand upward, dismissing the need for Rudi to make so much of so little.

Rudi took a long sip of beer, pleased with himself. He

tried to keep that sense of being in control, to tell himself it didn't matter, when—after returning with his uncle—Hermann pulled up a chair to sit down at the end of the table, joining them.

"So, Rudi!" Uncle August reached across to squeeze the young man's hand. "A long time we don't see you anymore. How goes it?" He used *du* also, but he was an old man speaking to one he had known as a child, so Rudi felt no hint of insult. And Uncle August had always seemed like Father Christmas. Everyone knew it was Uncle August in the costume, going from house to house, but the knowledge carried no disillusionment: The rest-of-the-year clothes were the disguise. As Rudi grew older, he heard stories, and as he learned about the world, he came to recognize a kind of narrowed look in August's eyes that wasn't just from the chuckling cheeks pushed up against them. But the memory of the candy-giver prevailed.

"Good, Herr Tobler. Thank you. And you?"

"Good, good. Always good. You don't live in Salzburg now?"

"No, Herr Tobler. I've been working in Bad Gastein."

"Beautiful, beautiful. Beautiful place, the mountains. Good air. Very healthful. My father and mother took me there once, before the war. Very beautiful. Very fashionable."

"Yes. Not like it used to be, I imagine."

"Nothing is like it used to be, Rudi. The work is good there?"

"Yes. People like to have their pictures taken on holiday."

"Ah. So. Good."

"That's what I wanted to talk to you about, Herr Tobler. I . . ." Rudi had thought long about what he would say, revising and practicing the words. His heart began to hammer and he felt sweat running down his back, but he went on with confidence. "I have some pictures that I'd like to sell. They're unusual and interesting, and—"

"What kind of pictures, Rudi? Postcard pictures? Like Hermann used to show? Ten groschen a look?" August chuckled indulgently and his red cheeks were puckered by a grin, not a leer; but his eyes had that look.

Although Rudi hadn't expected his point to be taken so quickly, it didn't faze him. He grinned back for a moment. "Yes and no, Herr Tobler. The special, interesting part about these pictures is the man. The man's face."

"Ah. So. And why do you wish to talk with me about such pictures?"

"The man, Herr Tobler. . . . I don't want to say too much, but the man is a person of importance. Of international importance. I am not someone who deals in matters of international importance. To sell these pictures—"

"You mean to sell the pictures?"

"Oh, yes. But I understand that such business is very risky. I want to conclude it as quickly as possible. So I need a. . . ."

"A representative."

"Yes, Herr Tobler. And I thought perhaps you would know. . . ."

Hermann had kept silent. The ideas might be his, but the business still belonged to his uncle. Now he broke in. "Gertmann. Gertmann and Grauber."

August turned with a look that warned of coal instead of candy in his nephew's shoe. But he reminded himself that the boy had to be taught. And furthermore, since Rudi had come to him for advice, he felt he ought to demonstrate his competence in these affairs.

"Small-time hoodlums, Hermann," he said. "The kind of men who have fur collars on the overcoat, and underneath—underwear with holes.'' He turned back to Rudi. ''For a matter of international importance, you must have a professional. It is good you came to me, Rudi. I know such a man.''

FRIDAY, JULY 15 16:15 HOURS—
OBER-FLATTACH

Ted Barstow was hungry. Feeling that seemed callous to
him, but he hadn't eaten since eight in the morning. They
had questioned him until after three.

At first all the restaurant patrons had been seated on
wooden benches, two rows facing each other, their backs
against the corridor walls. The policeman who brought
them there told them not to discuss the "incident" before
questioning, so they sat silently, apart as they had been in
the restaurant, separated into little groups of twos and
fours, or, in Ted's usual condition, alone. They were still
in shock. There was no clock and Ted did not recall seeing
anyone look at a watch. The shattering window and the
crack of the girl's head striking the hardwood floor seemed
to Ted original sounds, not yet echoes in his mind that
could fade. The walls curved inward just overhead into a
barrel-vaulted ceiling. There were no corners people could
tuck their stares into; a look upward slid over and down to
the person opposite. So they meditated upon each other's

feet. Ted felt they had been close, had been intimate with death, had been caught and brought to this place still naked, and now they were ashamed to be seen or to look at each other.

That reticence, perhaps, kept the others from looking often at him despite the interest aroused by his proximity to the barmaid. Without that particular interest, they probably would not have looked at him at all. If they had and had had to describe him, they might have said "average height, medium build, regular features, dark-brownish hair." Actually he was nearly six feet tall, and slender. He had prominent jaw muscles (from clenching his teeth) and some gray in his hair. But he kept his glance down most of the time, his head bowed. He tended to sit or walk not slouched exactly, but drawn in. Despite his posture, he observed the world around him acutely; but because he revealed no interest in it, it found him uninteresting.

Stone walls, ceiling, floor—sound carried. A fly buzzed and banged against the window in the farthest wall. Ted thought of it as refusing to be resigned to the pane. From time to time an officer would come from the room by that window, silhouetted—a dark shape, faceless, boot clicks echoing—and fetch them one by one. Ted saw each one turn with mixed hope and apprehension, as though being summoned to the Final Accounting, not entirely confident that his books balanced. After a while each would return, relieved but chastened, and ponder the questions asked and answers given.

When it was his turn, they brought the woman from the tourist office to translate for him. He always described himself as speaking menu-German; and they—just village cops—had only traffic-direction English. He had met her earlier in the day, when he had asked for maps. They had exchanged the usual few words but somehow had managed to find in them much to laugh about. Ted thought she was

attractive: bright, quick eyes; dark hair worn away
from her face and held by a tortoiseshell band. Quite a
nice figure. She was pretty but didn't seem spoiled by
knowing it. Perhaps she had been too fat as a child, or had
had a precocious nose out of scale until the rest of her face
and her character were formed. And he had thought she
seemed friendly—going beyond her job. He had wished he
might get to know her. But a pretty girl in a tourist
office—he imagined that every man who came in must try
to pick her up.

"*Name, bitte*?" The officer spoke sharply. Not with
hostility. But because of the language, the scene was
reminiscent of war movies Ted had seen, and he might
have felt intimidated except for the process of translation.
He understood the point of the questions—the simpler
ones—as they were asked, so he had time to think. And
the woman's voice was gentle.

"Your name, please?"

"Theodore Barstow."

"You are an American?"

"Yes."

"You arrived in Ober-Flattach today, Friday, fifteenth
July. Is that correct?"

"Yes. Just after noon. I came down on the train from
Salzburg."

"Where are you staying?"

There were two policemen who did the questioning.
One sat behind the desk. He was heavy but not fat.
Although he hardly moved, Ted thought he would not
have liked to stand in the way should the man decide to.
He was probably the senior officer of the village force. He
held a yellow pencil between his first two fingers like a
toothpick between sausages, and he bounced the eraser end
on the desk. From time to time he grunted questions—
repetitions and non sequiturs—to the younger officer's line

of interrogation. At first Ted had thought the man behind the desk must be stupid: he was beery looking, red-faced, his eyes almost glazed. Then he realized the look was anger. Ted wasn't sure of whether the anger was over the murder of the little girl or over the man's inability to solve the case. Probably both, he thought, and answered with thoroughness and diligence, transparently eager to please because he suspected the officer was hoping for some evidence that would allow him to break someone in half.

The other policeman, by contrast, seemed mechanically dispassionate. He was square-jawed and shaved up to the hairline at his neck and around his ears. Even his necktie looked starched. Possibly he was around thirty: When his superior interrupted, he seemed pleased with himself for being able to keep the fire in his stomach banked. He articulated questions precisely after referring to a note pad and wove the interrogation back and forth over the same points in an attempt to bring some hidden thread to the surface. Ted imagined him as a textbook example of thorough and efficient police procedure—except that when the man didn't clasp them together, his hands trembled.

Recognizing the effect the killing had on the two men, Ted was shaken himself. He had been giving his answers as though describing an abstract painting, but the shapes and colors resolved and began to make a picture. He didn't want to see it. He looked at Fraulein Stendler, gave his answers to her and thought about the mental processes that must be required for almost simultaneous translation, and how bright she must be, and in that way he kept himself detached.

All in all, Ted Barstow had sat on hard seats for three hours—thirsty, getting hungrier, stinking of beer and with a damp crotch. He had known his discomfort was insignificant compared with the senseless murder of a twelve-year-old girl. He had been miserable and then felt guilty for feeling miserable, until he had made himself snap it all off.

Now—at last released—he was washed and dressed and going for something to eat. He didn't want to think his feelings were calloused. Once he had seen a bull slaughtered, a huge, sleek, powerful, magnificent brown beast in an evening-green pasture. They had shot him in the head; he fell, kicked and was still. They tied his legs to the front-load shovels of two tractors and lifted him. The butcher plunged his knife in, almost hung there dragging the blade down. Ted was not revolted, nor morbidly fascinated either. The creature was the embodiment of male animal vitality one moment, beef the next. This was at a farm on the side of a mountain. The valley below was a deep, soft green, the mountains opposite a misty purple. An orange full moon rose through the haze overhead, and the body of the skinned animal glistened white in the hard-edged glare and shadow from the tractor lights. The colors of that evening could not tint the carcass, but neither could the carcass drain the colors. Two parts of one place, one moment, but separable. Ted had decided that separating them wasn't callous insensitivity. It was mental compartmentalization, and he had learned to consider it the secret of getting through life sane.

All of the village and half of the tourists were out in the streets exchanging theories. "Arab terrorists" was the favorite, "a madman" second. Each person in each group—in turn, in layer, edgewise—was telling the others what he knew, which was exactly as little as everyone else knew. But better a conjecture, a wild hypothesis, a theory demonstrably false, than the notion that catastrophe can happen without reason.

There was little they could say, really. The manager of

Ted's hotel had known as much of the facts as anyone.
"Bad, bad. How becomes the world?" He had "tsk"-ed
and shaken his head slowly, trying to play tragedy, but
melodrama was his true genre. "And do you know what
the police did find?" He paused, looking up from under
crepe-hair eyebrows so that Ted could register ignorance
and give him his cue. "They did the hotel across from the
Alpenrose search." With a gesture he built the hotel facade in the air before them, then poked a row of holes
across it one by one. "Every room with street window did
they search." He snatched at the last one, held it up
hidden in his fist. "And what did they find? *What*?" Just
before the suspense became so unbearable that Ted would
have had to seize the man's wrist and pry his fingers loose,
the hand was flung open. "Nothing! Two rooms with
windows open. *Sicher*, from one the shots must did come.
But all the guests were luncheon eating. So who did
shoot?"

Small towns: Ted wasn't surprised that the man knew all
the police knew. As did everyone else. As he wended
through the crowds—he was big enough to shove his way
but he preferred to slip through like a swimmer through
coral—some would hush and stare. "Him. The American.
His table."

The crowds filled the street. Automobiles had to push
through with their horns. Half of the tourists were leaving
town. If the Alpenrose Gäststube could be shot up at high
noon, even the Schloss Hotel might not be safe for supper.

Through sharpness of hunger and dullness of emotion,
that thought had penetrated to Ted too. But he wouldn't
leave; he was too stubborn; he couldn't imagine he could be
in danger. Although he enjoyed novels about spies and international intrigue, although he entertained himself during
his vacations in Europe by imagining the people he saw in

cafés as characters come to life and played out plots with them, he never believed his fantasies.

After all, he told himself, *I am not a spy or a secret agent. I don't run dope or carry diamonds.* In actual fact, he edited copy for two trade publications: *The Institutional Maintenance Journal* and *The Newsletter of the Floor-Covering Institute.* He took the material the engineers and sales directors wrote and translated it into English. He always said, "It's dull work and I'm a dull person." He was certain his being next to someone who was shot was pure coincidence.

TUESDAY, JULY 12 11:30 HOURS—
SALZBURG

"Danger, yeah. Life and death, sometimes, yeah. But such excitement! Ah, the old days!" August raised his glass of schnapps and drained it. The other old man touched his coffee cup with one bent forefinger as though joining the spirit—at least—of the toast. Rudi thought of them as two fat old hens on a narrow roost, crowded as they were into the side of the booth opposite him. Hermann sat again at the end of the table, his uninvited presence the previous afternoon clearly precedent enough for him.

It was late on Tuesday morning. Although baffled at first, light from the open street door found its way from side to side down the black walls to the men. And there were naked incandescent work lights here and there overhead. Even though the room had been cleaned and aired, the paleness of light in that place made Rudi think of old smoke, twisted sheets and a sour taste.

"Now everything is safe. Every day is the same and we all die old, in bed—from cancer if we are lucky, from boredom if we are not. Yeah?"

Rinehardt Erbacher touched his cup again and turned to look at August through bottle-bottom glasses. He did not like to talk about dying. August took the movement as assent. "But *then* . . . to wake up each morning and think, 'Maybe today I make a killing; tonight I go to bed rich and sleep with a beautiful actress. Or maybe somebody kills me—I sleep with a knife in my belly.' Sure, most of the time you go to bed as poor as you were when you woke, with whoever you can find for a bowl of soup; but you screw her like she was the actress because you're still alive and tomorrow she really may be."

Rudi was shocked—shocked to hear Uncle August speak so and shocked because that vision of days after the war was not the one his mother had given him. There had to be some talk about the old days, he knew; some talk about other things before they could talk about what Erbacher had been brought here to talk about. So he tried to appear interested and to be patient while he let his coffee cool and held the small manila envelope in his jacket pocket tight with his elbow.

"Of course I was involved only with local affairs. I was never involved in international operations like you, Rinehardt." August's tone and his use of the other man's first name succeeded in implying an association from which he gained importance even by denying it. "Rinehardt did business with all of them: the Americans, the Russians, English, French," he told Rudi, tapping his lip with a finger. "But perhaps I shouldn't say so much. Enough to say he was such a cat who always knew where to find a mouse. I hunted with him only perhaps two times, but tasty morsels we had." He grinned at Erbacher and nodded conspiratorily.

Erbacher nodded slightly, trying to remember. He could not. He assumed this Tobler was making it up, but ever since that little shock in his head last year, there were things he couldn't be sure about.

"But enough of old times, uh? Rinehardt and I could talk all day—"

Hermann Tobler's face was always unexpressive, so he betrayed no amusement now. Erbacher had said little more than "hello" and "coffee, please" since arriving.

"—but it is today's business that concerns us. Rudi, I have told Herr Erbacher nothing except that you have something to sell and that I believe it may have such value as to be worth his coming from retirement to see. Please, you begin."

"Yes. Thank you, Herr Tobler." The moment had come at last. In truth Rudi had imagined meeting a man in a crisp trench coat or a leather jacket, not one who looked like a sack of moldy flour giving at the seams. But Erbacher was someone, he was here, and there was no retreat. Rudi drew the envelope from his pocket and held it just above the edge of the table. "I am a photographer," he began. "I work in Bad Gastein. I know a girl. . . . Three weeks ago, you may have read about it in the papers, there was a conference of Ministers—Defense Ministers—in Bad Gastein. I guess they do not work too hard at these conferences, not all the time. My girl—this girl I know, met one of them. She . . . she lives in a little house outside the town. She . . . we were able . . . I took some pictures."

Erbacher had looked at Rudi steadily since he began speaking. The old man's eyes were pale and watery, magnified by the thick lenses of his glasses. Rudi had been unable to look away from them.

"Please," Erbacher said, turning his palm upward on the table. He pulled the envelope to himself, then exchanged his glasses for a second pair. Unbelievably, they were thicker than the first. He opened the flap of the envelope, turned away from August, drew out the photographs and held them six inches from his nose for examination.

Each of the pictures had been mutilated. Each showed the girl and the man—naked—in the various positions they had assumed, but in each picture the girl's face and part of the man's had been cut away.

"Why did you do this?"

"I didn't want to carry them with me. I was . . . they're too valuable. If you look at all of them together, you can see who he is; but I didn't think they would be of any use to anyone this way."

Erbacher's hands were palsied. He tried to control himself so their shaking would seem only that. He looked over the pictures again, holding them close but spread out enough that he could see the parts of the man's face in several simultaneously. Despite grimaces of passion, the composite could be identified. Then he abruptly gathered the pictures together, trying to make the gesture business-like—as though he were a teller used to shuffling fortunes. He slipped them back into the envelope, held it down and exchanged his glasses again. "How many copies?"

"One set. Besides these."

"Absolutely?"

"Absolutely."

"The negatives?"

"To be sold with the set. Herr Erbacher . . . this is not my usual kind of business. My girl and I . . . we don't do this. But the chance. . . ."

The chance. "You think *I* like it! *I'm* the one who's going to have to do it!" Ilse had stood by the window quivering with an anger that had overmastered and turned Rudi's to fear. Then she had whirled to look out, her long, blond hair spinning, gleaming for an instant. "Rudi, it is a bad thing, sure. But it is also bad to have men do what they do to me every day. They take off my clothes, they do things to me in every way they can imagine. They use me, and I feel every bit as dirty as if it was real and not just in their minds. And I have to allow them. I have to show I know what they're thinking and pretend I'm enjoying it. That's what the tips are for. For serving them drinks I get only the paycheck, barely enough to live on this week so I can go back to that for another week.''

Her fury had tempered to a bitterness that he knew covered deep hurt. He wanted to hold her, to shelter her. But that was foolish: He knew she was tougher and stronger than he although she was small and young—six years younger than he. They pretended sometimes that he was her protector. It made each of them happier. But it was only pretense. Rudi wept whenever he thought of how much he loved her and of how she loved him. It was her love, he recognized, that kept her from adding that there was no future for them, no escape to be made by his work either. "So one more time, Rudi. One more pretending. One more tip. The same as every day. Maybe worse, no different. Only different because it will be for the *last* time . . . and for that, we will take the chance!''

"Herr Erbacher, we just want to make some money from this—we just want to sell it—and that's all. We understand it might be very dangerous."

"Yes. How much money did you expect to make?"

It had come. Rudi steeled himself. He had never been able to bargain. But he and Ilse had talked it out and decided. "One million schillings," he said firmly.

Erbacher regarded him without change of expression. Rudi realized he had made a fool of himself. He should have asked for half. He had no talent for this business. Obviously the pictures were worth twice his demand.

Neither August nor Hermann had tried to steal a look at the photographs, but when they heard the figure, they gave up all pretense of being disinterested.

"So," Erbacher said at last. "And what sort of arrangement do you wish to make with me?"

"I . . . I don't know. What sort of arrangement is possible?"

"Usually you employ an agent to make contacts for you in return for a percentage of what you receive." Erbacher kept his voice steady. "However, I will consider buying this material from you direct and attempting to resell it myself, keeping whatever profit I can make."

"You would buy it yourself?"

"I do not usually work in this way but—to be honest with you—this is a valuable property and I think I can make something on it. I am an old man, Herr Bischl. I have retired from all this. I have no interest in lengthy or involved affairs. I have no interest in deceiving you. These pictures are worth more than you are asking to one who knows what to do with them. How much more is my business. I will give you what you ask. You will have that and then be done with all of this."

Rudi was stunned. It was beyond hope that it could be over so quickly, and without risk. "I . . . we would be pleased with such an arrangement, Herr Erbacher. Thank you."

"I can have the payment for you tomorrow . . . yes, it is time enough: Tuesday morning until Wednesday night. Can you deliver the material to me tomorrow evening?"

"Yes, of course. That is . . . not exactly. You see—"

"Not exactly?"

"Herr Erbacher, as you see, I am not a professional in this business. To be honest, I am very frightened about it. I— We thought it safer not to have the photos with me. They're hidden. In exchange for the money, I'll tell you where they are. Oh, you don't have to worry! Ilse— The girl and I wouldn't try to cheat. Honestly. We're too afraid for that. We know that if we cheated, someone would come for us. We know that in something like this, we'd never be able to take the money and hide.''

Erbacher looked steadily at the young man. In truth he could not see him well, but his gaze gave the effect of a soul-penetrating examination. He considered whether Rudi was attempting a confidence game. He considered how he might cover himself if so. Most of all, though, he considered the identity of the man in the photographs. To prevent a scandal, that man might pay extravagantly in money, information or influence. And not only he was involved. Such a scandal might even bring down the man's superior, bring down an entire government, change the policies of nations, shake alliances. Only an amateur such as this Rudi could expect to withhold such material and try to sell its *location*. Only professionals such as the potential buyers Erbacher planned to approach would appreciate that the value was worth a risk.

''Very well,'' he said at last. ''I will resell the materials—or their location—within a day or two. I will make clear our arrangement and guarantee that if the merchandise is not where you say it is, I will identify you and will return the payment should the buyer be unable to collect his purchase from you. I hope, Herr Bischl, that you are as frightened as you claim to be—for if you attempt any fraud, you will not be dealing with an old man. The people who will come for you will be of a kind to give any person on earth good reason for fear.''

FRIDAY, JULY 15 20:00 HOURS—
OBER-FLATTACH

When Ted Barstow left his hotel after supper for the Friday-evening band concert, the Russians' agents were waiting. Ted was blissfully unaware. He saw the one whose name was Brunner only as a pleasant-looking man with a mustache, standing to the left of the hotel door. He never saw the one called Janovich, who was across the street.

Ted came out of the hotel, then turned right—away from the band. He wanted to circle the Platz, to get the feel of it all. He slipped through the crowd. Everyone must have gone home for supper at some time, but now they were all out again. He didn't like crowds normally, but this was part of what he had come for: to hear the band concert in the village square, to see all the burghers out together, to absorb the sense of community. *Sentimentality*, he scoffed at himself. *Product of too many travel brochures*. The scent of the crowd should have been corrective: People here didn't seem to bathe as frequently as Americans.

29

But he found the human smell, mingled with the aromas of wurst, beer and cooking fat wafting from the open doors of cafés, somehow comforting.

The townspeople greeted one another, smiling. Then frowns appeared as there was head-shaking over the "tragedy," but finally music and the warmth of the evening won out. Except for the German tourists. Ted thought to himself that no one looks as glum as a German on holiday. He did not consider himself a tourist, of course. A "traveler," yes, but not one of those garish people who descend from air-conditioned buses and photograph each other.

Brunner followed him, trying to get closer, but Ted's move had put a family between them. Janovich paralleled him across the street. They knew that taking a man in a crowd is not as foolish as it may seem at first: The press of people gives reason for being close and hides what is being done.

Music carried over the heads of the throng, bouncing between the buildings at either side of the narrow street. It called Ted to come to see the show, but he was not yet ready to succumb. He dallied, looking around and up. *Tender evening*, he thought. *Sky like . . . evening sky*. The sun had dropped behind the mountains that surrounded the village; rays streamed up across the clear blue—

Eyes blue! He saw them. *Stop thinking about it! Golden-fingered twilight*; he made the image change.

A slight breeze rippled the banners raised around the Platz. He couldn't decide about the banners. The bright geraniums in wooden tubs placed at the foot of each pole were fine. Others just like them sat on balconies everywhere. But the banners were only for the tourists. Red and white, orange and black. They were meant to brighten the town, to make it appear festive. They didn't seem to him to be authentic. But they *were* festive. He stopped to take it all in.

Suddenly! In the small of his back: a blow, a sharp pain. His hips were thrown forward, his shoulders back. Half-turning to see, he nearly fell. He clutched at the arm of a man next to him. A woman screamed behind him.

"*Pepi! Enschuldigung, mein Herr! Bitte. Pepi! Was machts du! Langsam! Enschuldigung, mein Herr!*" She had a tow-headed boy by the shoulders and was shaking him like a mop while cascading apologies on Ted.

"*Macht nicht*," he said as he regained his balance. "*Nicht, nicht, nicht.*" Nothing, no problem. He was aware of the pun: His backbone felt as though the boy *had* made nicks in it, but he was afraid the mother would break the child in two.

The boy seemed terrified beyond tears. Ted's anger at being bumped vanished in reaction to the retribution falling upon the lad. He smiled at the mother to show it was all right. He smiled at the people around him. He smiled at the man with the mustache who was behind the woman and boy. Brunner smiled back.

Finally, after further begging his forgiveness for the totally unforgivable, the woman shifted her grip on the boy's *lederhosen* suspenders and swung him swiftly in an arc that terminated at the mustachioed man's stomach.

"*Enschuldigung! Mein Gott! Enschuldigung!*"

Ted smiled at the man again and started moving down the middle of the crowded street toward the band. Thirty feet away, Janovich reversed direction and began moving toward him.

Middle-aged women cradled bosoms on pillows in windows around the square. The window casings were great and thick; Ted guessed that the baroque trim around them was a recent addition, merely two hundred or so years old. He thought that most of the buildings were probably over five hundred years old, built when a wall was expected to keep things inside safe from things outside. The original stonework was now stucco-covered, painted ochre, cream, green or faded rose.

As he neared the band, Ted decided that it was very good: that is, not really very good at all. Strong on oompah-oompah but short of breath in the winds; an authentic village band. He had seen the bass drummer earlier at the chopping block in his butcher shop, where he had been mauling cutlets. The man brought to his music the same professional spirit and an arm as big as Ted's thigh. A boy of about eleven held cymbals stiffly in front of himself, staring through them in deadly concentration, trying to catch the bandmaster's hand with a crash every time it dropped directly into the center of his line of sight.

Ted worked his way closer. Janovich had approached to within eight feet to his right. Brunner had collected enough breath and apologies to free himself, and now he came up behind.

The crash of cymbals and boom of drums could cover the sound of a silenced gun. In a crowd, neither assassin nor victim would be known. Everyone is looking at the band. If a man slumps, few will notice at first; no one will remember who stood behind him.

To Ted the bandsmen resembled figures that parade in and out of a cuckoo clock: black knee breeches, white shirts, brass-buttoned red vests, black hats with little whisk brooms tucked in. They played a waltz now: oompah-pah, oompah-pah. Ted loved it. He recognized the local baker in the brass section, and one of the railroad attendants.

People were crowded together but he forgot to care. He wanted to get as close as he could. Like swimming in molasses, he moved up. The two men followed, chasing in slow motion. Then he couldn't slip any farther forward without actually pushing someone out of the way. He came to a stop. Brunner was directly behind him.

Snare drums rolled and syncopated between the ponderous beats of the bass. The slides of four trombones shot down deep and flashed up again in triumph, holding a quivering, high note.

A large man shifted position in front of Ted, blocking his view. He leaned to one side, trying to see beyond. Janovich managed to get to his right. Ted craned farther to the left, lost his balance slightly and jostled the person next to him.

"*Enschuldigung,*" he said.

"*Guten Abend, Herr Barstow.*" It was Fraulein Stendler.

"Uh . . . *Guten Abend*, Fraulein. *Wie gehts*?"

"*Gut, danke*. And you?"

"Fine, thank you."

She continued looking at him, and smiling. Brunner and Janovich developed a sudden, all-consuming interest in the music.

She had changed her clothes too. She wore a white blouse with handmade lacework around the collar. She was fresh and neat, prettier even than Ted had thought. And here they were, meeting outside, free of the constraint he had felt in her office. Perhaps he could. . . . Herr Bloch banged away at the drum; fortunately, Ted thought, that covered the sound of his heartbeats.

Not that he had never picked up a woman before. Actually, he did so frequently at singles bars established just for the purpose. The steps of the mating dance in such places are simple and he did not have to count his steps or think about his feet. But he was thinking about Fraulein Stendler—as a person, not as a pickup. How nice she seemed. What might she think of him?

She asked, "You are enjoying the concert?"

"Very much."

A slight smile, a touch of irony in her eyes. "You like this music?"

"I like most music."

"And you like *this*?"

"I like this. All of it. The music, the evening. I like seeing the butcher play the drum and the baker—"

"Ah, I see. It is . . . quaint."

"It's real. Authentic."

"So. But not very professional."

"That's the point. It's . . . It's the spirit, it's . . . you know, in Beethoven's Ninth Symphony, the *Ode to Joy*, all those magnificent giants of sound—the chorus, the orchestra— Suddenly this little German band shoulders them aside and marches right through the middle. That's *this* band."

"So? I had not thought about it in that way."

They paused and listened for a moment.

"How do you know about the butcher and the baker?"

"I located them as I came through town from the train around noontime. I need lunch when I go hiking."

"You are a climber?"

"No, just hiking . . . *wandern*. I go as high as I can simply by walking."

"Ah."

The piece ended and everyone clapped. Ted joined in. She did not.

"You don't like it at all?" he asked.

"Not tonight. I do not think there should have been any concert."

"You mean . . . because of—"

"Maria Tauschig is killed today and we have a concert ten meters . . ." She gestured toward the boarded-up window behind the band. "The mayor and my boss, they think it is better to have the concert. Everything must be 'normal' again. It is Friday night, there must be the concert.

Good for 'morale.' Too many tourists are leaving. We must all come out and make them forget."

"You must have known the girl."

"This is a small village. Everyone knows everyone."

"I'm sorry, Fraulein. I didn't know her." He saw again the pretty little girl, blonde, her hair in long braids down her back. She had been very serious about her job: being polite, remembering every order, quick to table to bar and back with a tray and half a dozen heavy steins—the weight of adult responsibility she would prove worthy to bear. Once he had noted that someone had complimented her and made her smile and he had felt that every bit of counterfeit sentimentality about childhood joy had been redeemed in gold.

Oompah-oompah, crash, crash, crash.

"Fraulein, there are people everywhere who . . . terrible things happen. If I let myself, if I dwelled on it . . . if you let yourself think about them, even just the ones you see. . . . You have to be able to put things out of your mind." He realized he was not being successful at conveying tough-mindedness. "I didn't know her. I'm sorry." He concentrated on the music, hoping the blare and bang would drive away the memory.

She stared at him for a moment. "*Ja.* It is okay."

With a trill from the piccolo, a swoop of trombone and a final crash of cymbal, the march and the concert ended. She turned to him. "So."

"Yes."

They stood silent for a moment. She was smiling slightly, an open, friendly smile. He took a breath—tried to take a breath—got only half of it. "Fraulein . . ." He felt that hot icicle right down the middle of his chest. "Would you . . ." *This is ridiculous! I am not afraid of women. I am thirty-six years old. I know I'm attractive to women. I know my way . . . I am not some goddam male virgin!*

Then the click came: his safety valve, his circuit breaker. He distanced himself from the moment, breathed deeply and easily. From just outside his head, he looked at himself standing there with her. "Fraulein, would you join me for a cup of coffee?"

"Thank you, Herr Barstow. That would be very nice."

The café was not wooden-beamed and paneled, and the waitress wore her apron over an ordinary blouse and skirt instead of a dirndl. But there were deer antlers mounted on the walls, and a rack in one corner held newspapers. And many of the customers obviously were local townspeople, making jokes back and forth across the tables. The place had its own special atmosphere that Ted decided was better—more authentic—than if it had been picture-book quaint.

He ordered coffee in German: "*Zweimal Caffee, bitte*." He turned and asked Fraulein Stendler: "*Mit Schlag*?" She made a face and shook her head. When the waitress left, he said suavely, "I wouldn't think you had to worry about whipped cream."

"Thank you. Perhaps so long that I don't eat it everyone will think so."

It was going nicely. He was glad he had met her. During the five minutes spent getting through the crowd to the café he had given her a sensitive appreciation of the village architecture, a couple of clever puns on words similar in German and English, a little light flattery. Shyness had been ridiculous, he decided firmly.

He relaxed into the noise and the warm aromas of coffee and pipe tobacco as though letting himself down into a hot bath. Then she looked into his eyes and spoke directly to him. "So, you like my figure?"

He blushed. He should have been ready. He should have kept pretending to himself that he was Cary Grant in a late-night movie; but she caught him being himself and he felt his face redden.

She chuckled, "I tease you."

"I . . . ah. . . ."

She laughed. "Do you know why I accepted your invitation to have coffee?"

"Why?"

"Because you were embarrassed. You were like a youth, a youth of fourteen years."

"I see." His insides were hollow and his voice seemed to echo.

A little shock came into her eyes and the laughter was gone. Had she really hurt him? She experienced the old fear. "No. No, forgive me. I do not mean to offend. You are not fourteen years, Herr Barstow. One sees that very well, so it is charming. I do not mean offense. Please. You see . . . I receive many invitations from tourists, Herr Barstow. Most of them are from men who think they are charming and they are not. You think you are not and you are." She looked at him steadily.

I should confine myself to bleached blondes and to women who laugh much, loudly, and to other types who never really look at you.

The coffee arrived. Ted stirred the heavy whipped cream into his.

She bit her lip. "Please. . . ." She reached across the table and gently pushed with her finger against his fist where he was clutching his thumb. "It is now okay?" She made him look at her again and smiled.

It was okay. It would be just fine if he were careful. "Sure. And, Fraulein—"

"Erica."

"Ted."

They shook hands.

"And, Erica, I must confess, I do like your figure."

"Good. You are supposed to."

He held the thought of coolness, but warmth was spreading through him anyway.

"Why did you come to this village? We have almost no Americans visiting here."

"That's why I came. I've hiked before in the Tyrol—I was there last week—but it's full of Americans. I heard that few of us come south to Kärnten. I looked on the map for a small place and took a chance. When I got here, I saw the castle on the hill. I went to lunch at the Alpenrose and nobody could understand English, so I knew this was the place."

"Why?"

"I wanted to immerse myself in the culture, I guess. I wanted a place that was uncommercialized, real. Not just for the tourists."

"Not for the trouists! Busloads of Germans. We have to have the concert for the—"

"I know. I guess I didn't think of them . . . because of the language. I could still be separate."

"Separate?"

"I mean . . . I . . . I mean, it wouldn't be as though I had come on the bus."

"Ted, do you know a dark man with a mustache?"

"No. You mean here? No."

"There is a man over there. He was behind us at the concert. He pretends he is not watching us."

"What do you mean?"

"He has a newspaper, as though he is reading, but he looks over the top. And if I catch him looking, he is just reading."

Ted turned, saw his fellow victim of the towheaded piledriver and nodded. The man nodded back, smiled and pressed his hand against his stomach. Ted told Erica the story.

"Why is he watching us?" she asked.

"I don't think he's watching us. Just coincidence. It's a small town."

"He is watching us."

"Okay, I can believe he's watching *you*. But people do not watch me. I hear there will be an organ concert in the church on Wednesday."

"*Ja*. But they will play only Bach."

"What's wrong with Bach?"

"There are other composers."

"Who?"

"You said you liked all music."

"Sure, when I can't get Bach. Who would you listen to instead?"

In another five minutes, Brunner stood up and left.

They had brandy with their second coffee so they would be able to sleep. Then they just had brandy. They agreed on Beethoven but not on Schubert; on Stravinsky but not on Schönberg; on Laurence Olivier and Maximillian Schell, but not on Robert Redford; on Orson Welles and Truffaut, but not on Goddard and Fassbinder. By obvious but unspoken agreement, they did not talk about the shooting. They had just edged into philosophies of life when the waitress locked the door, turned out all the lights but theirs and finally defied them to order more.

"Oh, and you must see the *schlucht*."

"Is that a waterfall?"

"Yes. No. It goes underground."

"In a cave?"

"Yes. Partly. It is a *bach* . . . a brook. It comes down from the mountain and goes between very steep sides. Like in a cave, but the sides do not meet at the top. A gorge." She remembered the English word.

"Is it dark?"

"No. There is much light. It is very beautiful. You must see it. It is very strong."

They were walking down the stone-paved street, along the wall behind the church. The clean air was good after the smoky café, refreshing despite an occasional waft from an open drain. Chilly. Erica had her arms crossed, held to herself. They walked slowly and close together. The streets were dark. It was the night of the full moon, but clouds had spread across the sky.

Ted felt that when sometimes Erica's shoulder touched his arm or the back of his hand brushed her thigh, those few people they passed might have seen sparks. They talked easily. They were comfortable with one another. Yet there was that high tension. To him it was like walking home a mile out of his way with his first great crush in high school, like turning the first page of a book of magical charms: an awareness of possibilities beyond any previous fantasy. He didn't mean just sexual possibilities, although that certainly was part of it. Erica felt it too, felt that he truly liked her, not only for her sex. She had felt that at the beginning. The liking had grown as they talked, and she was sure it was true for both of them. If there should be the sex, it would be part of that true liking.

"Beyond the *schlucht* the pathway goes up into a little valley. It is very nice too, for wandering . . . for hiking."

They came to a corner. There was a streetlamp above and light shone down sharply. It glinted on her hair band, highlighted her forehead and cheekbones and the tops of her breasts. Her crossed arms held her blouse tight and the light revealed her nipples, pointed. The chill, or excitement? Ted's mouth went dry.

They rounded the corner and started downhill, the church wall on their left. Their shadows were thrown against it at an angle, as though they were leaning forward. They were huge.

"Do you go hiking?" he asked.

"Oh, yes. On my holiday. I love the mountains. And in my job I must know all the places to tell visitors to see."

"Do you like your job?"

"Yes. I like to meet people."

"Why?"

"One always learns something. They come from many places. They have different lives. They see what I see every day, but not the same. We do not speak together very much, but sometimes they say things that make me see my world in a new way. You do not like to meet people, do you?"

"No."

"Why?"

"They . . . I don't dislike . . . I don't know."

"Are you not lonely?"

"No."

"You do not need to be close to anyone?"

What does she mean by that? How should I take it—with the two of us walking to her rooms late at night like this? "I like to be close to some people sometimes. Do you?" *Back in her court.*

"Yes. Always. That is why I came here. I did not like the city. Too impersonal." She spoke with her head down, thinking. "I like my job because I help people." She said it matter of factly; she did not think of it as something to her credit.

They reached the bottom of the street, a dead end. There were balconies across the front of the house at the end, and a stairway zigzagged up through them.

"Here is my flat. On the top floor. It is really only two rooms, but it is large and I have the balcony."

Ted detached himself and saw them standing there, she facing him at the bottom of the stairway with that slight smile at the corners of her lips.

"And my own entrance."

His heart was pounding again, his breath tight, but *he* was outside, and cool. No shyness now, he told himself; the pickup is made. He'd played the scene many times, he knew the lines. He'd say, "I'd like to see your place sometime." The girl would say, "Why don't you come up and have a drink before you go?"

"Thank you for the coffee, and for the talking," she said. "I have liked talking with you. You are a very interesting person." She was looking straight at him. He knew she meant it.

Quick, keep control. If you like my talk, baby, you'll love my screwing. I can have her, no doubt about it.

But it was no good. He liked her. Not *her*, but *Erica*. He couldn't pick her up because he wouldn't be able to drop her again. He had to get away. "Yes, this has been fun. Well. . . ."

He saw that she was surprised, then hurt.

Be away. Instantly. He extended his hand for the obligatory European parting. "I'll probably be seeing you at the tourist office." She took his hand. Her touch was warm and soft, but strong. He had to get away. "Well. . . ." Suddenly—he didn't know it was coming—"Erica, would you have dinner with me tomorrow?"

"I would like that very much."

She pressed his hand and went up the stairs. He stood looking after her. He felt anesthetized, like a panicked swimmer going under in a warm, pink ocean, holding that last breath.

He turned to go back up the hill. A tall man was standing just below the top, his shadow looming gigantic on the wall.

WEDNESDAY, JULY 13 08:25 HOURS— VIENNA

Tolz poured the measure of coffee into the top of the pot, then added the exact amount of boiling water to make one cup. He put kettle, coffee-box, and measurer back in their places and turned off the hot plate, all without having to think about what he was doing. For ten seconds he looked out the window at the tiny park and the baroque facade of the Vienna he knew and loved. By restricting his focus, he could ignore the glass and concrete it was becoming.

Then he turned and sat down again at his desk. The center of the desk was clear. Nonurgent reports and messages that had arrived at the end of the previous day, which he had glanced over and put aside for morning, had been read and put into appropriate piles. His memos and orders were in their baskets. That was what he did early each day between six-thirty and eight-thirty.

There was no requirement for him to arrive at six-thirty every morning. That he did so, and worked until six-thirty in the evening, was regarded as extreme dedication to

43

duty—with awe by his younger inferiors, who thought they were exceptionally diligent by arriving half an hour early at eight, and with annoyance by his superiors, who sometimes did not come in until nine.

In truth it was not dedication; it was avoidance of boredom. Tolz awoke at five each morning, not by decision or choice, but because as he grew older, he needed less sleep. There was nothing to do then but to get up; nothing to do then but to wash, shave and dress; nothing to do then but to have his first coffee and a roll; nothing to do then but to go to work. Each activity in sequence, each in its moment: riding to the office on the trolley, while reading the morning paper, coming up the stairs, hanging up his coat and hat, looking out the window for the first time, polishing his wire-rimmed spectacles, reading the reports and memos, at eight-twenty-five heating the water for coffee. At eight-thirty his assistant would bring in whatever had arrived overnight. One moment after another, each filled; until it was eleven o'clock at night and he reached the moment for going to sleep and another day had been passed without time to be aware of emptiness or boredom.

His name was Martin Tolz, and he had a rank; but his bureau worked in civilian clothes and all of his old colleagues—with only two exceptions now distant by status (one very high, one very low)—were dead or retired. His wife had been dead for thirty-five years. She had survived the war, but not what came after. They had had no children. So all he ever heard himself called was "Tolz" or "Herr Tolz."

"Good morning, Herr Tolz."

"Good morning, Johann. Is your cold better?"

"Almost gone, thank you."

"Perhaps you can get some sunshine this weekend. What have we this morning?"

"Not much, sir. Hammacher reported no activity when he went off at midnight. Strauss, nothing at eight. There is a summary update on the Algerian cell, but it seems only routine. No one thought enough of it to put it in the afternoon delivery." Johann did not mention the surveillances, wiretaps and so forth that were institutional. He put the small pile in the cleared area on Tolz's desk and took up the piles of "out" materials. "Anything special, Herr Tolz?"

"Not this morning. Thank you, Johann."

"Please, Herr Tolz."

Johann left, and it was the moment for the second cup of coffee. Tolz had no pastry with it because of his weight; the bureau physician had said that pastry was not good for his health. It was not clear to Tolz why he should care, but he obeyed his physician's instructions about food, if not about coffee.

He took his first sip, then sorted through the papers to arrange them in the order in which he would read them. All of the morning's moments had been passed through successfully. Now came the second work period, which lasted for two and a half hours, until the third coffee at eleven. This was the next-to-longest period of the workday, but because it was yet morning, not difficult to get through. And it was Wednesday. When the morning had passed, another week would be half over.

At nine-fifty-three Tolz reached the transcript of calls to the Russian Embassy. Since the Russians knew their public line would be tapped, there was seldom anything of value picked up over it. But it was inconceivable that the line not be tapped or that the transcript not be read. He scanned it quickly. Then he stopped at the third page and read it over again, carefully.

At the caller's request, the call had been switched to the Trade Section.

"My name is Rinehardt Erbacher. Some years ago I did business from time to time with Herr Gudanov in your office."

"Gudanov? There is no Gudanov here now. I don't recall—"

"Of, course, of course. This was perhaps twenty-five years ago. I have been retired. But, unexpectedly, I have come across a business opportunity of the kind that once interested Herr Gudanov."

"Perhaps you would care to send a letter to—"

"No. Please. One moment. Simply remember my name: Erbacher. Look in your records for my business with Herr Gudanov. I will call back later. Thank you."

Tolz put the papers down and turned to the panel of buttons on his desk.

"Yes, Herr Tolz?" Johann's voice came at once.

"Johann, please check the file on Rinehardt Erbacher." He spelled the last name aloud while flipping through the next page of the transcript. "It will be in 'inactive.' "

"Yes, sir. Do you want a copy made?"

"No. Simply obtain the last known address. It should be some village somewhere close to Salzburg." Tolz found Erbacher's second call. It was briefer than the first. The Russian trade attaché simply asked where Erbacher could be reached and was given a number. "Ah. Johann, we should have something on the code system Erbacher used for telephone contacts."

"Yes, sir."

Tolz sat staring at the window for a moment, pursed his lips and shook his head. He was still looking bemused three minutes later when Johann entered with the computer-retrieved material.

"Herr Tolz?"

"Who is Vassily Shamraev, Johann?"

"The KGB resident—in the Embassy Trade Section."

"Of course. And who is Alexis Lopakhin?"

Tolz's game usually had a point that Johann understood, but because Johann revered him, he played whether he understood or not. "Shamraev's predecessor."

"And Mikhail Novgorodsky?"

"Didn't he come before Lopakhin?"

"And Alestrovitch? Brodsky?"

Johann smiled blankly and shrugged.

"If you don't remember them, Johann, how could you possibly remember Serge Gudanov?" Johann spread his hands and dropped them in apology for incompetence. Tolz waggled a finger in admonishment. "You will have to be a very old man in the spy business to think of calling Serge Gudanov when you want to sell to the KGB." He nodded once, pausing to let the lesson sink in. Then he dropped the tone. "See who is available in Salzburg to do some legwork."

SATURDAY, JULY 16 01:40 HOURS—
OBER-FLATTACH

The paving stones were highlighted: light on the top edges, deep black in the cracks between. Arcs of stone, interlaced fans, rippled outward and up.

Ted assumed the man would be coming down; because he didn't want to see him, he stared at the stones as he walked slowly uphill. About two-thirds of the way up the street, he raised his eyes. The man stood there, his hands in his raincoat pockets, his back to the light. Ted couldn't really see his face. There was just enough reflection from the wall to reveal a heavy brow and high cheekbones. It didn't occur to him to be afraid. Backlit, standing above, the man might have seemed sinister. But in that village. . . . The idea of danger did not occur.

The man was looking at an angle upward. Instinctively Ted turned. Erica stood on the third-floor balcony, looking down at him. He could see her white blouse and dark hair. Seeing her eyes was imagination.

Electromagnetism: He felt he could have walked straight

up to her on the line of attraction between them. He stared at her. *Childish. Just met her. Romanticizing, like a shallow thirties' ballad: "Moonlight, love at first sight." Ridiculous. It wasn't love, it wasn't possible.*

He remembered the man and turned back. He was gone.

Ted looked at the wall. *I should go too. Wave to her, but go on.* He stood motionless, looking at the wall. *I can feel her presence.* The wall was of stone, stuccoed over, rough textured. He put his hand on it, pressed fingertips against a ridge. *I can feel her presence the way one can feel an object in the dark by nerves in the face. I should go.* The old wall had cracks along the lines of the stones. A chip fell from under his fingers. *I should go. It's like the way one can feel the presence of another person, silent in a dark room.*

He turned and went slowly back down the hill and then up the three flights of wooden stairs, forgetting to count each step. He reached the top. Erica stood midway on the balcony. She had turned to face him as he came up the stairs. It was as though they had not broken the look, as though there had been no stairs between them. She stood with her arms crossed; the light from the streetlamp showed her strong fingers, tensed. One of his hands was on the balcony rail. He rubbed the old, smooth wood once with his thumb.

Then he walked toward her and when he was a reach away, she turned and went into the flat, and he followed. She paused and breathed deeply, letting the air out in a rush. She took off her hair band, tossed her hair slightly. It fell about her face and she brushed it away with the back of her hand. He didn't breathe at all. He had even stopped thinking. Slowly, as one might reach to touch a sparrow, he raised his hand and touched her cheek—softly with his fingertips. She turned her head, her cheek into his palm.

He brought his fingers down the back of her neck. She moved to him, raised her face. They kissed gently, moved away, then together again, their arms going around each other. Very slowly, without thinking, not planning, just happening. Like a dance in slow motion, under water, on the moon.

They must have slept. Then she lay with her head on his chest, her arm across his waist. He stroked her hair and she sighed.

"I thought you were going away," she murmured.

"I thought so too."

"Why?"

"I . . . I don't know."

"I wanted you to come with me." She giggled suddenly and turned her face into his stomach. "Oh, that is *schmutzig* . . . dirty. I mean I wanted you to come here. . . ." She giggled again. "What can one say?" She raised on one elbow and looked at him, all embarrassment gone. "*Ja*, that is what I wanted. Did you not know?"

"Yes. I knew."

"Then why did you go away?"

"I don't know."

"I don't believe you. You are a person always thinking. You say you don't know because you don't want to say." She stared at him. He didn't answer. She put her head back on his chest. "Have you religion?"

"No."

She traced her hand across his stomach. "Have you a wife?"

He said, "No."

"You are not afraid of women. You have experience with women."

"Yes."

They were silent. Out on the highway at the edge of the

village a car going very fast whined up and away. Other than that, there was no sound. But the silence was not sharp and dry, like winter. The night was round; quiet at this moment but full of life.

He had to try to explain to her. It seemed as though he must. "I . . . I was married. Divorced. I guess that now . . ." He tried to make his usual joke. "I guess I've been vaccinated—you understand? I guess I've got antibodies against becoming involved."

She looked at him steadily for a moment. "*Ja*, I see."

Suddenly she kissed his chest and hugged him. "So you went away because you care about me." He didn't answer. "So what does it mean that you came back?" She looked at him with that little smile. "You no longer care? I had not that idea."

He laughed. Because of laughing, he was able to say it. "No, I cared. More than I wanted to admit." Then he had to go on and ask, "Why did you want me to come back?"

"Because I liked . . . I cared for you."

"How could you? We've only met."

"You can care for me, why cannot I care for you? We talk. We understand each other."

"There must be many tourists who like you." It was like picking at old scars. "How many do you like?"

She pulled away and sat up. She looked at him; then (he thanked God) she looked away. "A few."

A black hole in the middle of his chest pulled everything into it. "I see."

"What do you see! You go to bed with other women, *ja*? And that is okay, *ja*? But for me . . . ? For a woman, it is not allowed!"

"No. Yes. I mean . . . that's not the point."

"What is the point?"

"I don't *care* about them."

"Then why do you go to bed with them?"

"I like sex."

She clasped her arms across her breasts. "That is disgusting!"

"You seem to like it."

"Only when I like the man."

"How many do you like?"

"What does it matter? One, ten, if I *like* them?"

"Or a hundred?"

"Or thousand!"

"Your 'liking' isn't worth much if anybody can have it."

"So? Your 'caring' is so small you must give it in few little pieces, *ja*?"

A naked man and a naked woman, sitting now at opposite corners of a bed with their legs drawn up. One part of him saw them as ridiculous; one part of him scored the point for her. The rest of him ached. She looked at the headboard behind him. "I do not go to bed with 'anybody,' but I do not wait all my life for *you*. That is what you want, *ja*?"

"No!" But she stared him down. "Probably yes," he admitted. "Every man wants to be waited for, to be special."

"And woman."

He smoothed the bedcover. "I don't mean to hurt you, Erica, but how can many—however many—be special to you?"

"How can you like only one person? How can you want only one person to care for you?"

"I don't. But I don't go to bed with every woman I care about."

"*Ja*. Okay. *I* do not go to bed with men I *don't* care about."

"Erica, with you . . . I did . . . I do. . . ."

"But you didn't want to stay with me. Maybe you should have gone back with your friend."

"Who?"

"The tall man who waited for you."

"I don't know him. I thought he lived here somewhere."

"He waited, and then he went around the corner, and then when you were coming back here, he looked around for you. And then he went away."

"He couldn't have been looking for me. Could it have been someone looking for you?"

She brushed a strand of hair from her face. He thought she would tell him to leave. Instead she looked at him steadily and gradually her face softened. She was sorry for him. He wanted to bury himself in a deep hole and pull a heavy rock on top.

Finally she smiled. "Jealousy is not a good way to show that you care." She moved up the bed. "Going away was not a good way either." She was kneeling beside him now, her head to one side. "And you think going to bed is not a good way to show I care. But we must do the best we can."

WEDNESDAY, JULY 13 20:15—
SALZBURG

The woman in the doorway slid her hands from her hips, her fingers pointing downward, along the sides of her belly. "Love, darling? You want some love?"

Rudi never saw her, nor the couple ahead who walked with their arms across each other's backs, their hands on each other's bottoms. Nor was he aware of the music blaring from the bars and discos he passed, nor of the flashing lights—except as sensations that were part of the joy, the fear, the tension and relief that surged through him, making him dizzy with excitement.

Again he held his right arm close, pressing an envelope tight against his body. But a different envelope. His, with the sample pictures, had been given over and in return—handed to him, in his hands, in his pocket right now, felt with every step—was Erbacher's envelope containing one hundred ten-thousand-schilling notes. It was a fat packet, too large to fit inside his jacket. He had had to put it into his side pocket, where it bulged. He should have brought some kind of case. He had not really imagined the bulk of one million schillings in physical terms. It was the size in value that had obsessed him since yesterday, when Erbacher had agreed to the purchase. The amount was not vast. Rudi knew that there were people who made several million schillings each year. It was not a fortune for the rest of his life—their lives—but it was enough. They could break the chain of days. They could make a future where tomorrow was not just yesterday lived over.

Thrilled with a sense of unlimited possibility, Rudi had no consciousness of the people around him. He didn't notice the dark, stocky man who stepped from a doorway diagonally ahead to intercept him. He did not become aware of him until the man blocked his way.

"Herr Bischl?"

Rudi blinked. For the first instant he did not comprehend that he had been addressed. As he did though, his emotions clarified quickly through confusion to fear. The man said something else to him; all he caught was "police." The man took his arm and gently but firmly forced him over to a car parked at the curb. Another man sat in the rear. As he leaned forward to the open window, yellow light struck his face. It was a handsome face, middle-aged but still firm-jawed. The man nodded slightly in a formal, yet friendly greeting. "Rudolph Bischl?"

"Yes?" Rudi was still too stunned to think of what he ought to do.

The man in the car held up a wallet displaying a card. "I am Kurt Hartz, Special Bureau, State Security. I wonder if we might have a word with you?" He nodded again and gave a slight smile. "Please don't be alarmed. You have done nothing wrong. We want only to have your help in our investigation." He slid away across the seat.

The other man moved behind Rudi, exchanging his grip on Rudi's right arm for his left. In the same motion, he opened the car door, and with that soft but inexorable pressure, impelled Rudi into the back seat. Only then did Rudi's instincts succeed in communicating to him that he should either resist or flee. But the front seat was pushed back, locking him into the coupe as the man slid behind the wheel.

Rudi turned to Hartz, who was leaning against the corner of the seat to his right. It was a small car; they were a mere few inches apart. Hartz returned Rudi's stare. Rudi turned and looked forward, then through the window on his left.

Even on a Wednesday night there were people everywhere, crowding the sidewalks, crossing the street. Rudi suddenly was as acutely aware of them as earlier he had been oblivious. No one looked back at him. Their eyes were on each other and on what they saw of themselves in each other's eyes. But if he shouted—if he struggled— surely someone would hear and see him. All those people— those seekers of sensation, of excitement, out in this night in hope of some thrill—they would mob the car, they would—

"It will be in your interest to cooperate with us, Herr Bischl. If you are helpful, we will detain you only briefly."

"Where are you taking me?" The car moved out from the curb, forcing pedestrians to let it by, with the same quiet irresistibility the driver had used on Rudi.

"To a place where we can talk."

"Am I under arrest?"

"Not yet. We hope that won't be necessary, Herr Bischl. I know this is disturbing to you, but I assure you it will be possible for you to avoid any serious unpleasantness. We are quite decent people and—to be frank—you are not the sort of person with whom the bureau is concerned." Hartz kept his lips together but gave another smile: a serious man, a stern one perhaps, but not unkind.

Rudi was afraid of what he might look like as he stared at Hartz, so he turned and dropped his eyes to stare at his clasped hands. It was several minutes before he looked up again. To his surprise, the car was heading out of the city rather than in to any of the central municipal offices. He twisted abruptly to face Hartz.

"I have told you, Herr Bischl: We are from the Special Bureau." The man seemed to know what he was thinking. "We have our own places for interrogation."

Interrogation! The word was horrific. To be asked questions was bad enough—he was already weak with fright—but to be *interrogated*. . . . He clutched his hands and pressed his lips together to keep them from quivering. He must not appear cowardly.

"Sure, Rudi, it is dangerous. Dirty and dangerous." Now Ilse sat across the table from him. "You don't get something for nothing." She sipped her coffee for punctuation. She took it black and strong. He used cream and sugar.

He couldn't let her think he was weak. "I only mean that we have to *recognize* it's dangerous." Masculine practicality, not fear. "We have to take precautions." He put his coffee down, leaned back casually and looked out the window. "That's all I meant."

He saw only the lights of scattered farmhouses. They had left the outskirts of the small city and passed through a village. They turned from the secondary road onto one surfaced with gravel. Rudi leaned forward, trying to make out where they were going.

"Almost there," said Hartz.

The road led into a forest. After a short distance they came to an even smaller track to the left and turned in, went a hundred meters and stopped. "Here we are." Rudi turned again. To his surprise, his panic was fading. Hartz smiled at him. "You expected an office. No. It's such a beautiful night we thought we'd talk alfresco."

It was a fine night, the moon two nights from full. Rudi could see deep blue sky and a bright planet before they left the track and led him under the trees. There it was dark but shafts of moonlight came down through the boughs, dappling the tall trunks and needle-covered turf. Despite everything, he could appreciate the beauty of it. All the tree trunks were bare, stripped of branches to two or three times a man's height. The trunks were pillars separating solemn sylvan aisles. It was a young forest though, still a decade away from harvest, so it was no stretch for him at all when they stood him against a tree, his arms around the trunk in front of him, and handcuffed him.

The short man searched him. Rudi closed his eyes and leaned his head forward when the money was pulled from his pocket, but his regret was not bitter. As his hope was taken, so was his caring. He heard the men step back and speak in low voices. Then Hartz came around where he could be seen.

"Now, Rudi, here we are. As I have told you, we are not from the regular police. We do not use the same methods. We are not interested in making arrests or in having trials. We really are not interested in *you* at all. We are interested in the pictures you took. Oh, yes, we know. We've been keeping in touch with Herr Erbacher's activities. Where are those pictures?"

"I don't know."

Hartz studied him for a moment, stepped behind him again and then returned with the packet of money. He waved it in front of Rudi's eyes. "Rudi, Erbacher gave you this money in return for the location of the pictures. You didn't tell *him* you don't know where they are." Suddenly Hartz clenched his jaw, slapped Rudi's face with the packet. Instantly he stepped back, shook his head and sighed as though the act had been from an impulse he could not control and now regretted. "Where are the pictures?"

Rudi licked his lower lip. "We knew this business would be dangerous. I didn't bring the pictures with me. Ilse hid them. I don't know where. She didn't tell me. When Herr Erbacher gave me the money, I called her on the telephone. I gave her a special word and then I let him talk to her and she told him where they are."

"Are they in Bad Gastein?"

"No." Rudi had no thought of deception. He was resigned. He had understood even before Hartz struck him that they could do anything they wished to him. And would. Everything was lost; nothing mattered now except avoiding immediate pain. "Ilse comes from Kärnten—on the south side of the Hohe Tauern. She said she would find a place there."

"So she told Erbacher to go to her grandmother's gravestone."

"No. I showed her how to locate whatever place she chose by finding its coordinates on a map. She gave Herr Erbacher the coordinates. I don't know what they are. That was our plan."

Hartz stared at him for several moments. "So," he said at last. "And who was the man in the pictures?"

Rudi told him.

Hartz took a deep breath and let it out in a whistle. "Well, Rudi, that was a big fish for such a small angler to catch." He went away again, and again Rudi heard him talking to the other man.

The moonlit forest was so lovely. Rudi could smell the tree's resin. He looked down the passageway between it and the next row of trees. Enough moisture hung in the air to catch the light so that the trunks could be seen to some distance in black contrast; and where direct light dappled those trunks, they glistened. Capturing it would require a long exposure and would be especially difficult because of the difference in light qualities. And the picture would need a subject. A nude? Ilse, kneeling in the center of an aisle or half-hidden behind a tree? But she would have to be very still, and it was chilly. Rudi shivered at the cool waft of the gentle breeze.

The men seemed to be arguing. Their voices rose enough for him to make out the words, "no chance." Each of them said it, with some difference in meaning between them. But he didn't attend further. There was nothing to be gained. The whole of his life was lost. What mattered the next moment?

Then Hartz returned. "So, Rudi. You have been very helpful. I will underscore your cooperation in my report."

"Are you going to kill me?" He was past fear, only mildly curious.

Hartz looked at him blankly for a moment. "Kill you? Rudi, we are from an agency of the state. Our methods are irregular, and we are not above frightening people to get information quickly, but we do not kill people like you. We must keep you from causing trouble for a day or two, but after that . . . who knows? You have not actually committed any crime. My superiors may even decide to let you keep the money. Sergeant Schimmel, come release this boy."

SATURDAY, JULY 16 09:00 HOURS—
OBER-FLATTACH

Brunner and Janovich followed Ted Barstow's bus on Saturday morning and when they saw where he got off, they went ahead of him while he was walking up from the highway. The side road turned to dirt and after a quarter of a mile or so, it climbed into the narrow valley. Farther on a footpath diverged from it and led to the *schlucht*.

Ted felt good, walking in the cool, crisp air. The clear blue sky reminded him of the little barmaid's eyes, as perhaps it always would now. But he had developed the ability to shut out pain. He saw the eyes for a mere instant and then only the sky.

It was a fine morning for hiking, he thought. Although it was chilly, strong sunlight promised warmth at lunchtime. By late afternoon, lack of sleep might weight his pack and doubts come stumblefoot downhill with him; but for now he would remember the heat he and Erica had shared, not the chill when they had argued. He would believe that he was in love with her, be assured that he would see her in the evening, and keep himself from thinking about yesterday and tomorrow.

He put a schilling in the box and passed through the turnstile. He got a cheery "*Grüsse Gott*" from the dumpling woman who was chastizing two grains of sand for having had the temerity to fall upon her path. "*Schön Tag.*"

"*Ja,*" he agreed. It truly was a beautiful day. "*Schönes Wetter.*"

"*Sinds Sie Englander?*"

"*Amerikaner.*"

"Ah!" Her smile broadened as the valley did when the sun cleared the mountains over it. "*Amerikaner!*"

Had his uncles liberated her from the Germans? Had they shielded her from hordes of Russian ravishers? He couldn't think that his countrymen here before him could have kindled that warmth simply by burning dollars. It melted some of the icicles on the north side of his heart. Foolish of him, of course, but she seemed so exemplary—her hair braided on the nape of her neck, her generous bosom under a flowered apron—and so genuinely pleased to see him that he felt accepted and welcomed by Mother Austria herself.

America is a wonderful country. Austria is beautiful. But America is so large. Austria is so peaceful. Americans are good people. Austrians are warm and friendly people. Neither of them could outcompliment the other. He felt that at any moment she might offer him a piece of homemade blackberry *kuchen*; he would gladly have given her Manhattan, Niagara Falls and the Grand Canyon in exchange.

He became embarrassed and finally reminded himself that he was going hiking. She gave him Godspeed, and good weather, and good traveling, and it was becoming more than he could carry. He backed his way up the trail from her, waving as he went.

"*Und passenauf den Fussweg auf wo nase ist*," she called after him, still beaming and waving.

"*Ja. Ja. Danke viel mal.*" He waved back.

The path led along the side of a rushing mountain stream and then rose above it toward a narrow gap in the cliff ahead. The *schlucht*. At first it didn't seem very impressive. Its rock walls were about fifteen feet apart, perhaps seventy feet high, moss-covered, yellow-green. The wide stream at its bottom cascaded over stones. Pretty. Typical.

At the entrance to the gorge the trail was continued by a wooden walkway roughly three feet wide that lay on triangular wooden braces jutting out from the wall. The walkway twisted with the contour of the cliff. There was a handrail made of smoothed saplings. He took hold of it and started in.

Ted tended not to be afraid of things, but he had to admit to some anxiety about the path. He told himself that Germanic thoroughness would assure the soundness and good repair of the structure (even if this was Austria), that the rail would not break and that he could not slip under the lower rung unless he lay down and tried very hard.

At the point where the path turned out of sight of the entrance, one wall climbed over the other so that although light filtered down, he could not see the sky. The pitch of the stream's bed also rose, the gorge narrowed and the current was swifter.

He made the turn. Ahead he saw curved walls of striated rock: yellowish ridges against deep, blue-black gouges. The gouges seemed to him to have been made by great fingers clawing the sidewalls as something huge and alive was swept downstream, screaming unheard over the tumbling rush of the water, helpless against the current.

The air was full of mist. The walls and path glistened with it, and there was a green slime underfoot. Suddenly he remembered what "*Passauf*" means: "Watch out." "Watch out for the footpath where it's wet." He slid his foot back and forth on the boards. It slipped easily. He thought again about the space between rail and floor.

He decided that he was being ridiculous. As long as he held to the rail, as long as he didn't run or dance around, he couldn't possibly slip. He got ahold of himself, took the rail firmly—not clutching it, but firmly—and started on with care.

The sound of the stream was loud at that place but there was a great roaring around the next bend. Coming out of that bend was a torrent of white water. It no longer fell over stones: No stones, no rocks, not even boulders, could stand to that force. Now he knew what Erica meant when she had said, "The *schlucht* is very strong." He was glad he had come to see it.

But he hadn't seen it yet.

Moving up toward the bend, peering farther in with each step, he began to see. He moved half a step at a time, shuffling along the wet boards, holding the rail with both hands—hand over hand, then hands sliding, never released. He was not in fear of falling, not in fear of anything so rational. It was not really fear he felt, but awe. The torrent coming out of the bend now seemed a trickle. Coming into it—the top much higher than the bottom, draining. . . . Draining a lake, draining all the glaciers in the Alps—he could have believed anything. Into and through that bend, pouring, hurling, hurtling, crashing down, fell all the power of the old gods under the earth. Nothing he had seen—not Niagara (too vast and open), no storm, no hurricane, compared to it. Never before had he felt such concentrated force as in the white rage of that white water tearing into the entrails of the mountain. All at once he sensed the hatred water must have for anything solid. The roar almost physically pressed him down to kneel, to cover his head in the terrible Presence.

Edging farther, his eyes fixed on the stream to his left and under him, suddenly he was aware of a shape in the center of the concaved bend. For the first instant it seemed only an outcropping of the wall obscured by mist. Then, as his brain comprehended what his eyes registered, it seemed to be transformed into a man—as still and solid as the rock, but a man. A man he had seen before, the man with the mustache.

The man looked at Ted steadily; he must have been watching him ever since he came around into the bend. Ted felt foolish, let go of the rail and stepped back with a deprecating shrug: He wasn't *afraid*.

Brunner smiled. The mustache seemed not to move but the corners of his mouth drew apart and the full lower lip went down, revealing large, regular, white teeth.

Ted smiled back. He gestured toward the stream, nodding his head in appreciation. Brunner raised his hands wide apart and nodded back. They had considered the *schlucht,* individually and jointly, and found it worthy of note.

Why is he here? Why is he just standing there? Why doesn't he go along so that I can just stand there? I hate being in crowds!

Ted took two steps toward him, toward the very center of the bend that Brunner occupied. *I'm only eight feet from him: Surely he'll move away. I would if someone came this close.*

Brunner kept on looking at Ted, kept on smiling. He did not move. Ted had a flickering memory of childhood stories about trolls and bridges. Brunner stood relaxed but solid, his feet firmly apart, his weight even, his fingertips just inside the pockets of his brown-suede jacket. He was big-chested, and broad. His shirt was open at the neck and Ted could see the upper tufts of what he knew would be a mat of hair. Again a memory of legend: the King of Under-the-Mountain. He would not go away. He would not let any stranger pass into his domain.

Well, if he won't leave and let me be here alone, he'll have to go too. Ted took another step toward him.

Brunner still did not move. Ted looked at him. Brunner leaned back, smiled and nodded for him to squeeze by. To squeeze between him and the rail. Between him and that rushing, crushing roar.

Ted was not normally afraid of things, and the man seemed to be only another tourist—one whom he had seen before. Now suddenly he was afraid. Because he ordinarily avoided close contact with people, when it did come, he was especially sensitive to every nuance of expression. Brunner smiled with his teeth; his eyes were watching.

Ted halted. He was close enough that the man could have touched him at arm's length. Brunner drew his right hand from his pocket, rotated his palm upward in a gesture that seemed a further signal for Ted to pass by, but a gesture that also flattened the hand into a blade. Ted became very frightened.

Ted shifted weight and took a careful step backward. Brunner turned to face him, bringing his left hand out and up to chest level, his palm down and flattened like the other. Ted stepped back again, his own hands coming up defensively. But since he was too amazed and frightened to remember any of the spy movies he had seen, he didn't think to knife them or to hold them across himself protectively. He simply let them rise, palms outward, in front of his shoulders. Brunner took a step toward him and Ted stepped back again.

Brunner smiled more broadly—with real amusement this

time. Although he had hoped he might have some advantage from surprise, he hadn't counted on it. Highly skilled in hand-to-hand combat, he was prepared to meet another professional head-on and was confident he would win. But now it seemed that his opponent was incompetent in this part of the business. Unless he were faking.

All at once Brunner jabbed out his hands in a mock attack. Ted jerked back and against the wall. Brunner was sure now: The reaction, the look of fear, was instinctive and true, and no one who knew what he was doing would have thrown himself off balance that way. He took another step forward. Ted backed. Again Brunner feinted and again Ted jerked away. Brunner was certain the natural movement to the wall would be repeated. He lunged, his left arm shooting out in feint and parry, taking a big step; then, using the acceleration of the step, he thrust from his cocked right arm to drive the bladed palm toward Ted's stomach. Ted flinched to the wall again, and Brunner would have hit into soft flesh trapped against unyielding stone. But as his heel came down, it slid forward on the slick planking. He began to slide into an impromptu split.

Ted Barstow was not a trained fighter, and he was very frightened. But he was not paralyzed by terror. Instantly reacting to his attacker's predicament, he thrust his raised palms forward from shoulders braced against the wall. Their force striking Brunner, who was falling backward anyway, spun the man and threw him—slammed him—back down across the walk.

Brunner slid for three feet, struck a railing post and spun against it. His head and shoulders shot under the lowest bar, his weight dragging him along. He started to fall to his left, with his head down, but his right arm whipped up instinctively, his wrist striking against the bottom bar. He grabbed it and held on.

Ted watched in frozen horror. He had acted automatically.

Now shock and fear swept over him with the force and icy suffocation of the torrent below.

Brunner hung over the edge. He was motionless for a moment, assuring himself that his hips and legs were secure. He felt the post against his hip and squirmed against it to give himself purchase.

Ted could not move; he could neither help nor hurt the man or run past him.

Veins on the back of Brunner's hand popped out, knuckles and tendons bulged as he pulled himself up. He lifted high enough to reach the bar with his other arm. He hung there for a moment more and then began to slide himself back onto the walkway.

The last dam of self-control inside Ted burst and fear inundated him. He ran. Not down the path past Brunner, but away from him—away up the path toward the top of the gorge.

Run! Run! Nightmare running over wet, mossy boards; his legs stiff and leaden. He slipped down on one knee, scrambled upright, slipped again careening off the rock wall.

Out into the open but still in the gorge. A deep pool below reflected the sky. *Her eyes sky! Death eyes!*

No! Free blue sky. Above, below—free blue!

He was caught, hanging in a vise of black rock that seemed to close as the gorge narrowed again. The pathway twisted around points of rock, a chasm walled with blades. The catwalk rails were like the bars of a trap. *Must go into it! Monster behind! Don't look back!*

His legs drove so slowly. He heard Brunner just behind him, his steps crashing, shaking the walkway. *Don't look back!* He heard Brunner's breath, hoarse, panting. *Don't look back! Run!*

Running, still running, *keep running*! Halves of logs—stairs—ran up one wall. *Up, up, get up, get out*!

He reached the top, stumbled off the walkway and onto solid earth. The path doubled back above the stairs. He grabbed the post and swung, almost falling around.

He isn't there! He wasn't there at all. He hasn't come out of the schlucht!

Ted stopped, gasping, ravening air, his legs twitching, his hands shaking. He could rest. He was safe.

But he might come out at any second. Get away! Get help!

He started running down the road that paralleled the stream above the gorge. He ran, then walked to catch his breath, then trotted as fear came over him again.

He came around a bend in the road. About fifty yards ahead, in indigo shadow under the great pines lining the bank above, a car was parked. Ted didn't see it at first, a gray car against gray rock. A man stood beside it, looking down the hill. Ted's fatigue vanished. He breathed deeply and smoothly. He was safe. He would go to the man, tell him . . . anything, get him to drive him back to the village, to the police.

The man was facing away, his hands in the pockets of his raincoat. A tall man.

Ted stopped moving and stood very still. Although his chest was still heaving, he did not gasp. What had just happened in the *schlucht*, now the same man waiting here who had waited for him the night before, and the shots that had killed little Maria Tauschig just as she leaned her head close to his—suddenly all these things made a single picture.

Quietly he turned and began trotting back up the path, looking over his shoulder as he went. The tall man did not move. Once around the bend again, he increased speed, running steadily but no longer in panic. He came again to the exit from the *schlucht*. He could see Brunner just starting up the stairs, his eyes down at that moment. Ted continued running up the road.

THURSDAY, JULY 14 15:50 HOURS—
SALZBURG, VIENNA

It was like following a narrow path through a forest and suddenly emerging at a summit. Erbacher had held his breath for so long that he panted afterward. He had barely endured those days in the Toblers' establishment, but now the pieces fell into place and he made himself stop and look again, step by step.

Two men representing the Russians had come as arranged to examine the sample pictures an hour after he himself had received them Wednesday night. They had been impressed. Although they were professionally noncommittal, Erbacher could tell they had recognized the power those photographs could bring. He didn't know the men, but then he hardly knew anyone in the business anymore. One was broad and hairy, with a mustache, jovial, Austrian. The other—tall and bony—spoke German well but probably was Polish. They were intermediaries: The Russians were not risking one of their own men in contacting a ghost from the past like himself. He was not offended. The Austrian had returned at nine on Thursday morning with a bid of three million schillings.

There had been a pause then. The American's flight had been delayed and he hadn't arrived to examine the pictures until after ten this morning. He did not even try to hide his evaluation of them. But when he reported the identity of the Minister in them to New York, there was disagreement among his employers as to whether it was patriotic to use them for blackmail. Some felt that the existence of the pictures should be made known to friends in the CIA, who could work through the Minister's government to have him removed quietly. One of Erbacher's former associates—who had been young Corporal Perone of the Quartermaster Corps—achieved another of his famous compromises: They could carry out a straightforward business transaction, selling the photos to the Minister to save him public disgrace and then leaking knowledge of the man's indiscretion for the government to use however it thought best in the national interest. New York offered three-fifty.

The Russians went to four; the Americans went to four-fifty and final; the Russians went to five. Erbacher actually would have preferred selling to the Americans.

He stared at the telephone now, looking over the panorama of possibilities open to him. There—directly ahead—he could see Morocco. He squinted against its brilliant color, felt the sun there, hot even in winter. He watched discreetly from behind sunglasses the girls in bikinis lying on the beach; and then—no need for discretion in that country—he lay himself to be caressed by the little girls one could get so cheaply. Yes! Old he was, ill, his sight almost gone, his hands shaking, becoming twisted from arthritis made more agonizing by winters in the snowy mountain village he had once thought picturesque.

Soon he would be dead. But not yet, not there! A man is always a man, age never takes that need. He had not thought about that, or about how the cold would feel when he was old; he had not thought he could ever tire of that village created magically from his childhood storybooks. And when he did, it was too late to change. The million schillings he had paid for those pictures was most of what he had owned. But now, with nine and a half million schillings (over five hundred thousand U.S. dollars, over a million and a quarter good Swiss francs). . . . Because that was what it came to: the total. That was what the wet-eared boy had given in exchange for a paltry one million, what his combination of cleverness and naiveté had handed over.

Erbacher suddenly saw what he would do, felt it with the sensation of gulping a glass of brandy—the instant burning in his stomach and then the warmth and well-being spreading through every capillary. If the boy had given him the pictures, he would have had to hand them over to the buyer—to the Russians with their five-million high bid. But the *location* was a tale that could be told over and over and be ever new to each listener. The location was a *place* that had to be reached, a journey that would take most of a day. The one who arrived second would be unhappy but would direct his displeasure, initially, toward the children, whom he would believe had tricked them all. By the time he got back to Salzburg, Erbacher would have vanished into the blinding southern sun. He himself had advised Rudi Bischl against deception. But dazzled as he was now by that glare, drunk with imminent wealth, he was absolutely confident that—somehow—he could elude pursuit.

And so he lifted the receiver again, completed his call to the American and—for the second time—enjoyed the pleasure of giving joyful news.

*   *   *

"All is good, Herr Erbacher?"

"What? Oh, yes, Hermann, all is good."

"You sold the pictures?"

"The business proceeds."

"Good. Good. Who did you sell them to?"

Erbacher paused for a moment, the way out of the little alcove blocked by Hermann's belly. "The highest bidder," he said finally.

Hermann ducked his head and threw up a hand as though warding off an undeserved blow. "Not to pry, Herr Erbacher. Not to pry. Uncle August and I have only interest in your success."

"Yes, Hermann, thank you. I am grateful to both of you." He would show his gratitude tangibly when he left—as the Toblers obviously expected in every protestation of disinterested friendship. He would have to think about how grateful to be; however much (he was sure) would be less than they hoped for. But it had been convenient to use the bar as his base, to be fed from the kitchen, to stay in a room on the third floor—although he had not been able to sleep through half of each night. People using the other rooms and noises that escaped through the doors had not troubled him if he didn't think about them; but the incessant pounding of that abomination they called music had been almost intolerable.

"So why do you stay there?"

"I'm afraid to leave."

"If you're afraid, why do you take no precautions—not the simplest—to hide your business?"

Johann Zimmerman thought. His role was to think of the answers, all possible answers, even those that might seem absurd and make him seem stupid. That was the basis of the game—that he was a dolt. But Johann was not a dolt. He was intelligent enough, first of all, to realize that although Herr Tolz was notorious for not explaining to others what he thought or did, he liked to teach. He did not expound, did not like to answer questions (which he seemed to confuse emotionally with attack), but he did like to guide the thinking of someone less experienced. Second, Johann understood that Tolz was a good teacher because he made his student think out answers himself rather than receive them. These understandings had come to Johann soon after he began working for Tolz, when he had responded to one of his superior's occasional rhetorical questions with an answer both logical and ridiculous and was asked another question that suggested a truth by contrast with that reductio ad absurdum.

Tolz rubbed it in. "You call the Russian Embassy direct. You use the same code for your telephone contact that you always did. You make all of your calls from the same location. You actually live there while conducting your business." Johann sank farther into the chair on the other side of Tolz's desk. "In short, you violate every rule of the craft of your trade. Why?"

"I know it's wrong, but I feel I'm safe there. I'm playing a very dangerous game—I've decided to sell to two parties. I'm afraid to go out."

"But you are going out! You have just agreed to meet your American buyer at the railroad station tomorrow morning."

Johann shrugged, then straightened himself and smiled with foolish brightness. "I guess I'm not afraid. I'm overconfident. I don't think anyone is tapping my phone."

"Indeed." Tolz's scorn was withering.

"I guess I'm really not very good at this business," Johann said despondently.

"Second rate. *Third* rate, Rinehardt, that's all you *ever* were." Tolz shook his head in sad exasperation. Then he paused, nodded abruptly, and the scene was over. "So, good. We will require three teams there tomorrow morning. Brunner and Janovich are to come to the bar at nine to receive what they have bought. They are to be taken when far enough away so that Erbacher should not see. He is to be followed to the station, and after he hands over to the American, both he and the American will be taken also.'' That was all he might have said, but he liked Johann. The young man was bright, he learned. There actually seemed some point in investing time with him. ''And why do we wait until then instead of picking up poor Rinehardt now?''

The relationship did not require Johann always to seem stupid. ''So we will have something incriminating on all of them.''

SATURDAY, JULY 16 10:05 HOURS—
OBER-FLATTACH

One: get distance between. Two: hide, or get help. Help better if possible. Who? Valley leads up into mountains. Hikers maybe. One: get distance between. Two, find help if possible, hide if necessary. Three: figure how to escape.

The panic was gone. Ted's body was still in a state of animal terror but he was thinking fast and clearly—one, two, three. Somehow, recognizing the cold calculation of his hunters calmed him. Escaping from them became a problem to be solved. Why they were trying to kill him was secondary; he could consider it later.

A footpath branched to the right, climbing the hillside parallel to the road and rising rapidly above it. He took it. To the left of the road there was a steep drop, perhaps thirty feet down to the stream, with an equally steep rise on the other side. If he could have crossed that way, he might have been able to climb up among the trees. His pursuers would never have known exactly where he crossed or have been able to search the whole forested hillside. But he might have slipped—the bank was sandy. He might have been exposed while still trying to climb. So it seemed wiser to take the footpath on up into the valley on the less forested side, although it meant they could follow in their car and see him.

It was bad judgment. There was a third alternative. He should have climbed steeply to his right, then turned back and gone into the trees above the road and headed down again. But he couldn't do that. He was past blind panic but he wasn't totally rational. He couldn't turn back toward them. His instincts wouldn't let him even consider that a possibility.

The valley widened between mountainside and stream. As he went up the footpath, the road curved away to the left below, making a wide brown loop through the dandelion-spattered meadow. He slowed to a walk to catch his breath, then resumed jogging. He was in good physical condition and knew he could continue at that pace for some time, even uphill. Without stopping he slipped off his backpack, put his water flask and some chocolate into his jacket pockets and then dropped the pack.

After a series of switchbacks, the path climbed along the grassy skin of the mountain. The road, by now more than a hundred feet beneath, wound back and forth. He saw the car moving along one of the lower bends. He had almost allowed himself to hope they were not coming after him. He was completely exposed. Tufts of forest sprouted above—black firs with good thick trunks and deep shadows underneath—but he would be seen scrambling up to them, visible if he left again.

Quickly he dropped down and lay on the path. Hikers had worn it down so that it was lower than the grass along its edges. The road must be half a mile away. At that angle, looking up, they might not see him.

The car moved slowly in second gear over the rough

surface. Ted was sure the men inside were searching carefully. *But they may not see me. They might go past and then I can double back, and then.* . . . He lay there, trying to hide behind grass three inches tall, trying to press himself into the hard-packed earth.

The car stopped. Janovich got out and stood beside it. He looked around, slowly and carefully. He started by looking to his side, across the stream. He turned up the valley, then back down, scanning the other side. Ted held his breath, unblinking. Surely, at that distance, at that angle, with him lying so flat, so still—surely the man couldn't . . . *surely.* . . .

Janovich's eyes traversed along, over, past the place where Ted lay.

Before leaving for this vacation, Ted had discarded his old gray windbreaker and bought a new one. His color choices had been either neon-red or electric-blue. He had taken the blue.

Janovich looked back now, directly at him, and shaded his eyes with his hand. Ted tried to contract his body. He willed the grass to grow. Janovich pulled back, leaned down to speak into the car. Brunner got out and raised his hands to his eyes. He was using binoculars.

Ted had long ago made himself an expert at being inconspicuous. People remembered him vaguely, if at all: "Oh, yes, there *was* someone else; what's-his-name, who sat in the corner." When he walked in the woods, he rolled his steps on the outer edges of his feet and chipmunks were startled to find him standing only three feet away. *Why didn't I go to another store?* What insane aberration had made him buy an electric-blue jacket?

Brunner gave the binoculars to Janovich, who stared upward too, and they talked for a moment. Then Brunner started to walk across the meadow. Ted sat up. Brunner proceeded steadily, beginning to climb slightly. He would have a hard climb as the slope became steep, but he seemed to have the necessary energy. He didn't waste any of it by hurrying.

It seemed absurd, totally absurd. Ted Barstow was sitting in all the vastness of the Alps and the sky overhead, just sitting, one lone figure on the side of a mountain, and half a mile away a man was starting to walk toward him, a tiny, lone figure also, growing larger almost imperceptibly with each step—walking a straight line through the dandelions and up the hill, not deviating from that straight line, just walking up the side of a mountain to kill him. Ted had the sense that it didn't matter whether he waited there or ran. If he ran, Brunner would come after him—up the mountain and down again, under the oceans, to the poles, to the center of the earth. He wanted to shout, "This doesn't make sense! There must be some mistake!"

Ted got to his feet. They had seen him and they weren't going to pass him by: now he would have to do something. Maybe he could still double back. He waited until Brunner was two hundred yards from the car before he started down the path. He ran a little distance and then looked over his shoulder. The car was facing across the road. It reversed. It was turning around. Brunner was standing still; he had not returned to the car as Ted had expected he would.

He calculated quickly. The car would be able to catch up with him and get ahead of him. Whether he followed the footpath back down to the road or struck off from it toward the trees above, the driver would see where he was going and be there first.

Ted turned back up the path. The car stopped, waited and began to make the shuttles back and forth across the road necessary to face it up valley again. Ted had a wild urge to start downhill once more just to make them turn around another time. In context it was ludicrous, but he had a vision of a Mack Sennett routine with the film running backward and forward. He was brought to reality, though, as Brunner resumed climbing toward the path.

It still seemed absurd, but Ted understood. They would not accept his winning by default—with them on the road and him on the path, just sitting and looking at each other. If he wanted to sit and wait, the walking man would reach him. More likely his progress would force Ted to move: Action would continue; there would be no stalemate. He and the man walking toward him could go in any direction, but slowly. The driver could go rapidly, but only back and forth along the road. The possible combinations were limited. The only one that seemed to offer any hope was for him to continue up the valley, the two men following behind.

Ted jogged up the path, past the place where he had stopped earlier. When he looked back, he saw that the man was returning to the car. Ted concentrated on his jogging, breathing carefully and in rhythm.

Ahead he could see the end of the valley. The mountains on either side were joined by a col. There seemed to be painted on its face the roots and trunk of a huge white tree: a single shaft of water falling several hundred feet, breaking on the rocks below. Between him and the waterfall lay a group of wooden buildings, huddled together as though hoping the great mountains above might not consider them significant enough to step on. And there were cows.

I'm saved!

He knew that in the Alps the herds are taken up each summer to pasture in the high meadows. They stay there all summer and someone stays there with them—usually the grandparents and the young children of the family. There would be people in those buildings. They would hide him. They would protect him, get help.

The footpath led directly to those huts. The road, keeping to the shallower grade near the stream, swung far away to the left before winding back and forth to reach the same end. Even on foot, he could get there well ahead of the car.

He trotted faster. In another three minutes he reached the buildings. There was no one in sight; there were no sounds. The buildings were old, weathered and coffee-brown. They were lichen-covered, with roofs of thick slate held down by heavy stones. The first group consisted of barns or sheds, and there was no one in them.

He called, "Hello!"

Silence.

"Hello, *ist man hier*?"

What if no one's here? What if they're away somewhere? Can I hide in a barn, under the hay? That's the first place they'd look, stupid!

At the end of the row of barns he noted a building with a window. A cabin. Smoke came from its chimney. Its door was open. The inside was dark.

He went closer. Inside, to the left of the door, a huge cauldron hung from a tripod set over coals. Something bubbled in it; there was an old cheese smell. A twig broom leaned against the jamb inside.

"Hello?"

Nothing. Silence.

Louder, "Hello!"

He banged the door frame. His eyes were conditioned to the bright sunlight outside. He couldn't see well into the cabin, but he made out another doorway leading to an inner, darker room. Shuffling out of the gloom came a figure, bent over, head thrust forward. He saw a shirt once red, now stained; a man's black jacket, ragged. It was an old woman with beady eyes, sunken cheeks, a pointed jaw and hooked nose. She wore a bandanna over her head, gypsy style, and a gold earring. She even had a wart on her nose.

Can she hide me in her oven, make me disappear, turn me into a cat? Desperate as he was, he thought of all that as she took form before him.

She cocked her head to one side, squinted up at him and croaked in a voice like a parrot, "*Grüsse Gott.*"

"Can you help me . . . *Bitte, können Sie mir hilfen?*"

"*Was?*"

"*Hilfe. Hilfe.*"

She leaned closer, just under his nose. "*Was?*"

She was deaf.

"*HILFE! HILFE!*"

"Ah. So." She rocked back, caught his meaning. "*Wie?*"

How? What was he going to tell her, what could he ask in the hundred words of German he commanded?

She sucked her lips and the wrinkles around her eyes became crevices as she strained to learn how she might help him. Alone at the end of that valley, she had waited for someone to need her. She had waited for years, for generations, charmed and cursed. She had waited for ages for someone to come and make her young again by asking for her help. She would help him gladly. He had only to tell her how.

But she was deaf, and he didn't know the German words for "killers" or "escape" or "hide."

He looked back down the valley. Less than a mile away, as the road turned, the little gray car wound itself around a bend.

He shouted at her and pointed.

Because the road at that point was only for use by cows and tractors, the car was in first gear, moving at about ten miles an hour. One mile in six minutes.

He spoke loudly and slowly, exaggerating his lip movements. Her eyes beseeched his face. He needed, she needed; but between them there was a spell like a wall of crystal. What magic word could break it?

One half-mile in three minutes.

Moving carefully so as not to break its springs, the car reached the second turn.

"*TOD!*" That was all he could think of. "Death." "*TOD, TOD, TOD!*"

One hundred yards closer every twenty seconds.

Slowly a light spread across her face. In twenty yards it went from eyes to mouth.

"Soooo!" She nodded in understanding through another ten yards. The importance of his plea had been comprehended but not its urgency. She peered at him and at the car that loomed closer with each split second. Then she wrung her fingers. Her eyes watered. She understood, at last, but the curse remained. His imminent death was a problem beyond her. She referred him to a higher power: "*Der Mann.*" Ted could hear the car whining now as she explained—looking upward—that he must find "The Man" for help.

"*Los.*" Up there. She gestured toward the sky. He expected no help from there, but he looked upward too. Far up on a shoulder of the mountain he could see a hut.

"*Los.*"

The car came to the nearest bend. Ted took her hands and thanked her. Then he ran up the trail into the woods, toward the hut.

The path climbed through belts of tall, blue-black firs. Their roots, partly exposed by erosion from rainfall down the hillside, clutched the slope like talons. The path was clear, marked by tracks of hoofed animals; here and there Ted saw the print of a hobnailed boot. That gave him hope. Hikers wear shoes with lugged rubber soles. His own boots left a clear print in the moist earth. Only a true man of the mountain would be hobnailed.

The path was steep. Frightened as he was, Ted was in

control of himself. He did not try to run, which he knew would exhaust him quickly.

When he was a boy, he had often played "chase" with the other boys. Usually he was the quarry. He preferred running out alone to being one of the pack of hunters. It seemed more challenging, outwitting a gang of pursuers more exhilarating, the satisfaction of success greater for being undivided. Now remembering some of the tricks of the game, he considered jumping away from the trail and trying to hide. The woods had no underbrush though. He'd have to chance standing behind a tree. That might hide him from one person, but two would find him if they fanned out. All the tree limbs were too high for climbing. It was better to go on.

He came out of the last section of trees, went up a grassy rise and onto a knob. The path ran nearly level for fifty yards, then zigzagged up to the higher shoulder where the hut would be. He could see over the trees to the valley floor, from the waterfall clear down toward the *schlucht*. It would have been a wonderful place for a picnic.

He looked down and back to the buildings. The gray car had reached them, the men were outside with the woman. Ted hoped she would be all right.

Suddenly he was swept by a wave of fear and guilt. *They might hurt her!*

Why should they hurt her? She doesn't know anything. Why should they want to kill me? They're killers! If I ran back. . . .

But they didn't seem to be harming her. They were all talking together. They seemed to communicate easily, as he had not been able to do. They seemed to be getting on very well. The woman gestured, waving her hands beside her head. The men laughed. She waved at the sky and bobbed up and down. They all laughed. She turned and pointed to the hut; the men turned and looked up at it. Then she pointed to the trail he had just taken.

The hut was one of the crude but solid buildings herdsmen use when forced by work or weather to shelter high up. It was built of logs, its thick timbers squared to make flat walls and tight joints. The timbers had been sturdy and whole once, but now checks and twists lined them like the back of an old outdoor man's neck. The roof shingles were grayed, split and curling. Ted thought of a derelict huddled on a park bench.

"Hello," he called.

A goat peered out from the open door and regarded him with a look of superior, amused and detached curiosity.

"Hello! Hello!"

Nothing.

My God, what will I do if no one's here?

Then the man stood in the doorway. Smiling, he came forward to meet Ted. He looked to be a storybook Alpine peasant herdsman: Heidi's neighbor, waiting for his cue to walk on in *Willam Tell*. He was dressed in loden knee breeches, high gray-wool socks, a collarless shirt, and wore a conical-crowned, green felt hat on the back of his head. His age could have been anything between twenty and forty. He had about three weeks of black stubble on his face. As he came closer, still smiling, Ted could see that his teeth were crooked and blackened.

Ted was not quite sure of what he expected the man to do; possibly he would lead him over some hidden path and down the other side of the mountain or hide him in a cave behind the waterfall. It didn't matter. The man would know some trick.

Ted reached toward him. "*Bitte, können Sie mir hilfen?*"

"*Was?*" The man said, cupping his hand behind his ear.

Ted too went deaf. It seemed so. For a very long time

he looked at the man, hearing nothing but a pounding like a bass drum beaten far off at the end of a cave.

"*Was*?" the man said again and giggled.

Ted studied his face intently. It was unlined except for around the mouth, where it was creased in curves. Ted looked at the man's unfading smile, at his gentle brown eyes that seemed to focus just past the back of Ted's head. Saliva appeared at the corner of the man's mouth. He remembered to swallow, wiped his chin with the heel of his grimy hand, giggled and smiled at Ted again. Ted turned and continued up the path toward the mountain's peak.

THURSDAY, JULY 14 22:50 HOURS—
VIENNA, SALZBURG

On the whole it had been a good year, Tolz thought—
the year of 1742. The war was going well (never mind
how it would end; it was not necessary to know that yet).

The idea for his hobby had occurred to him twelve years
earlier when, over the course of one week, he had happened separately across the facts that Schiller's *The Robbers*
and Mozart's *Abduction from the Seraglio* were produced
in 1782, and also in that year Pope Pius VI had visited
Vienna to argue against the religious reforms the emperor
was making. Tolz had wondered what else had happened
in that particular year, then about what conjunctions of
events had occurred in other years.

At first he had merely consulted encyclopedias, making
out file cards on contemporaneous events. He imagined
that he would draw some kind of chart based on them. But
then the thought came to him of attempting to more fully
relive the past. He began with 1700. He read all he could
find of original material—poetry, plays, essays; he read

every kind of account or history; he listened to the music composed, looked at the pictures painted, visited the buildings constructed during that year. His progress through the past reversed the sense of time of real life: The first years passed quickly because there was less material to assimilate; the later ones more slowly. Soon, he estimated, a year of the past would take longer to live through than one in the present. He felt secure that he would die before reaching 1914.

He had finished the last book on 1742 and sat sipping his hot milk while listening to Goldberg's *Variations* on his phonograph. When the music ended, he turned off the machine, wiped the record and put it away, rinsed his cup and went to bed. Thought of the Erbacher operation in the morning did intrude momentarily, but he closed his mind to it.

The thought was mildly exciting of course. Any operation involving action presented challenges and broke routines. Minutes, even hours, might go by uncounted; not only unboring, but actually interesting. Yet the thought of action was repulsive too. It brought a feeling close to fear. Not a fear of failure—Tolz was expreienced, he was very good. He made mistakes sometimes, but he never failed; not in other people's terms at least.

But beginning an operation meant setting a goal. Achieving the goal meant discovering once again that no action has real purpose; nothing changes except for the worse. Tolz had read Camus; he agreed that the myth of Sisyphus describes man's condition. Being called again to take a turn at rolling the rock filled him with almost overwhelming fatigue and a sense of futility.

He had done what he could to prepare, working even later than usual to clear his desk, going over plans once more with Johann and the people in Salzburg. Then he had put it out of his mind for the rest of the evening—except for that moment before going to bed and once during the night when he awoke from a dream of which he had no remembrance other than that it had been unpleasant.

Rinehardt Erbacher slept poorly too; but it was hope, not despair, that troubled him. He alternated visions of life in Morocco with reviews of the steps that would take him there. He would give the coordinates to the Russians' agents, go to the station for his train home—meeting the American briefly in passing. Then he would pack quickly, hire the local taxi to drive him back to the Salzburg airport and vanish into the sky.

As he had done a dozen times since making his decision, he went over the list of things he would pack. There could be but few, and choosing them was difficult. Clothes were relatively simple since he would buy new ones for the warmer climate; nonetheless, he changed his mind four times about which would be the best to take. More of a problem was in determining which of his books, photographs, letters and souvenirs must be left behind. He was ready to begin a new life—thrilled that he had a new life instead of only death ahead of him. Yet. . . .

The watch given him by his grandmother on his confirmation sixty-some years ago: its crystal scratched, its numbers faded, laying idle for years—could he leave it behind? What about his medal for excellence in geography? Could he become a man without family, childhood, distinction? The picture of Margaritte, who had died of tuberculosis, and her letters from the sanatorium: He had not looked at them in a decade; they were in the back of a bottom drawer. But they were—she was—still with him. Would it not be infidelity to abandon them? Every event or moment or person important enough in his life to have been kept near and tangible to him had to be taken up and then either discarded or found some corner in the one suitcase he would carry. Mentally he packed and repacked.

Then he imagined writing the letter of farewell to his landlady. And rewrote it. He would doze from the effort, awaken with a start and do it all over again to be sure or because he had forgotten what he had decided to say.

The men who for this operation were using the names of "Hartz" and "Schimmel" discussed their plans once more after receiving the call that Erbacher had gone to bed early. They would be employing a sub-agent as backup, and Hartz telephoned him to confirm things while Schimmel checked the car and gear. Except for its speed, the car was not really suitable for this action—a coupe, and red (dark, yet not inconspicuous). But they decided not to bother to arrange for another. Picking up Erbacher ought to be simple.

While both men were excited at the prospect, they were experienced enough to diffuse their nervousness. Hartz poured himself a large portion from a bottle of Martel Cordon Bleu he saved for special occasions and went to bed with a spy novel. Schimmel went to bed with his latest girlfriend. She was as dark-haired and muscular as he, and they wrestled to a mutually satisfying conclusion.

Hermann Tobler required both alcohol and sex. After the bar closed, he took a bottle of American whiskey to his room and ordered two of the girls on his string to come up and do a show and work on him together until he was stupified.

Only Johann Zimmermann was able to think about coming events and yet sleep soundly. He was always happy when Herr Tolz went into action. It was a thrill to see the old man work, and he always learned something. At the same time, he was apprehensive. Herr Tolz was taking a chance by not pulling in Erbacher now. Now they had him. In the morning all the pieces would be moving. Johann understood. In his five years with the bureau—three with Tolz—he had learned that effectiveness is the result not only of knowledge and skill, but of capital as well: nuggets collected and treasured until needed. Favors were such, but incrimination was better. Tolz wanted something on Brunner and Janovich (perhaps to turn them against their KGB employers?) or on the Russians themselves, on the American agent or on his employers. Waiting so as to take them all was clever, but it was dangerous. Johann thought through all of the instructions, going over a street map of Salzburg, until he felt sure there were no flaws. Then he did his push-ups and sit-ups and went to bed and slept until six.

Brunner and Janovich napped in turns, one of them always watching the disco bar. They had been watching ever since their first meeting with Erbacher. They had identified the competition—the dark-haired American—and were prepared to hijack him if his bid won. They continued to watch—ready to protect Erbacher should the American prove a poor loser, ready to check Erbacher should *he* prove false. There was no reason to think he would, except that the possibility was always present with such a man in such a business. And the arrangement *was* peculiar. Neither of them felt any degree of excitement.

SATURDAY, JULY 16 11:20 HOURS— *OBER-FLATTACH*

Hundreds of peaks—black rock, white snow—faded to blue in ranks as far as Ted could see. He knew the names of some of them: brooding Hochalm, serene Sauleck. Behind him was angry Rotzahn, then Kreuzeck. And—back across the main valley, half-veiled in northern cloud, mysterious, ancient and mighty—loomed Ankogel.

He looked out at the mountains to try to calm himself, to keep his eyes from the men climbing after him. He estimated they were about eleven minutes behind. It had been fourteen minutes earlier, but now he needed rest. He had decided it was better to let them gain quickly while he was getting stronger than gradually as he weakened. They were game, he had to give them that. Not dressed for hiking—one of them had at least left his raincoat somewhere along the way—and without proper shoes, still they came along steadily.

He sat just off the trail, leaning against the almost vertical bank of the mountainside. The trail moved up across the bank, back and forth—climbing, not yet scaling. It was the sort of place he might have come to for pleasure. Soon, though, he knew the trail would lead to bare rock. There the technical climbers would begin their sport and he—ordinarily—would have congratulated himself on his better sense and turned around for home.

His despair at not being saved by the half-wit had dissipated in the exertion of the climb. He really felt nothing about the incident now. The futility of depending on someone else was clear once again, but he didn't bother to berate himself for a mistake made under unusual pressure.

The little valley of the *schlucht* was to his right. He could see the road. There was a red car moving up it. *Now the hikers come!* He looked ahead again, across the main valley toward the ranges on its northern side. It was just like a miniature model. Below the peaks, the grass was like soft, yellow-green velvet. Then came patches of evergreens; they might have been made of bottle brushes. There were toylike farms here and there, with tiny humps of haystacks in rows. He looked on down to the highway, fully a mile below. Chips like confetti moved along it.

Suddenly fear shot through him. He clutched the clumps of grass and leaned back hard against the bank. He did not usually have acrophobia, but at that instant he feared he might throw himself off the mountain. The urge to try to fly was almost irresistible. He held tight and looked down at the ground beside him, concentrating on the wild flowers that grew by the hundreds in every square yard.

This is ridiculous! Get ahold of yourself!

He clenched his jaw, relaxed his grip on the grass, pressed firmly against the ground and made himself relax. Then he shifted his gaze down the slope.

They were on schedule. He would rest for three more minutes. He took another drink of water, ate another piece of chocolate. Raising his head, he looked farther out and down, clear to the village on the valley floor. He could see the Platz. He thought of the concert, of band music in a tavern. He thought of people sitting at long tables on long benches, their arms across each other's backs, packed together down the row, swaying with the singing: hot, sweating, close. He longed to be among them.

He saw the church and tried to locate Erica's apartment. Closing his eyes, he felt them nestled together in bed, their arms and legs wrapped around each other, the covers pulled over their heads.

He shook away the vision. It was time to go.

Twenty feet beyond where he had been sitting, the trail leveled. He had reached the ridge leading up to the rocky base of the peak. It was knifelike. The side to his left, going down to the little valley, was steep—probably seventy to eighty degrees. If he had been going to try to escape that way, he should have done so sooner, when the slope was less extreme. That side was grassy and flower-covered. The trail, a groove not two feet wide, ran along about eight feet below the top of the ridge. That top, to his right, was like a saw. Through a gap between points he could see the other side. It was a sheer cliff of red rock. As the ridge rose over the course of the next quarter-mile or more, the saw points became great teeth.

What will I do when I reach the end of the ridge? I'm not a climber! He had no equipment. He knew nothing about mountain climbing. Anger began to replace his fear. *Letting them drive me!* They could kill him as easily that way. He might as well wait and save himself effort. *If I could fight them! But they'll probably stand ten feet away and shoot me.* But even without hope, he could not simply wait for them to come and kill him. He went on.

A hundred yards farther the trail jogged to the right to avoid a place that had been eroded. Passing between two of the teeth it went along the side of the cliff. A steel cable was pinned to the rock as a handrail.

As he went through the teeth, he felt a wave of fear at the height. The path was hardly more than a foot wide, obviously hacked out of the cliff. Beyond that tiny ledge there was nothing—only a straight drop down and an open view to the next ridge a mile or more away. He clutched at the cable and froze. Then fear melted before a flame of hope. Once through that gap and on the cliff side, he couldn't be seen—not until the moment his pursuers came through it too. If there was no escape, at least he had found a place to stand and fight.

He looked around. Loose stones lay on the path, chipped by erosion from the cliff. *Find one—a good heavy one. No. There's more control with a lighter one, something just a pound or two.*

Find the place. About six feet farther along the path from the gap. Back up against the cliff. Look to the right, back the way I came. I'll have to throw the stone to the right with my right arm, overhand.

He stood with his feet apart, holding the cable with his left hand. He rested his right hand, with the rock in it, on his head. He practiced the throw mentally.

Focus on the gap, on a spot on the wall beyond it. Feel what it will be like to throw—my arm whipping out from over my head, my fingers releasing.

Again and again he imagined the action, sensing when his fingers must release the rock to hurl it precisely at that spot.

There was a rush of wind through the grass above his head—not a shrieking or moaning, but a gentle, lonely sound. He looked up to the great peak to his left and then outward again. He had a vision of himself as he might be seen by an eagle soaring high over the ridge—a tiny figure, precarious, perched on a scratch across the vast, sheer cliff. The immensity of the mountain, of the space around him, calmed him.

Then, *They're coming*! He heard a grunt, footfalls. They were moving quickly. They had been fast before but now, having reached nearly level ground, they came on more rapidly. While they were intent on catching him, obviously they didn't expect to do so just then. He heard their heavy breathing.

Brunner rushed through the gap. Earlier, below, he had been prepared to deal with a fellow professional. That his opponent was incompetent but yet had escaped him created a combination of contempt and chagrin that made him reckless.

Ted's leg stiffened; he threw his weight from left to right and whipped out his arm. His fingers released and spun the stone, hurling it across the span of three feet from their tips to Brunner's head. He couldn't miss. Brunner did not have time to register surprise fully, much less to duck, before the stone smashed into his forehead. He just crumpled against the cliff and bounced away, dropping a thousand feet or more.

Janovich had been immediately behind. He jerked back, simultaneously flattening himself against the bank around on the other side and drawing his gun.

Ted had hoped for something like that. In the brief moment when the second man did not foolishly rush into peril, he was going to run farther up the path. Instead, he did something unplanned.

He felt as though his reactions had been speeded up while the rest of the world barely moved. Even as Brunner was drifting down along the face of the mountain on his progress to the rocky debris below, Ted studied the side of the cliff back down the trail beyond the gap. With no sense of urgency he took note that although the ledge upon which the trail was laid narrowed, it actually extended for about three feet over there before disappearing back into the cliff face. Without giving the matter much thought, he stepped past the gap and onto the extension.

Janovich waited, gun ready. His back was pressed hard against the bank, his neck strained as he looked over his shoulder. His arm was extended, fingers rigid, gripping the pistol.

Nothing happened. Ted did not jump through the gap at him, and Janovich was certainly not going to rush through himself to discover firsthand what had hit his partner.

Ted expected him to do something eventually—to come through or go back. Either way, he was sure he would hear him.

But he heard nothing. For a long while he heard nothing. His legs began to shake. He was standing on less than a foot of ledge over that thousand-foot drop, looking over a wide gulf. His back was tight against the cliff. There was no cable there—he had nothing to hold to.

Still he heard nothing. Perspiration ran down his body from under his arms and the wind chilled him. *Why doesn't he do something? What if he's slipped away and I didn't hear him? What if I'm standing here needlessly, getting shakier, my leg muscles cramping, until I topple over?* It seemed absurd to stand there hiding from no one, not really in danger, and then to fall and die only because of something that didn't exist. *He's gone. He must be gone. I should step around the ridge and look.*

But what if he's right there, just on the other side, his back five feet through the ridge from my back, waiting for me to break first?

It was a test of wills, he decided. He would be the stronger. He *would* be. His legs began to quiver from tension; after his exertion, they were stiffening in the cold air. He would have to relax. He tried to put more weight on one leg, to let up on the other. He couldn't. The ledge seemed to be growing narrower under his feet, and his body would not obey a command to move in a way that might put him off balance.

Still he heard nothing.

No! There's something! Hard breathing. Where is it coming from? Automatically he looked left and right.

It was from above! Janovich had waited on the other side as Ted had waited, listening, wondering like Ted, until an idea had occurred to him. He had turned to the bank and—watching carefully to ensure that Ted didn't spring out to surprise him—had clambered up the few feet necessary to allow him to peer over the edge and along the path. Ted heard him grunt, and there was a scratching sound as he hauled himself up with his elbows so he could look out.

The top of the ridge overhung the cliff slightly and the trail was cut in. Ted tried to press himself farther back into the rock's face. He wedged his fingers into the cracks behind him. There was nothing to grip but hurting fingertips against rock edges made him feel more secure. Above him Janovich scooted himself farther up, leaning on his right arm. His hand, holding the gun, projected out beyond the edge, scarcely more than two feet above Ted's head. It swung from side to side as he shifted weight to climb and seemed to threaten the entire range of mountains. Ted might have grabbed for the hand but he realized that he would more likely throw himself off the cliff than pull his enemy over. He could only stand there and stare up.

Janovich had looked up the path first but had meant to check below too. The gun dipped as he put weight on his arm to pull himself higher. A pebble was loosened, dropping just past Ted's nose. Janovich's hand pushed farther out; half of his forearm cleared the cliff as he moved in preparation for pulling himself up to look over the edge. Ted heard him grunt again as he leaned on the arm. Suddenly a piece of rock cracked and fell off; clumps of dirt and sand showered down. Janovich jerked back. He deliberated. Those falling stones had struck nothing that he could hear. As far as he could see, the cliff dropped sheerly below him and there were no places along the path where Ted could be hiding: He must have run ahead.

Janovich was not keen to follow alone. On the other hand, he was not keen to return to his employer and report that he had not followed. Ted heard him slide down the bank.

Silence again.

I should be able to hear whatever he's doing!

Silence.

Across the gap Ted saw a left hand appear, sliding along the rock's face; then a wrist, with a watch of many dials; then a forearm. Fingers curled into a crack to gain purchase. Suddenly Janovich sprang around onto the path, his back to Ted, firing three shots straight up it. Echoes ricocheted from cliff to cliff.

Ted was four feet away. He took a gigantic step, brought his right knee up as high as he could and smashed his heel into the base of Janovich's spine. Janovich's arms flung out. His legs buckled. He fell to his knees, one knee on the edge of the path, the other missing it, throwing him off balance. He started to fall, caught the cable with his left hand, dropped and hung at full length. He twisted himself around, his chest against the cliff, his feet scratching for a toehold. He looked at Ted across his left arm. Instinctively he had kept the gun clutched in his right hand.

Ted looked at the man suspended there. Janovich's lips were pulled back—stretched to white lines framing his teeth. His eyes looked up, and although they seemed to say many things, pleading was not one of them.

Even as Janovich raised the gun, Ted smashed his heel into the man's face and then kicked with the steel toe of his hiking boot against the back of the man's left hand. Once was enough.

FRIDAY, JULY 15 10:00 HOURS— *SALZBURG, VIENNA*

"Taxi pulling up." Janovich nodded to the left. Brunner sat up, pressing the lever to bring the back of the seat upright behind him. He had been awake but with his eyes half-closed. He looked along Janovich's line of sight across the corner of the street where they were parked, toward the Toblers' disco bar where the cab was drawing up. "Good," he grunted. "I was beginning to think he got Tobler to get him a girl to celebrate with. Then we'd have had to wait all day for him to move."

"No. We'd only have to wait until the ambulance got here."

"If he called a taxi, he probably *is* going to the station to go home."

"Fine. Then I'm wrong," Janovich answered without turning his head. He was behind the wheel. He always did the driving; Brunner's temperament was too variable. Usually he was good-humored but sometimes other drivers angered him, and then he became aggressive and reckless.

107

"Maybe after all he *was* so nervous only from thinking about all that money."

"You ever been down to Kärnten?"

"No."

"It's the sticks. Not as bad as Steirmark but— The girls don't shave their legs. Klagenfurt's not too bad. Then there's this Kreuzeck area. They got valleys up in the mountains there; you talk to the people, they want to know who's emperor now."

"How long will it take us to get there?"

"With the autobahn, two hours to Bad Gastein. We have to put the car on a flatcar there and go through the mountain by rail. Twenty or thirty minutes. It all depends, then: We get a map, see where the coordinates are. If we have to go around to the south side of the *gruppe*— If we fart around with Erbacher all morning, don't get there until night. . . ."

"We'll know about Erbacher pretty quick. He gets into his taxi, goes to the station, gets on his train—or. . . . We know, we move."

"Still not moving, sir."

"Thank you." Tolz sat in a molded plastic chair, the weight of his upper body resting on his arms crossed on the table in front of him. He nodded his head slightly in silent affirmation, and reflections from the dim down lights glinted off the rims of his glasses. Johann Zimmermann sat a meter away to his right. Two junior officers, friends of Johann, had—by his influence—been allowed to observe. They were behind, very quiet. Also present of course were the three operators for the room's systems. Six men besides Tolz, none of them his equal or superior in rank. Although Tolz was universally respected for expertise and exuded confidence in his trade, he could not tolerate the presence of any who might presume to question or criticize him while he was working.

"Confirmation from the agency: Taxi has been ordered to take the fare to the railroad station."

"Thank you."

A detail map of the area of Salzburg that lay between the disco bar and the station was projected on a large screen that Tolz faced but he didn't seem to look at it. Johann did occasionally, only to confirm the one he carried in his head.

"So." Tolz decided. "Attention. B team will depart position, on command, ahead of subject. Lead to the railroad. As instructed, take Erbacher on command to be given immediately after he completes contact with the American."

"Understood, sir." The voice of one of the men in the sedan parked around the corner from the bar came over the speaker as though he were sitting next to Tolz.

"Tell the taxi agency to instruct the driver that any change of destination must be reported instantly, but that it may be made."

"Yes, sir." One of the communications men spoke into his mouthpiece.

"A team, continue observation of your subjects. I expect they will follow Erbacher to the station. If so, you will join the procession. Take your subjects on command, to be given with command to B team."

"Understood, sir," came from the A leader, who controlled two cars, each with three men. One was parked a block behind Brunner and Janovich, the other around the corner to their right.

"Attention. C team?"

"No change, sir. Subject remains seated on bench farthest south of station entrance."

The American representative had arrived at the station

forty-five minutes early. He was rightly sure he hadn't been followed: The man selling newspapers, the one handling baggage, and the third, who dispatched taxis, were there before he arrived.

"Good." Tolz nodded once more. "Very well, my friends. It now remains only to wait for poor Rinehardt."

Erbacher drew out the long envelope and extended it. "In appreciation of your assistance and your hospitality, dear . . . August." He had decided to be generous. In the first place, it was wise to leave the Toblers well-disposed toward him. Second, he enjoyed being a multimillionaire who could tip generously.

"Oh, Rinehardt, no, no! This is not necessary," August protested as he took hold of the other end. "It is enough to have been of service to an old friend; to have relived, a little, the old days. No, please."

"I insist." Erbacher released his grip.

"Rinehardt, truly . . ." August left the thought dangling, not quite sure of what he could say, truly. He still held the envelope out before him. It did not feel very thick between thumb and forefinger. He shook it as though about to thrust it back at Erbacher. Of course it might contain only few notes but those of large denomination. Unfortunately, he would not be able to look inside until after Erbacher had gone. "Rinehardt, Rinehardt, I thank you." He waved the gift once more as though he might yet throw it down, then crammed it into his pocket.

Hermann stood behind his uncle, both of them facing Erbacher. He noted the place of deposit and the singular thanks. They were as expected, so he had no sudden disappointment to make smiling difficult. Actually, his smile came with uncharacteristic ease, as he anticipated laughing last.

"Must you go, Rinehardt? Now that your business is

finished, why don't you enjoy Salzburg for a day or two?''

"Thank you, August; but no. All of this has made me very tired. I wish to go home to my peaceful little village and rest. Perhaps another time. . . .''

Rinehardt Erbacher and August Tobler had been brought up in an age of manners, so despite the fact that each of them wanted the parting ended instantly, they were obliged to go on for several minutes more. Finally, though, Erbacher managed to get out of the bar and into the taxi. He slammed the door and settled back, serenely unaware that the act had sent flashes of electromagnetic energy to Vienna and back and caused explosions in the cylinders of automobiles all around him.

SATURDAY, JULY 16, 15:40 HOURS—
OBER-FLATTACH

When Ted came again to the site where he had experienced the acrophobia, he looked up and outward. He had walked back along the ridge to that point directly, steadily, in a state of shock. He had watched his footing, step by step, on the narrow path. When he looked up and saw that expanse again, suddenly he had to sit down. Not from fear of height this time, but from fear of feeling the horror of what had happened. He was being successful at keeping that horror away. While walking back, all of it had seemed distant, outside himself. Perhaps that was because it was so inexplicable and had happened so quickly. More likely it was because he was well-practiced at withdrawing himself from any unpleasantness. But when he looked up, the view seemed to force reality upon him.

The afternoon sun slanted at a low angle and its yellow light made the contours of the mountains deep, the colors rich: yellow-green on western faces, dark blue-green on the other sides. In such contrast, so molded, they were vivid beyond ordinary reality. Sensuous. The vibrant glow of every ridge against deep valley shadow seemed an inner light. The air was absolutely clear; no haze or heat wave gave an illusion of motion. There was no wind to sway tree tops. No cloud drifted. Every peak, every rock—he felt aware even of blades of grass—was as still and intense as a moment when breath is held and heart races. The very stillness seemed to testify to surging life within. It was not scenery, not background in an illustration for a fairy tale. Real, real—it had all been real!

He clamped his hand over his eyes to shut it out, but those men moved behind it, chasing him still, and he fought for his life again, and they fell. . . .

No!

He looked once more at the mountains. The little farm buildings and amber haystacks on the nearer slopes stood out in sharp relief. He could even see a farmer at work— defined as much by his long shadow as by his true figure; he was probably mowing grass with a scythe as his ancestors had mowed grass on that hillside for a thousand years past. Ted sat watching silently . . . and suddenly he found himself weeping. He was very glad to be alive.

After a while he rose and went on. Going down was as hard as climbing up had been. He was tired. And now, in addition, there was a psychological reaction to contend with. He couldn't deny it. He had enough control to suppress it, but it was there.

He kept on at an even pace, one foot after the other. A chain of thoughts seemed linked to his steps. *Why* had this happened? He didn't know, couldn't imagine, and that was the greatest horror of it. What should he do? Flee, go home, hide and be safe! But what if he couldn't get away? What if there were more than two men after him? Although he couldn't begin to find the reason those two had hunted him, they must have had one. That reason might still exist. Someone else might follow him. He might be in danger yet.

He stopped to scan the slopes around him, wondering if he did want to reach the woods again—wondering what might be concealed within them. But he knew there had been only two chasing him. *On the mountain, yes; what about back in the village though? How can I know? I must have help.*

He had to go to the police. *But what do I tell them? "Bitte, Ich habe. . . ." What's German for "kill?" Missed that one in my language guide. "Good morning, Mr. Police Officer, how are you today?" "Fine, thank you, Mr. Tourist. And you?" "I am very well too, Mr. Police Officer. I have just killed two men."*

Just killed two men! He had never in his life killed anything larger than a mouse, and today he had killed two men!

He didn't feel guilty about it. Not that he had expected to. He had fought in self-defense. But he would have expected to feel something stronger than he did. He supposed he didn't because their attack had neither the calculation of a crime for profit nor the logical irrationality of revenge or passion. It seemed more like he had deactivated machines than killed men.

But they must have had some motive. Why were they trying to kill me?

Back to the beginning again, and on around with suppositions and variations all down the mountain.

There were two cars at the bottom of the trail: the gray one and the red one he had seen driving up later. He assumed the red one belonged to hikers and hoped he might see them to ask for a ride. But it seemed they must still be up on one of the trails. He expected to see the old woman, but there was no one around the buildings. He did not want to meet her and have to try communicating again.

He resigned himself to trudging all the way down the valley—another hour's walk. At least it was less steep than the trail behind him. He passed the cabin and was walking along the row of barns.

"Mr. Barstow." It came from behind him.

Ted threw himself to the right, into the space between two barns. He hit the ground with his shoulder and rolled. He didn't think about it. The realization, while he was coming down the mountain, that there might be more people after him had been enough.

Keeping low, running on all fours, he dashed to the end of the barn, crawled around behind it, stood up and flattened himself against the rough wood. He thought about breaking for the woods. He estimated them to be about sixty yards away. And he would have to keep running— uphill—once he reached them before he would find real cover.

A man came out of the cabin. "Mr. Barstow. Mr. Barstow, it's all right." He walked down the path toward the barns. He was tall, well-built, athletic-looking. "I mean you no harm. Really." His voice was not particularly deep but it was rich and warm. "Truly."

He was almost to the barn. The woods were too far away.

"Hold it right there!" Ted thought about it before saying it, so his voice wouldn't squeak. "Take another step, I'll blow your head off!"

The man stopped, turned toward the sound of Ted's voice. He grinned in that direction. "I certainly wouldn't want you to do that, Mr. Barstow, especially as we haven't been introduced." He raised his arms slowly, forearms leading, hands dangling at first, then brought up with a relaxed flip. He was bareheaded and his hair was golden in the late afternoon sunlight. "I understand your concern,

Mr. Barstow, but this really isn't necessary. I'm on your side. I'm a policeman.''

Ted didn't believe him. He was too handsome. He might have been James Bond, but he did not look like a policeman.

The man stared directly at the place where he thought Ted was. The openness of his countenance modulated. He tipped his head forward as though he sought to beam to Ted some light from the star of his sincerity. "I am on your side," he repeated.

Ted was almost ashamed of himself, but he was still suspicious. "I want you to turn around and lie down with your arms stretched out ahead of you." He would get the man into that position, then run like hell for the trees.

The man lifted his head again. "I couldn't do that, Mr. Barstow. My tailor would never forgive me." He spoke lightly, the tone of mock seriousness making it a joke between them instead of defiance. Yet clearly he was serious. Fawn-colored trousers, a lightly checked hacking-jacket, beige turtleneck pullover: Even from a distance the crispness and the care of cutting were obvious. The path was dusty, there were cow droppings. No one of any taste and intelligence could ask him to lie in that path; it was unthinkable. Ted felt like an oaf.

And the man seemed to be such a gentleman. "I will lean up against a wall if that will make you feel better, or turn out my pockets, or whatever, to show I'm not armed. If that will put your mind at rest. I want you to have confidence in me, Mr. Barstow. There really isn't any need for you to hide yourself back there behind that barn. I'm sure you've been through a great deal today, and naturally you're a bit nervous."

Ted was amazed. The other man was totally exposed, supposedly under a gun, and yet he was the one giving assurances!

He went on in that manner, serious and sincere but with a shading of benevolent mockery: the tone one uses when talking to an old friend who—uncharacteristically—is behaving like an idiot. Ted thought he should try to be decisive, to bark commands. But it seemed rude to interrupt. He tried to determine what he should do. He couldn't show himself and reveal himself to be unarmed. And he couldn't make the man go away. He couldn't *make* the man do anything, except to the extent that he felt threatened.

And the man didn't seem to feel threatened at all. He seemed quite relaxed, standing still and keeping his hands up only to humor Ted so *he* wouldn't feel threatened.

Ted was just beginning to suspect that the man was holding *him* in place when suddenly he heard a crunch from behind. He jerked his head around. A second man stood fifteen feet to the side. He had a sub-machine gun aimed at the center of Ted's chest.

This man looked like a wrestler. Not "athletic," a true jock. Close-cut hair made his head seem small despite the width of the brow and jaw. His neck broadened from behind his ears, flowing with only a slight change of angle into shoulders as wide as the length of an ax handle. Ted felt his eyes looking at him as though X-raying his insides for the exact location of vital organs.

The jock called out, *"Hier."*

"Gut. Ich komme," the other man answered.

Involuntarily Ted looked back. A pistol had been produced from somewhere under that skillfully cut jacket. The man moved in an arc that kept the two men free to shoot without endangering one another. He stopped a dozen feet away.

"I really hope you'll forgive my little fib about not being armed, but you understand, under the circumstances . . ." He gave a tiny nod that was almost a wink. Of course Ted would forgive him. Obviously he would have done the same thing himself. Obviously he had—in reverse. "You seem to have been fibbing too, Mr. Barstow. You don't have a gun at all. You're an old wool-puller yourself!" The man's grin was full, his eyes wide with delight. Ted felt he was expressing joy at finding that the two of them, in this remote place, were fraternity brothers.

"It's all right, Schimmel." The pistol vanished. "We really are on your side, Mr. Barstow. Allow me to introduce myself properly. I am Colonel Hartz of the Austrian National Security Bureau."

Ted had a glimpse of a slim alligator-skin wallet that appeared, opened to show a card with black-letter printing and the Austrian eagle and then disappeared. The man *was* James Bond.

"And this is Sergeant Schimmel."

Schimmel clicked his heels and touched two fingers to his forehead. "It is my pleasure," he said, giving identical weight to each syllable.

Hartz said, "We've come a long way to help you. We thought we were too late. But it seems we could have saved the trip. Ah . . . exactly where are Janovich and Brunner?"

"The men who followed me?"

"Yes. We assumed . . . that's why we were under cover when you came down. Should we be watching still?"

"No."

"They won't be coming down?"

"They're already down. They're at the bottom of the cliff below Rotzahn."

Hartz's face went blank with surprise. "My compliments!" To Schimmel, "Janovich and Brunner!" Then he drew the corners of his mouth apart to make dimples at the sides of his even, white teeth. "Mr. Barstow, I'm beginning to suspect that you are one hell of a fellow. You must tell us all about it.''

Hartz was a professional, competent to judge, and his straightforward manner made false modesty impossible. Yes, it was clear to Ted, he *must* be one hell of a fellow. Speaking as such he said, ''Colonel Hartz, if you will just get me a cold beer and a sandwich, I will tell you everything I know. And what I don't know, I'll make up.''

''Intelligence, Mr. Barstow. Pure intelligence.'' Hartz grinned. ''My father had the intelligence to get us to America in thirty-seven. I had to learn German when we came back. They tell me I speak it with an accent. I still visit the states regularly.''

So that was why he spoke unaccented and idiomatic English.

''We were trailing Janovich and Brunner. We made the usual inquiries; the tourist office was on the list, naturally. Fraulein Stendler identified Brunner, connected him with you and told us where you had gone. Fraulein Stendler seemed very concerned about you.'' He looked at Ted and smiled knowingly—not with a leer, but with an appreciation by one man of the world to another. ''She's a very attractive young woman.''

That was his explanation of how he knew who Ted was and why he and Schimmel had followed him.

''That's the mystery. Obviously you had no connection with those men. You're some sort of an innocent bystander. Probably a case of mistaken identity. The most we can do is to ask some routine questions about your activities since you arrived in Austria and hope something you say may tie in with other information.''

That was all he offered Ted as to the ''Why?''

They had driven back out of the valley. They sat in the car now, just above a country *gästhaus* screened by a hedge. "If you don't mind, it might be best not to be seen for a while." Schimmel was sent for Ted's beer and sandwich. He brought back food for all of them. "We don't want you drinking alone. And they also starve who only stand and wait."

It was very jolly. Ted had two bottles of beer. He told them about the chase up the mountain and the fight. He sat in the back seat of the car. He was impressed by it, a BMW—one of the expensive ones. It had comfortable seats, padded all around with dark-gray velour. He thought the car smelled like the ink on money. There wasn't much leg room so he leaned against the left side with his legs across the seat, his boots off. Schimmel sat behind the wheel. Hartz leaned back against the right door, his arm along the back of the seat.

Hartz's hand was suntanned. No, Ted thought, Hartz's hand had been bronzed by the sun. Although his nails looked to have been manicured, the fingers were too strong to tolerate any suggestion of effeminacy. Hartz was older than he had first appeared to be. There were many silver threads among the gold. And the dimples, the cleft in his chin and the little lines around his eyes were there always— not just when he opened that smile. There was a slight sagging and some fat. But he looked the way Ted would like to look at fifty. He looked the way Ted would have liked to look at any age since he was fifteen.

They had sausage sandwiches and Schimmel had brought a round cut from one of the good Austrian smoked cheeses. They broke off pieces, passing it back and forth between themselves. When Ted was finished with his story, they made him tell it again and asked questions and made jokes. He fleshed out the facts he had already given by adding his impressions. He imitated the old woman, which they thought was very funny; and the half-wit, which they thought hilarious; and the goat which brought tears streaming down their faces. When he got to the battle on the ridge (as he thought of it), Schimmel stopped him several times. His English seemed slow and he asked for parts to be repeated. He appeared to be extremely interested—professionally, Ted assumed. Ted didn't do or say anything funny when telling them about that part. When he finished, they were all silent for a moment.

Hartz was looking at Ted, his head on one side. He shifted forward, staring more intently. "Mr. Barstow," he said, "I told you we were on the same side. I'm very glad of it. You truly are quite a man."

There in the car—warm, comfortable, relaxed—Hartz's compliment seemed plausible. Ted let it settle over him and it felt good. He resolved to think about it dispassionately and in detail later. For the moment, though, he gave Hartz's evaluation the benefit of the doubt. He took another swallow of beer, looked the man straight in the eye, and said, "Thanks, Colonel. I thought myself it wasn't a bad morning's work." They grinned at each other.

Hartz stretched his arm to reveal a thick gold band and a very thin watch. The previously blank face glowed at his touch. He grimaced, shrugged at Ted and nodded to Schimmel.

The sausage and cheese were spicy and Ted must have been dehydrated anyway, so that last swallow of beer he took was from his third bottle. And he was very tired. And he was relaxed after a day of strenuous physical exertion and emotional tension. And the car was so warm. And he felt himself to be among friends . . . companions. All this may explain why he fell asleep and didn't question where they were taking him.

FRIDAY, JULY 15 10:10 HOURS—
SALZBURG, VIENNA

"The taxi is pulling away."

"Attention, B team: Go."

"Yes, sir." The blue VW pulled away, turned right and was traveling toward the thoroughfare at the end of the street of bars even as the taxi driver tipped his flag and checked the rear-view mirror. He could see a tan Ford Escort at the intersection behind, but it was far enough away that he did not hesitate to pull out.

Janovich let the taxi get a block ahead, then turned the corner. When *he* was a block ahead, the brown Audi Fox came out from behind and then the black one turned in after it. Once on the thoroughfare, the black Audi dropped back for the first third of the way, then overtook the brown one and let it fall back for the second third. The brown Audi would come up again when they all approached the station.

Mid-morning traffic was not so dense as to make the operation difficult; to the contrary, there was just enough movement to screen it. Janovich checked his mirrors regularly. He had no reason to suspect that he was being followed; he did it unconsciously as professional routine. Nothing in the pattern of cars behind troubled him.

"Yeah, you see?" Brunner had accepted the necessity of watching Erbacher, but he hadn't liked it. Back in Vienna there awaited a possible deal for the sale of a case of MPi 69 machine guns to some Hondurans. An assignment from the KGB took precedence, but he wanted to finish it and return. "He's going straight to the station. He's just an old fart. It was just the idea of having to get it up again that gave him the shakes."

Erbacher was shaking. He clutched the small valise on the seat beside him, but trying to use it to still his hands seemed only to drive the tremors up into his whole body. He shook with joy, with exhilaration over his success. He had pulled it off! It had been confirmed by his bank. In this one last transaction he had acquired more wealth than he had in years of grubbing in the garbage heap of black-marketing and petty espionage. It was not a profession his background had prepared him for. He had endured the sordidness, betrayed his family—Muti's hope, Vati's pride, Margaritte's faith in him. He had debased himself to build his hoard so he could live at last under the pure, sugar-crystal snow in his village. And now, when that had turned to ash and he himself had seemed like the burned-down butt of a cheap cigar, he had proven to be a phoenix.

And he shook with fear too. Anyone might who was attempting such deception, taking such risk. Anyone might fear—even the most confident agent imagined by the cinema, and Rinehardt Erbacher knew he was not any such.

To him, the drive to the station was a purgatory. If he could reach his destination safely, control himself and conduct the final business, he would be admitted to paradise.

He quivered. He perspired. He chewed his lower lip continuously. His pulse pounded, his ears rang. Shapes, colors, sounds flashed past him without distinction.

"B team here. We are at the station. Taking positions."

The VW pulled to the curb in front of the station's entrance. One man emerged from the back carrying a small case, another came from the front. The supposed traveler and his associate chatted together easily and strolled southward.

The taxi dispatcher spoke into his radio. "B team in place."

"Thank you."

"Erbacher's here. Taxi at entrance. Paying driver."

"A team here. Subjects pausing at north end of pull-in to station."

A-1, the black Audi, had no option but to wait as Janovich halted. In the through lane, A-2 held back out of the subject's mirrors. There was no apparent reason for such pausing, and drivers behind sounded their horns and mouthed imprecations as they pulled around.

Back in the Vienna control room, Tolz sat without moving, staring at the projected map as though seeing through it to the station itself. Behind him a young man came into the room. He tiptoed to the table, handed Johann a message and backed away. Johann glanced at the paper, then sharply at Tolz, then put it down on the table to one side.

"Erbacher leaving the taxi now. Just standing, looking around."

The news dealer came out of his booth to check and rearrange his stock. The baggage handler moved down the platform, pushing an empty cart before him. He parked it halfway between the entrance and the south end of the

platform, where the American agent was sitting, not looking at Erbacher.

Erbacher stood facing the entrance, momentarily be-
fuddled. Had he said north end or south end? South, yes.
Which direction was south? He swung his head from side
to side, squinting. *Ah, yes. There.* He turned toward the
bench where the young "average-sized," dark-haired man
sat alone, staring ahead, ignoring the people around him.

Erbacher turned and lumbered to the bench.

"That's him! The Ami! You were right!"

"Are you sure?" Janovich leaned over, trying to see
past his partner.

"I'm sure. Drive!"

"Erbacher has gone to the wrong—"

"A team here. Subjects moving away from station!"
Cutting over the dispatcher's report.

"A team, take them!"

"—way. He went north! He's talking—"

The brown Audi shot forward. A Peugeot that had been
attempting to pass it screeched its brakes and blared its
horn as it scraped the Audi's side. The Audi driver braked,
then accelerated again. Janovich glanced into his side mirror;
when he saw what had happened, he instinctively went
into second and floored the gas. His eyes swept the road
ahead, took in his chances. Tires shrieked and burned off
blue smoke as he darted away, then spun left toward the
opening of Ferdinand Porsche Strasse opposite the station
entrance. He cut across two lanes of oncoming traffic. The
driver of a heavy Mercedes in the near lane was able to
brake, swerve, and avoid collision. The smaller car in the
far lane also swerved but still hit the right rear of Janovich's
Ford. The two vehicles glanced apart, Janovich's fishtailing.
He kept the gas down, got traction and hurtled into the
side street. The other car bounced into the side of the

Mercedes and both screeched as a single barrier into the path of the Audi.

Crash of sheet metal, shatter of glass. And crump and smash again as the Peugeot hit the Audi's rear. And then again as someone else stood on his brakes, managed to stop inches from the Mercedes before being hit himself by another driver with slower reflexes.

SATURDAY, JULY 16 19:50 HOURS—
OBER-FLATTACH

Slam!

Ted started awake, frightened and confused. The car had stopped. He saw the back of Schimmel's head. Hartz was gone. What was going on? The car moved forward again, through shadow. Ted swung himself up, trying to peer through the rear window. The clear evening sky seemed torn away, ripped along a jagged line halfway down, with a black void below. Then he realized they were in some kind of walled enclosure.

Hartz came back and opened the door. "Had a pleasant nap?"

"Yeah. Well, I guess I did drop off." Ted felt embarrassed, awkward. He fumbled for his boots and tried to get them on in the narrow space behind the front seat. He had to twist his foot and he banged his head against the back of the seat.

"Here." Hartz tipped the seat forward. "Easier?"

"Thanks." *Why didn't I think of that?* Ted managed to

get his boots on the correct feet finally, and more or less tied. He jackknifed out the door, half-tripping on the sill, and blinked around him.

They were in a courtyard surrounded by crenelated walls of dark gray-brown crudely dressed stone. At one side was a stone building—a tower—a castle! They were in *the* castle, the one on the hill over the village. Ted had seen it only from a distance but he recognized the tower at once. It was a square column with gabled turrets high above that projected out at each corner, and there was a pyramidal roof over all. That roof was unmistakable. It looked to him like the crude crown worn by some dark lord of the Dark Ages, who wore a cape of black bearskin and had a hawk perched on his shoulder.

"Wow."

"It isn't much, but it suits us."

"I never expected to get . . . I thought it was privately owned."

"It is. By a dentist in Salzburg, I understand. They tell me he's seldom here. As you can appreciate, we'd like to keep this affair among ourselves. This place may be a little on the theatrical side, but it's the only one we could find on short notice where we were sure no one would notice us."

Ted was amazed and delighted. Ever since poring over the illustrations in his childhood books of fairy tales, he had loved castles. He had looked up wistfully at this one—perched high on a crag above the village, rising out of the dark forest, protecting, commanding. He had thought about the Black Knight who must have lived there all alone. He had never expected to be inside of it. He was about to say all that to Hartz but decided it seemed romantic and childish.

Schimmel had gone to the door. Later Ted realized he must have been picking the lock. He got it open.

It was a fine castle door, with herringbone panels of deep-brown wood between massive strapping timbers studded with wrought-iron bolts. It made a heavy grinding noise as it swung on its leaf-shaped hinges.

They went into the two-story structure that contained the living quarters. It was built into a corner and along one wall of the courtyard, and from it the tower rose to a height of sixty or seventy feet.

Ted had expected—hoped—to find standing suits of armor and swords on the walls. Disappointingly, the room they entered was furnished in a contemporary style. There were soft leather couches, a glass-and-chrome table and a few antiques for accent. There was an oriental carpet on the floor. The floor, at least, was stone.

Perhaps something about the smartness of the room reminded him. "Erica! I'm supposed to be having dinner with Erica—with Fraulein Stendler."

"Indeed?"

"Yes. What time is it? We said eight o'clock."

Hartz gave life to his watch again. "It's not quite that yet. We certainly wouldn't want you to miss one glorious moment with the delightful fraulein. We'll make this as brief as possible."

"But— Is there a phone? I'd better call her. She'll be worried. Especially since you asked about me this morning."

Hartz's grin faded. He looked at Schimmel. "*Hast gehört?*"

"*Ja.*" Schimmel raised his head slightly. Hartz went over to him and they spoke together. They were turned away from Ted but Hartz kept him in view the whole time.

He came back, smiling reassuringly. "Yes. Well, we don't want the lovely lady worrying about you. We'll give her a call." Schimmel glanced around and started to cross the room to the telephone he had spotted.

"I'd like to talk to her myself."

"Schimmel will give her your best. Why don't you just sit down and—"

"I'd just like to—"

"Sit down, Hollings."

Ted had turned to follow Schimmel. The tone of Hartz's voice stopped him, although the sense of the words didn't register. He turned back.

Hartz was giving him the full display—his upper and lower teeth together in what passed for a grin. "That's what I said: Hollings."

Ted stared uncomprehendingly for a moment, then started toward him, his hand moving out in a questioning gesture. "I don't under—" This time he saw it. It came from under the vent at the right side of Hartz's jacket. Ted didn't know much about those things, but he recognized it as a European type: Luger, or Mauser, or Walther.

Hartz's dimples deepened. "Sit down, please. I insist."

Blocks of stone, heavier than two men—some that six couldn't lift, some that must have been stacked by a giant—Ted felt them all on his heart.

Hartz spoke as smoothly as ever but now his voice had a cold ring. Ted wasn't sure whether that was his own perception or reflection from the stone. His head to one side, Hartz gestured to those walls, to the heavily beamed ceiling. "We really don't have to play out this setting— with Schimmel coming back in a black hood, bringing tongs and pincers."

Ted tried to speak. He wet his lips so that he could say something. He was still in shock; he couldn't understand— no, without even trying to understand, he couldn't believe the simple facts. He would have thought it was a nightmare except for his hands. His wrists were wired to the thick chair legs at his sides.

They had guided him through doors and along passages to this room in the bottom of the tower; guided him without touching him—just nodding and pointing with the pistol—and he went like a sleepwalker.

"If you insist, we probably can find an old iron boot around here somewhere. But it will be so much easier . . ."

The numbness in Ted's wrists had become a throbbing ache. The emotional and mental numbness was passing too, ballooning into a pain greater than that in his wrists. *How could I have let this happen? How could I have trusted them?*

He was afraid, but he gave Miss McCartney his painting and she said it was beautiful. But later she had shown it to Mrs. Baker and they had laughed and laughed.

Then Bill Whittlesey complimented him for a new idea on an account. He offered to take it upstairs for Ted. His eyes sparkled, he slapped Ted's back, and Ted went out that evening and got a little drunk, and planned new campaigns, and reorganized the agency, and imagined being rich. And he got a five-hundred-dollar bonus for suggesting an idea that made Bill Whittlesey a vice-president.

And Janice. "Yes, I've been seeing Jerry Spasky. You noticed. You finally looked up and noticed. Well, as a matter of fact, I've been *sleeping* with him. What do you think about that? You always have to *think* about everything. What are you going to *do* about it? Are you going to *do* anything? Do you really care? Do you really care about *anything*?"

Ted had thought he could protect himself, but he had been caught once more. He had to understand that so he would never let himself be caught again. How had it happened? *Why did I trust him?*

". . . your situation and simply tell us."

That's it! I trusted. It doesn't matter why!

"Hollings, you really must take hold."

I really must take hold.

Ted pulled against the wires to get the pain back into his hands, and then ignored it. He looked directly at Hartz. "My name is not Hollings. My name is Ted Barstow. You've made a mistake."

Hartz regarded him for a moment and then grinned. "You do that very well."

"Go to my hotel room. Get my passport."

Hartz tipped his head, then looked up ruefully. "Which one? I have six myself."

"I am Ted Barstow."

"It isn't going to work."

They looked at each other in silence. After a while Hartz spoke as one demonstrating infinite patience in dealing with a naughty and very stupid child. "We know your name. We knew Erbacher would make contact with you at the station. We were there. We saw you together." Pause. "We're not guessing, Hollings, we know."

"Who is Erbacher?"

Suddenly Hartz took a step forward and kicked with the side of his shoe against Ted's left hand. Then he stepped back, shaking his head regretfully. "Sorry. I've been trying to give up that sort of thing." He gave Ted that little nod and smiled. "You really know how to get to a guy's weak spot." He smoothed down the front of his pullover. "Now, we saw you there. Brunner and Janovich must have seen you. God knows who all saw you. Erbacher is not up to standard anymore. When he went out to meet you, there must have been so many people following him they should have chartered a bus. We saw you together on the bench. He left you. You got up directly and came here to Ober-Flattach, the same as Brunner and Janovich did. It really is pointless to pretend."

Ted could think of nothing to say. He was afraid Hartz would kick him again.

After staring at Ted seriously for several moments, Hartz came closer, changed his tone and went on like a used-car salesman. "Now this situation may turn out better for you than it seems. Consider it this way: You are better off now than you were earlier today. Brunner and Janovich knew where it is; they had to kill you since you know too. We don't care that you know. We haven't paid for it, we don't feel cheated. It's not our secret. You tell us, we get it, we have no reason to hurt you. Once we've made use of the information, we'll set you free. Make a deal, Hollings."

Hartz grinned, jabbed lightly at Ted's shoulder with his fist. "Come on, guy. Make it easy on yourself. You know, I have that nasty streak (though I try to fight it), and *Schimmel*—he's a direct descendent of Attila the Hun. So you really had better give us the coordinates as old Erbacher gave them to you."

FRIDAY, JULY 15 10:25 HOURS—
SALZBURG

Several railway attendants in blue coveralls, presumably off duty, leaned against the counter of a kiosk drinking glasses of dark beer. They held their heads together in intense, inaudible conversation, then broke away laughing raucously. Dirty jokes, Ted supposed. He thought about having a bratwurst and beer. He really wasn't hungry and it was only around ten-thirty, but it seemed to be in the spirit of things. Everyone else was eating. At the bench beyond him an old man had a length of sausage. The odor of garlic drifted down the platform as thick as smoke from a smudge pot. He had spread a blue and white bandanna across the years of good eating between his chest and thighs and carefully unfolded what any policeman might call a lethal weapon. Slices fell away as he allowed the edge to pass through the sausage against—but amazingly not into—his thumb, and he ate the rounds off the back of the blade.

About thirty feet down the platform an eye looked around

at a height of three feet from behind a stack of luggage,
watching Ted intently. When he became aware that he was
observed, he stared back. The eye disappeared, returned,
disappeared, returned. Two solemn brown eyes, hair in
long braids, a wide nose, the rest of the face obscured by a
very large bread roll held in pudgy little fingers. Ted
smiled. Her head disappeared, returned. He winked. The
face disappeared, returned. He winked with the other eye.
She froze. He winked again with the right eye, then with
the left. Both eyes blinked back at him. Then her mother
came and dragged the girl away before such flirting led to
harm. She glared at Ted; he flushed and stared straight
across the busy street.

An old man appeared and sat down beside him, clutching a valise. Ted was annoyed. The platform was not
crowded; there were several empty benches. Ted did not
encourage the man by looking at him; he had only an
impression of wispy light-gray hair and baggy dark-gray
trousers. A sour smell. The man also stared into space.

Good. At least he won't talk, Ted thought. He was
wrong.

"*Schönes Wetter heute.*"

*The weather is only an opener. You concede it's raining
and they tell you about their gall-bladder operation.* "Sorry,
I don't speak German."

The man twisted abruptly to look at Ted, his head
thrown back at first, then thrust toward him. His pale eyes
were magnified by thick glasses. Ted felt like a bug on a
microscope slide.

"*Mein Gott!*" the man muttered under his breath. Then,
"*Enschuldigung.*" With quivering, liver-spotted hands
he gripped the valise handle, stood up, nodded "*Auf
Wiedersehn*" as German strangers do when leaving a space
they have occupied coincidently, and started to sweep like

a windblown newspaper down the platform and out of Ted's life—so Ted had thought.

Then suddenly there were shrieks and screeches and crashes. Ted snapped his head around and stared incredulously at the junk pile that had appeared in the street before him. It was like a monster snatching cars to itself from all sides, growing by concrescence. Despite its horrific noises, Ted realized it was less dangerous than it seemed. The traffic was not fast, no collision seemed sufficiently violent to give serious injury. He needn't think of helping. His instinct for self-protection warned him, though, that witnesses might be sought and detained. It was almost time for his train. While everyone else seemed to be focused on the accident, he moved quickly into the station.

He barely noticed the old man who had spoken to him, now halted halfway down the platform, turning his head from side to side in bewilderment.

SATURDAY, JULY 16 20:30 HOURS—
OBER-FLATTACH

Ted considered his situation. He tried not to feel anything about it because it *felt* hopeless. He thought about it only as a problem to be solved. It was like Dustin Hoffman in the movie *The Marathon Man*: tied to a chair, the villain about to torture him for information he didn't have. Ted had thought about that predicament for a long time after seeing the film. How *would* a person save himself? He had never thought he would have to learn whether his answer would really work.

"Hartz. I don't want. . . . Is it Hartz?"

"It might as well be."

"Okay, Mr. Hartz, we have a problem."

Hartz threw back his head and roared with laughter. He came over and slapped Ted's shoulder. "Mr. Hollings, you are superb. You are tied to a massive wooden chair in the bottom of a stone tower in the depths of a walled castle; you are being threatened with the most hideous of

tortures by a pair of sadistic villains—and you tell me *we*
have a problem.''

"We do have a problem, Hartz. *We* do. It's the same
for both of us: How can you be convinced I'm telling the
truth? Look . . . imagine I *am* telling the truth. Come on,
Hartz, imagine it! This is one of those intelligence tests
where you have to look at the picture upside down. Imagine that I am Ted Barstow and this is all a mistake. I look
like someone else. Erbacher made a mistake. Everyone's
made a mistake. When you were trying to reassure me,
you said yourself it must have been mistaken identity. You
were putting me on, but it was a natural thing to say
because it's so easy to believe. Believe it for a minute.
What does that mean to you? It means that even if you do
whatever you want to me, I still won't be able to tell you
whatever it is you want to know. You can kill me. You
can torture me till I die. I won't be *able* to tell you. But
you won't know if I *couldn't* tell you or if I just had the
strength *not* to tell you. Imagine I'm not this Hollings.
You kill me, but I haven't told you anything. Is the secret
gone or is Hollings away somewhere else, perfectly safe
now that you think he's dead? *We* have a problem. So you
had better help me think of a way to solve it."

Hartz had stopped laughing. He looked at Ted intently.
Ted looked squarely back at him.

There was a wooden packing case at one side of the
room. Hartz got it, brought it over and dusted it off with
flicks of his handkerchief. He sat down on it, crossed his
arms. "All right, what ideas do you have?"

"Ask me about myself. I have a life. I have a job. I live
by myself in an old farmhouse in North Andover, Mas-
sachusetts. Ask me about it. See if you can prove I'm not
me."

"It won't do. For all I know, you *are* Ted Barstow and

Hollings is the cover name. Who you are when you're at home doesn't matter.''

"Ted Barstow couldn't be involved in this, whatever it is.''

"Mild-mannered accountants embezzle millions and blow it all in Tangier. The Sunday-school superintendent is arrested in a teenage brothel. We could establish beyond question that you are Barstow, Hollings or J. Churchwarden Upright and still not prove you innocent of a predelection for adolescent ducks.''

"Get a lie detector. Try truth serum.''

"We are resourceful but we are not the CIA. We must do the best we can with what we have here.''

"You're not helping.''

"Tobler.''

Ted looked at Hartz blankly. Hartz leaned forward, looked directly into his eyes. Even at the end of the day, Ted could still smell the man's cologne. Hartz kept his eyes on Ted's. "Disco-bar Cutie.''

Ted did not twitch.

Hartz leaned back, bit at his lower lip. "Let's get this straight. You meet Erbacher at the train station in Salzburg purely by accident. Brunner and Janovich mistake you for someone else. It's possible. I accept that much as possible.'' He nodded slowly to himself, then once sharply to Ted. Ted felt a surge of hope. But then Hartz looked away again, tipped his head and thought on. "You come here, to the same village as they, again by coincidence. Increasingly improbable. Brunner and Janovich try several times to kill you. They are professionals, but you elude them. Single-handedly and unarmed you dispose of them, *two* of them; throwing them off a cliff as a matter of fact!'' He focused back on Ted. "And now. Although taken prisoner, you sit calmly in the face of torture, playing intellectual games with your captor. And who are you really? Ted Barstow, mild-mannered accountant and Sunday-school superintendent.'' He grinned. ''It strains credulity.''

''But it's true.''

''How can we know that? Ah, Mr. . . .'' He smiled and shrugged. ''The age-old questions: Who are we, what is truth?''

''Try to catch me. Do what you were doing before.''

Hartz nodded. He moved behind Ted, put his hand around Ted's neck, his fingers against the artery in the throat. After a moment he began to list people's names. ''Schmid, Alvarez, Seidel, Walther, Weinberger, Poiret, Cadogan.''

Ted did not react.

Hartz switched to the names of mountains. ''Ankogel, Hochalm, Jungfrau, Matterhorn, Rotzahn. . . .'' Involuntarily Ted caught his breath as images of the ridge and the fight flashed into his mind. ''Goldeck, Glockner, Reisseck, Kreuzeck.'' Pause. ''Kreuzeck.'' Pause. ''Weisskopf, Grüneck, Kreuzeck.'' Pause. ''Interesting but not conclusive. You may just be very good.''

''I may just not know anything.''

Hartz came around to the box again, sat down, crossed his arms, cupped his chin and thought.

Ted was beginning to sweat. Clearly he had made Hartz doubt but equally clearly he had not convinced him. His pulse was heating, the lid was lifting and whisps of fear were rising around it from the bubbling terror underneath. Hartz continued to stare at him. Ted stared back, afraid that any shift of his eyes would seem to be evasion and to the man opposite that would be the same as confession.

Finally Hartz said, ''If you do know, I advise you to tell me.'' His voice was low and calm and even. ''I mean that sincerely, for your benefit as well as ours. You're right: If we killed you quickly, we'd never know; so we will have to make sure you don't die quickly. Ponder on that for a while.''

FRIDAY, JULY 15 10:25 HOURS—
SALZBURG, VIENNA

Hartz stood just inside the entrance of the railroad station, where he could watch arriving taxis through the glass-paneled doors. Schimmel was outside, parked in the narrow area that separated the pull-in to the station from the street beyond. Little Putzi Schroeder, whom they had contracted for by the day as backup, sat on a bench to the right, from where he could be directed by either of the other two.

It was a wonderfully clever scheme. After contact was made with the American, they would take Erbacher; the "National Security Bureau" approach was infallible. Assuming they could move fast enough once they frightened the coordinates from him (allowing about fifteen seconds to do so)—and speed was what the BMW was for—they would find the pictures before either of the betrayed but legitimate buyers. They would see that Erbacher's duplicity was known and leave the competition blaming each other, or Erbacher, or Rudi Bischl. The fortune they would

extract from the hapless minister—in cash or secrets or
both (and perhaps they could follow Erbacher's example
and turn the profit several times)—would make them independent for life.

Independent. Hartz was especially pleased with the
thought. Schimmel was a good business associate: percep-
tive, clever, ruthless. Hartz accepted the necessity of working with someone who was ruthless. He himself found
being unpleasant to people distasteful. Charm was much to
be preferred. He could become quite angered by people
who did not respond to charm. Schimmel responded to it
at least by recognizing its value, even though he possessed
none himself. Hartz would part from Schimmel with respect but without regret. There was an island he knew, off
the west coast of Greece, where a man with capital and
charm could establish a small, elegant resort hotel. It
would be the sort of place where the best people would
come to visit as one's personal guests. One could live at
leisure, as though in retirement, and grow richer at the
same time. It was a magnificent future to contemplate.

He would enjoy being rich. Spending money was an art
he practiced well, philanthropically. Tailors, restauranteurs,
purveyors of fine wines, crafters of exquisite artifacts—all
would benefit. He had apprenticed the mystery of wealth
for a decade, first observing masters as he held their coats,
opened their car doors, then made appointments for them,
brought them messages and carried their commands. His
father had had little left but reputation and a few old
friends when he had insisted on bringing the family back
to watch him die, Austrian again. That meager inheritance
had been enough, at least, to secure young Kurt appointment as a novice. After those ten years, he journeyed; but
the paths he took—though often to minor treasures—never
brought him to a golden city. Now he saw one shining not
far off. He squinted at the light over the street named for

Ferdinand Porsche and decided he might begin by buying one of the man's cars.

Hartz checked his watch once more. His ship should be coming in at any moment: It was ten minutes since Hermann had called in to the pay telephone in the station's lobby. Sure enough! A taxi drew up and Erbacher stepped out.

As the cab pulled away, Schimmel saw Erbacher standing irresolutely, looking around in a daze. Schimmel folded and laid down the newspaper he had propped against the steering wheel. Putzi saw the signal and nodded.

Erbacher threw his head back, evidently recognizing the man he looked for. He went over to the bench, sat down and spoke a few words. Then he rose again, started to walk away and there began the screeches and slammings of multiple collisions. The sound shocked Schimmel and broke his concentration for an instant. But he snapped back, caught Putzi's eye, jerked his head to set him onto Erbacher's contact. If there was any problem with the old man, they would let the American lead them.

"Attention. Attention. Attention!" Tolz was required to raise his voice. The shouts from the two A-team cars and from the dispatcher ceased.

"Controller!"

"Traffic accident. A team immobilized! Subjects escaped!"

"Erbacher?"

"Went the wrong way. Coming back—no, he's stopping. He's looking around. *Our* subject—Hollings—he's getting up. Should we take him?"

"No! Let him go. Take Erbacher. Take Erbacher!"

Erbacher thought the noise was in his head. He never looked at the collision. What had he done? Who had he . . . the man looked like . . . where was . . . which way . . . ?

The noise *was* inside, the pounding thudding faster and faster, the ringing rising. He staggered as he turned about trying to see his man. All was blurred, more than usual, but he did see all the men—the baggage handler coming up close to the building, the two behind spreading to the side, the taxi dispatcher crossing the platform. He saw them and he knew. He lurched around. He saw the tall blond man come out of the station. He was trapped. The pounding increased to a roar, the ringing to a scream.

Hartz was quick. He took in the convergence on Erbacher, understood, swerved aside a step and continued as though headed out to the accident all along. He was aware but far enough away to be able to pretend he hadn't seen Erbacher stagger and collapse.

Johann slammed his fist down on the table, instantly catching it on the bounce with the other hand. He massaged it as though trying to rub away anger and frustration with the pain. The two younger agents looked at each other and at the floor, not certain whether it was better to leave quietly or to remain seated and pretend they were not there at all.

Only Tolz showed no reaction. He sat staring ahead as he had been except that he puckered his lips as though about to blow out a candle. But Johann was unsuccessful at soothing his own anger, and it exploded again in words of outrage. Tolz turned with an expression that suggested amused amazement at the unlikely combination of organs and activities that Johann was describing. Johann caught himself.

"I'm sorry, Herr Tolz. Forgive me." He paused for a moment. "I'm sorry, sir, about the whole thing. But there was no way you could have expected he would go to the wrong person."

Tolz gave a silent chuckle. "I should have been certain

that Rinehardt would exercise his incompetence somehow.''

''But you couldn't have known he would *die*.''

''Only the masterstroke of an entire career. I should have expected it. So. Perhaps a bird in the hand would have been worth three in the bush.''

''*I* think it was worth the gamble, sir. If we had . . . if only that . . . it was worth the chance, and no one ought to say—''

''Johann, when you are as old as I am, you will have made so many mistakes that one more such as this will not trouble you greatly. You must understand: The value of experience is not that it prevents you from making mistakes, only that it teaches you what to do afterward. Now, first put out an alert through the regular police for Brunner and Janovich.''

''Pick them up?''

''Without Erbacher we have no charge but reckless driving. Nor can we pick up the American.'' He threw up his hands. ''We know Hollings now. Perhaps in the future there will be other business. Since Rinehardt did not reach him, he doesn't have the information. He surely is aware—he surely saw our men close on Rinehardt. I think he will try to fade away and advise his principals there is no hope in pursuing the matter. We'll watch, but we have no ground on which to charge him. Nor the Russians' men either. We can't charge them, we can't bluff them. We must hope to find and follow them. Undoubtedly they will change automobiles, so they must be found by personal description alone. In the meantime we must continue to try to find Rudolph Bischl; we can begin that search with Tobler.''

''Oh.''

''What?''

''This was brought in just before. They have found Bischl—the Salzburg police have found him.''

"Yes?"

"He is dead. They found a body in the forest, and it took some time. . . ."

Tolz pushed out his lips again and sighed. "So. Tobler, then. I think we go ourselves, Johann."

SATURDAY, JULY 16 20:40 HOURS— *OBER-FLATTACH*

Kick out, high, hard—directly into his crotch. He doubles over in agony. Kick him again, knocking him off balance. He falls. I raise myself; stand, all bent over, weight of the chair on my back. Twist myself, fall on him. My weight, weight of the chair, crash down on him. Then. . . .

Then what?

What if I can't rise up onto my feet? This chair must weigh as much as I do. Solid oak.

But I do it right. I put Hartz out, and then. . . . I lie there and Schimmel comes back. Try another.

A character in some thriller Ted had read had been tied to a chair. How had he escaped?

Hartz leaves the room. I can move my legs, my feet. I push myself across the floor, only inches at a time, but enough. I reach the stone stairway running up the back wall, lean forward, get the weight onto my back, lift, get the back chair legs onto the step, push. Terrible pain, yes,

*but I can endure it. Three steps, four, six. High enough.
Scrape over to the edge. Take a breath. Throw myself off
backwards. Crash onto the floor. Chair breaks. One hand
free. Untwist wire on the other. Grab a piece of chair
back, stand behind the door. . . .*

*The chair won't break. I'll crack my head open against
the floor. Break my arm. Break my back.*

*Hartz isn't leaving the room anyway. Breathe deeply.
Slow the heartbeat. Good.*

Ted looked at his situation as Hartz had described it. *My
plan of escape is. . . .*

Clunk! The latch lifted and the cross-battened plank
door swung open. Schimmel was back.

Hartz turned to him. *"Das Fraulein?"*

Schimmel nodded in affirmation, then glanced in Ted's
direction questioningly. Hartz went over to him. They
turned away, spoke together softly, looking over their
shoulders toward Ted from time to time. Ted's pulse raced
again and he felt cold. He stared at them, fascinated
by their every tip of the head and shift of a shoulder. He
felt as he imagined a mouse might feel staring at a snake.

*Stop it! Get back outside again! Think! My plan is:
one. . . .*

They approached him. Hartz put one foot up on the
packing case and crossed his arms on his raised knee. He
looked directly into Ted's face. Schimmel stood to one
side.

"We have decided to offer you a choice. I want you to
think about it carefully. First understand this: We are
going to kill you—no matter who you are. You know too
much even if you don't know anything . . . even if this is
a case of mistaken identity. We can't have you running to
the police and telling them about us. So we *are* going to
kill you. Give up all hope of living." He paused, continu-
ing to stare into Ted's eyes. "Now, here is your choice:

You can die quickly—a bullet in the back of the head, you'll never feel it. Or,'' he spoke slowly and deliberately, ''Schimmel will get the propane torch from the car and we will burn you inch by inch. We will do it carefully and slowly so you will not pass out in shock. And if you do pass out, we'll bring you around again and then go on.'' His voice was soft, even. ''You appear to be in good health. You will probably stand it for many hours. Even for a day. But long before the end, you will have lost all sense of time. You will be in hell; it will be an eternity. You will expect to die, then pray to die, then forget death is even possible.'' The calmness of his voice, the matter-of-factness of his tone, made what he said more horrible. ''When you give us the coordinates, we'll shoot you and end the pain. If you finally die without telling us, we'll know you didn't have them; anyone who did have them would have given them to us in order to stop the pain.''

Perspiration ran down Ted's face and into his eyes. It was salty, burning, and he blinked. Without shifting his stare, Hartz took a folded handkerchief from his breast pocket, leaned over and wiped Ted's forehead and eyes.

''Have no illusions. Have no hope. We are not bluffing.''

Ted knew they weren't bluffing. He felt fear; it was like an electric current generated in his chest, vibrating through his body. He tried to speak. ''I . . .'' It croaked somewhere in the back of his throat. ''I believe you.''

''Good. Then tell us.''

''Please,'' Ted said. ''Please. Oh, God, please. I don't know.''

Hartz continued to study him, then leaned back and nodded to Schimmel. Schimmel nodded once in return and left the room.

Hartz dragged the box farther away. He sat down on it, his legs thrust out in front of him, watching Ted all the while.

Ted wondered if he would scream. Of course he would. He decided not to consider it a sign of weakness. He decided not to review his life. He tried to keep terror from over-whelming him completely.

The door opened again. Erica came through. Schimmel was behind her. Surprise threw her back, her eyes wide, her hands up to her cheeks. *"Was ist?"*

Schimmel grabbed her right wrist, twisted her arm be-hind her and pushed against the small of her back so she could neither struggle nor kick at him.

Hartz spoke to her in German. Ted couldn't follow what he said. She stared at Hartz, at Ted and back to Hartz uncomprehendingly.

Hartz stood up and walked toward Ted. "We are going to try Plan B. Many people have amazing strength of will and can bear amazing amounts of pain. Pride, I suppose. Some people would rather die of pride than admit defeat. You might be one of them—you have impressed us with some of your personal qualities. However, it's different when one has to watch someone else suffer. Someone whom one cares about?" He raised the question with his eyebrows.

Erica stared at them, white-faced. Hartz tipped his head and Schimmel put pressure on her arm. She screamed.

Ted went mad. He screamed too. He roared. Blood pounded in his head and his pulse leaped through his body. He heaved forward, up onto his feet. Bent over, the huge chair on his back, the weight of it on his wrists, his arms out behind him, wires cutting into them with searing pain—he felt it and yet he didn't feel it; he felt it only as rage. His face was twisted with fury. His mouth was open, still roaring, his teeth bared. He ran at Hartz, charged at him like a bull, ran to smash and trample and crush him.

He took three steps and fell. Shocking agony flashed through his knee. He tried to rise and toppled, his legs were sweeping, trying to right himself. He was screaming, howling.

Hartz came over to him and tried to lift the chair. Ted kicked at him, his legs driving like pistons. Hartz went behind him; Ted beat his head against the chair back, trying to hit Hartz's hand. Hartz held on and began to tip the chair up, but to lift the weight, he had to shift his grip, his hand neared Ted's head. Ted bit him. Hartz yelled in pain, released the chair, and Ted's head struck the floor.

FRIDAY, JULY 15 20:00 HOURS—
BAD GASTEIN

Tolz studied the photographs, moving from wall to wall as though in a museum, finally stopping before those enlarged and displayed on easels facing the shop's window. Johann, behind the small counter, went through the appointment book, the ledger and other papers—an activity more appropriate for a police search in the opinion of the uniformed policeman who remained by the door. His opinion had not been solicited, so he retained it. He knew his function was merely to present a facade of legality for what was an irregular proceeding. He had presented it outside while Johann picked the lock. He stood ready now to face anyone who might wonder what was going on behind the drawn blinds.

Everyone in the front-room pictures was smiling. Some seemed self-conscious, or even displeased that strangers might see such an expression on their face. Some seemed as though trying it on for the first time in their lives. But they all smiled. Rudi had been good at getting them to smile. Those taken outdoors, usually in front of the waterfall, did it the best.

The people in the rear of the inner room did not smile. Tolz and Johann continued their search there after Johann failed to find what they were looking for in the outer room. They did not know exactly what they were looking for of course, but they hoped to recognize it if it was there. The inner room was divided by a curtain; the front was the portrait studio, the rear the work area, with counter, filing cabinets and dark room.

Again Johann searched methodically while Tolz studied the pictures. In one, a tall, elegantly dressed gentleman—he had given up wing collars but kept his pince-nez and homburg—stood erect, distancing himself as far as the leash would allow from a long-haired dachshund that looked embarrassingly toward the camera as it arched, defecating. In another, beneath the outstretched arms of sorrowing Christ, one toddler bawled as another, holding his teddy bear by one leg, swung back to deliver a coup de grace. In a third, two lovers walked toward the viewer, their private bliss drawn around them in a soft-focus veil, oblivious to the woman behind them—with frowzy hair, her bulbous bosom sagging on her fallen belly, her fat lips slack—who stared after them in sullen hatred.

Tolz suddenly thought of Hermann Tobler. "What is this?" he had asked.

"Only an inquiry, Herr Tobler." Johann had handled it. He had stood in the middle of the dance floor. Hermann had come over to him. Tolz had been sitting in a booth to one side, and Hermann at first thought he might be a customer. "We are investigating a matter of national security and we would be grateful for your help," Johann had said. "Only a few questions."

"Yeah? Okay, what?"

"You are acquainted with Rinehardt Erbacher?"

"I want to call my lawyer."

"You certainly may, Herr Tobler. But why? You are not being accused of anything. Does my asking about Rinehardt Erbacher upset you?"

"No. Why should it?"

"That was my question, Herr Tobler. Why are you upset about Rinehardt Erbacher?"

"I am not upset about him."

"Then you're not afraid to answer questions about him without a lawyer present?"

"I'm not afraid, I only—"

"Good. Then we will begin."

Hermann had kept his mouth open for a moment, then clamped it tight, pushing out his lower lip.

"Shall we sit down?" Johann indicated a booth to his right, diagonally opposite from where Tolz sat staring into space. Johann slid into one side, Hermann berthed himself into the other.

"What do you want to know about Erbacher?"

"Actually, Herr Tobler, we know all we need to know about Herr Erbacher. What we want to know is, what was he selling?"

"Selling?" Hermann shrugged and wagged his head. "Is he a salesman?"

"Herr Tobler, I think we should be honest with each other. Let me be first. We have had the telephone here tapped since Wednesday morning. We have had surveillance outside also."

Hermann might have revealed no reaction at all but for the blue-green light coming from above. Its angle picked up the film of sweat that formed, making his forehead reflect more brightly than its normal oiliness warranted. "Is that so?"

"Yes. So we know about Erbacher's business deals."

Hermann tipped his head, conceding the advantage. "Then

you know more than me. Erbacher is a friend of my
uncle's. He said he had some business, he could stay here,
meet some people, use the phone. I personally know from
nothing about it.''

"You know about Rudi Bischl?''

"Rudi who?''

"Bischl. He came here Wednesday night, gave something to Erbacher, got money for it.''

"Oh, Rudi Bischl. Yeah. Little cat shit. I went to
school with him. Yeah, I saw him. I didn't have anything I
wanted to say to him. If he sold something to Erbacher, I
don't know about it. Look, you better talk to my uncle.''

"Who's Kurt?''

"Kurt who?''

"You called him this morning. At the railway station.
Just after Erbacher left.''

"I did not.''

Johann stared at Hermann for a moment. "You want to
hear the tape?''

"Yeah, see if whoever you got on it really sounds like
me. I know all about tapes. I got a friend—you give me
until tomorrow, I'll give you a tape sounds like you asking
if you can suck me off. Now, you got any other questions?''

"Let him go, Johann,'' Tolz called from the other side.

Hermann jerked his head around in surprise. "He with
you?''

"Let him go. We'll talk with the uncle.''

"All right, Herr Tobler. That will be all. May we speak
with your uncle?''

"Yeah, sure. Yeah, you want to know anything about
Erbacher, you ask him.'' Hermann extricated himself from
behind the table. "Maybe he knows something.'' He
shrugged to express his doubt. "I'll get him.''

"Herr Tobler . . .'' Tolz called as Hermann started
away.

"Yeah?"

"Perhaps you would return with your uncle."

"Why? I told you, I know from nothing."

"Yes. So we will ask you no more questions. But perhaps your uncle will have questions to ask you."

"What do you mean?"

"One moment, Herr Tobler . . . let me find it . . ." Tolz lifted an attaché case from the seat beside him, rummaged through it and brought out a sheaf of papers. "Where is it . . . ? Ah, so. Here."

Hermann had been drawn back. He stood by the corner of Tolz's booth. "What?"

"These are the transcripts of calls from your telephone. Naturally most of them were of no interest to us. We attended only to those that seemed to arise from this Erbacher business. Yes. Here. Friday, fifteen July, at twelve minutes past ten in the morning. The call that was made this morning to the railway station saying that 'he' had just left. 'He' must be Erbacher, at least one would think so since Erbacher did leave at just that time. And here . . ." Tolz shuffled back through the pages, ". . . Wednesday, July thirteenth: Rudolph Bischl calls at three minutes past eighteen hundred, speaks to Erbacher; they make an appointment for twenty hundred. Seven minutes later there is a call made by that same person who has a voice that sounds like yours: 'He will be here at twenty hundred.' "

"So?"

"Did you know that Rudolph Bischl has been murdered?"

"No!" Hermann's surprise was genuine.

"Yes. Sometime Wednesday evening. Unfortunately we had not been able to locate a photograph of him at that time. Had we been able to recognize him among your other customers. . . . Did you know that Rinehardt Erbacher is dead?"

"No!"

"At the station this morning."

Despite the shocks, Hermann regained his customary stolidity quickly. "So. I'm sorry to hear, but so?"

"Your uncle owns this establishment, I believe?"

"Yeah. So?"

"As you yourself know, Herr Tobler, such transcripts . . ." Tolz rippled them, ". . . would not be admissible in a law court. But that does not matter since we are not charging you officially with any crime. Nevertheless, they do give rise to interesting speculation, don't you think? Would you like to call your uncle now?"

The old man glared in fury, his brush of white hair standing as though charged with the anger that wrenched open his mouth to vent some curse past twisted teeth. The object of his rage did not appear in the photograph. Perhaps Rudi meant for it to be understood as death. Or life.

All of the pictures were in black and white. Rudi could not afford color for his personal work, but even Tolz would not have inferred that as the reason since his subjects and medium were so well matched. As he made his way around the room, Tolz saw only one photograph in color. No, it was not in color. Johann had turned on the light table and was looking at negatives taken from the file and spread out on it. A bluish light through frosted glass shone upward, tinting the photograph mounted on the wall over it. Tolz came up beside Johann to look at it. The illusion of color must have been intended in placing the picture there because it so well-suited its subject.

The girl knelt by a pool of water. The picture was taken from above, her head was down and her hand in the water made ripples that broke the reflection: It was impossible to see her face. She was nude, her modesty preserved by the angle of the camera and her long, light-colored hair. There was a wreath of flowers on her head. Tolz looked closer.

Forget-me-nots. He would have expected that. The picture was technically excellent, if trite. The wash of light was the right color, its direction suggesting reflection from the pool.

"Officer," Tolz called.

The sound of music reached them even at that distance from the square, possibly through some trick of the breeze or an echo from a cliff. Tolz knew the name of the day; that was usually the only way he distinguished one from another. But had he forgotten, he would know now that it was Friday. On Fridays, for the tourists, there is the band concert.

He and the driver had to leave the car by the roadside and walk up a lane around a knoll to the cottage.

It was a charming cottage, a tiny hideaway, a love nest. Even the openings cut into the shutters were heart-shaped. Had it been built as some nobleman's toy, a retreat where a lord and his mistress could escape the decadence and falsehood of the court for a few days' idyll as shepherd and shepherdess? It was old—the wood now a deep coffee-and-tobacco brown. There were the obligatory geraniums but there was no running water or electricity. Just the thing for a young couple who were poor but in love.

Tolz went through it alone—he asked the officer who accompanied him not to help—and as carefully as Johann was going through Rudi's studio. He found little. There were some clothes—not many, cheap, what everyone their ages wore a year or two ago. He came across some bits from which the personality of Rudi might be reconstructed: an album of family photographs; odds and ends turned out of pockets and left in corners when they should have been thrown away; a half-dozen worn science-fiction paperbacks. But for the girl—nothing. Her clothes were folded carefully in the drawers so as to take minimum space. There was nothing personal—no pictures, mementos, magazines, candy wrappers, stuffed animals, postcards—nothing to reveal a person except the lack of things. She had not carted everything away—some clothes remained, and the butter and cheese in the small icebox showed she intended to return. All in all, Tolz found little, and in that, much. He began to see her. Her face was turned away as in the photograph taken by the water. But he began to see a girl who would put flowers in her hair and pose in naked innocence for a photograph sentimental enough to sell bath soap to maiden aunts . . . but also a girl who traveled without baggage by whatever route was the shortest.

"Ilse Katernig."

"Yes, sir," the officer confirmed again.

There was nothing in the cottage relating to the pictures or to the identity of the man in them, or to where Ilse might have gone.

"Yes. So. Nothing for us here, it seems. We will return to the station and see if the police in Ober-Flattach have answered our request for information about her there."

"Yes, sir. Perhaps there will be something, although they are having their hands full today."

"Yes?"

"Yes, sir. A bizarre crime. Someone shot through the window of a café at lunchtime today and killed a young girl."

SUNDAY, JULY 17 00:35 HOURS—
OBER-FLATTACH

"It's hard to get rid of a body. Two bodies, even harder."

"Lucky for us the problem doesn't arise."

Ted imagined Hartz's reassuring smile but kept his eyes closed. The throbbing was bad enough that way. Erica had put her sweater behind his head and he tried not to move. A point of stone pressed into his back and the floor was cold, but moving was worse.

His voice was unusually deep from fatigue and he had to concentrate to put words together. "Your fingerprints are all over things here. Places you don't remember touching. You can't clean them all." What clues did the detectives in mystery novels search for? "Tire tracks from your car. The police may not notice, nobody take any trouble, if it's a break-in with nothing stolen. Think it was kids, tourists. But bodies, blood: They'll check carefully."

"Mr. Barstow, you have nothing to fear."

"I'm not afraid, Hartz. You got me past that."

"Good. We're convinced. The man we thought you were—Hollings—might or might not have borne his own pain, and it could have taken us longer than we'd like to decide whether you were ignorant or resolute. And—as you suggested—if we'd . . . lost . . . you too soon, we'd never have known either way. But there's no doubt that a professional would have been able to watch someone else suffer. You could have been faking earlier, but not when you came at me. Someone in our trade doesn't lose his head that way over a . . . a recent acquaintance. We accept that you're Barstow, and that means you're safe. Believe me."

"I do believe you. I believe what you said before: I know too much. I know what you and Schimmel look like. Your car. I know the names: Brunner, Janovich, Erbacher. I know you want coordinates, whatever they are. And I'll tell the police."

"*Nein!* Ted, no! We won't tell anything. We will promise."

"No, Erica, we won't promise. They wouldn't believe us. Why should they? Think as they are thinking. Why should we keep our promise once we're safe? We aren't going to get out of this by pretending. We're only going to get out by showing them it's to their advantage to let us out."

Erica sat next to him. She had tried to comfort him and he was glad she was there. He could smell her and feel her warmth. He moved his left hand and touched her leg with the back of one finger. It hurt him to even move his wrist.

He wondered if he was concussed. *What are the symptoms? My nose hasn't bled. I think that's a good sign.*

They had released him from the chair and propped him against the wall while he was still stunned. He had opened his eyes and seen Schimmel in the chair by the door, Hartz sitting on the box, holding his handkerchief around his hand. Closing his eyes, he had thought: *I have to find the angle; look at it from their side, not mine. What do killers do? How are they caught when disposing of bodies?*

"So it will be better for you not to kill us here. You will need to take us someplace and do it there. You'll want to do it there, not along the way, so you won't have to carry our bodies. That would be risky and messy. And you wouldn't want to be stopped for speeding or have to change a tire with us in the trunk. But if you take us out of here in your car, someone may see you."

"Mr. Barstow, if I ever do decide to kill anyone, you may be sure I'll hire you as consultant first."

"My advice is not to kill us at all. We'll be missed. Even if our bodies aren't found, we'll be missed. Both of us will be missed tomorrow. Someone may have seen you with us. With me, this afternoon—some hiker in the valley. Your car stands out. You talked to Erica this morning—yesterday morning?"

Hartz touched his watch. "Yesterday. It's just after midnight."

"All right. Someone may connect you with her. Schimmel . . . Schimmel picked her up this evening."

"Outside the village, Mr. Barstow."

"You still can't be sure that no one saw. A nosy old woman looking out from behind her curtains in one of the farms between the village and here. Someone walking a dog. Even if no one saw Erica get into the car, maybe one person saw her walking and someone else saw the car in the same area. The police here are very thorough. They'll get the stories and put them together. You'll never be sure you're safe." Ted paused, then said it again. "Killing us does *not* assure your safety. All you gain for sure is a little time. But you can gain time without killing us. Leave us here, tied up. Or put us on a back road. We won't be able to contact anyone for a full day. And then—if the police

ever do catch you—it won't be for murder. Kidnapping?
You haven't asked for ransom. You haven't hurt us very
much. Alive or dead, we're a danger to you, Hartz. But
we're less danger alive.''

''What is your profession, Mr. Barstow?''

Ted told him.

''You should have been a Jesuit. If we needed persuading,
you would persuade us. But truly, Mr. Barstow, although
we are not above frightening people, we are quite decent.
We never intended to kill you. That was just for effect.''

Ted opened his eyes, blinked and focused on Hartz,
who tipped his head and looked directly back at him. ''I
mean it.'' He leaned forward. He radiated sincerity like
heat from a red-hot stove. ''Truly.''

Ted was certain then that they were lost.

Evil needs no illumination, and honest and honorable
people—the righteous, upright and God-fearing—are all in
bed by midnight. That's why, normally, streetlights are
turned off at that hour in Ober-Flattach. Tourists are a
class between the extremes of dark and light: Their money
is good, their ways are questionable. To accommodate this
ambiguity, lights glow until two A.M. in the summer but
tolerance stays up not one minute later. Hartz and Schimmel
waited for the dark hour. They would not acknowledge it,
but Ted knew.

They were silent for the most part. Finally Erica asked
''Why?'' again and Ted gave her the absurdity that passed
for explanation.

She shook her head, unsatisfied. ''But what are they,
these coordinates?'' She turned to Hartz. ''What is it you
want?''

He stared at her, blank-faced.

She shouted at him, ''For what? You kill, you *hurt*
people! For what? For money? Innocent people you hurt

for money? You are that kind of a man? For how much? I would like to know what my life is worth!''

Hartz dropped his look to the floor but hers battered him; he felt it and seemed to cower. Finally he cleared his throat and spoke in a thin voice. "The coordinates mark a location. At the location is hidden something—"

"Kurt!" Schimmel's voice broke in like a whip snapping.

Without looking at him, Hartz shook his head slightly. "I won't say what. Something that various people think has great value. It's not money, though having it can bring money. Other people value it for other reasons. That's all I'm going to say. The coordinates—they represent opportunity: the sort everyone dreams of but never really expects. You must have some dream, Fraulein Stendler, everyone does: living happily ever after. At those coordinates lies the gate to Happily Ever After."

"I want no opportunity that must be taken this way."

"Perhaps. You will know for sure, Fraulein, when it is offered to you." Hartz paused, risking a veiled look at Erica. "We would not be here if we did not feel this was an opportunity greater than any we've ever . . . I'm sorry, Fraulein. We don't usually. . . . It has not been our wish to hurt anyone. We have been forced by special circumstances."

Ted felt the apology may have been as genuine as anything of which Hartz was capable, but even in making it, he began to make his way out. He put on self-justification like armor. "Our line of work is not an easy one. We try to do no harm. But for a mistake—a pure quirk of fate—we would never have harmed you. We didn't intend . . . it's not our choice."

Except for that one word when he cautioned Hartz, Schimmel had not moved. He must have blinked from time to time, but Ted's sense was that his eyes were always fixed and open like the end of a shotgun. Ted hadn't really taken notice of him at first—he seemed only to move the props around while Hartz did the tricks. The more aware of Schimmel that Ted became, however, the more he was afraid of him. Hartz might kill them or do anything he thought he needed to, but he would feel bad about it. Or rather, he would feel that he *should* feel bad. He would want people to think he felt bad. "Feeling anything is dangerous" was one of Ted's mottos. Not that he thought emotion was always bad, but he knew that to feel is to be vulnerable. And he knew that nothing would move Schimmel.

But *Hartz*. . . .

"We aren't insensitive." Hartz actually said it: "You don't know how much this hurts us—"

"So." Erica's stare was like a scythe through a hayfield. "Maybe *we* should apologize." She twisted the blade for another moment, then looked up and studied the ceiling as though it were an object of far greater interest than Hartz could ever be.

He had the look on his face of a small boy who has wet his pants. There was no doubt about truth of feeling at that moment and Ted thought he saw an opportunity. The pain in his head had subsided to no more than one of the eddies in a tide of aches and he could think with less effort. Not better perhaps, but faster.

"I accept it, Hartz. You know, for what you do, you really aren't a bad guy."

"Thank you, Mr. Barstow." Ted thought the man's gratitude was pathetic. "I like to think I'm a professional."

"No, I mean more than style. Some people—from what I read in the newspapers—some people would have gone ahead and tortured us and enjoyed it. You found a way of getting what you wanted to know with as little pain as possible. I'm grateful for that."

"Good of you to say so. May I say in return that my compliments to you were not empty flattery. We're all here because Schimmel and I believed you must be a professional too." Ted had thrown him a lifeline and he was back on solid ground again. "I guess we've deceived each other." He gave Ted another smile for a merit badge.

Ted smiled back. He was a beginner, but he learned quickly.

Erica was outraged. "What do you do? You speak to each other as though you are friends—brothers! He is a . . . a gangster. Maybe they yet will kill us!"

"Fraulein, we are not going to—"

"You don't understand, Erica. This is man to man."

"Man to man! He will kill me too! How can you smile and—"

"You don't understand."

"No! I do not understand!"

Ted looked at Hartz. *They* understood. There is a code among real men, even when they are adversaries. Ted looked at Hartz to show that he understood. She was only a woman. *They* understood she wouldn't understand. What could he say? Ted shrugged, Hartz nodded his wink.

"Erica. . . ."

She had turned away. She brushed a tear away with the back of her hand as she had brushed at her hair that night. Last night. The image flooded over Ted. He nearly wept too.

He used the memory. "Erica, I'm sorry you don't understand. I would like for you to understand. I would like to be able to tell you . . . I'd like to tell you . . . everything. I wish . . ." He reached out to stroke her hair. She pulled away. He studied her profile, her breasts. He thought of her in bed as she had been last night. He imagined making love with her; he could feel himself flush. Truly felt passion made his voice rough.

"Hartz, can you lock that door—from the outside?"

Hartz looked at him blankly for a moment, turned to the door and back again.

"Hartz, I think we respect each other. You *have* been as decent as you can about this whole thing. I know you're going to kill us—"

"Barstow, I've told you . . ." His forehead furrowed, hurt showed in his eyes.

I think he is really hurt that I don't believe him. Doesn't matter that he's lying; it hurts him not to be believed. "We're helpless. We can't get through the walls. The nearest window must be seventy feet above the ground. You don't have to watch us." Ted looked at Erica, then back at Hartz. "Give us this time alone. You know what I mean. I'm asking you as one man to another."

Hartz looked at Ted and then at Schimmel. The partners deliberated silently; but how can a man who cares about impressing people refuse a request put to him as a test of his manhood?

"I suppose the warrior has earned his recreation," Hartz said, grinning at Ted.

Schimmel continued to stare for a moment from the eyeholes left when his face was cast in concrete. He shrugged, stood up and left the room.

Hartz followed but paused at the door. "We'll be leaving in about an hour." He clicked his heels together and actually gave Erica an Old World bow in parting. Instead of the usual grin, Ted got a nod of well-bred impassivity with only a hint of sophisticated amusement.

I guess he's being an Austro-Hungarian baron or a Junker knight. Ted nodded back and Hartz closed the door behind him.

Ted wasn't sure that Erica had followed his meaning at first. As she began to comprehend, she drew back with a look of shock and disbelief. He reached over and grasped her arm.

"*Nein*! What do you mean, Ted? Not here . . . !"

He spoke above her protest. "Yes, Erica. We have only a little time to live. All right! Let's make love in the face of death."

She tried to push him away.

"Erica, I want you. I need you. Love me now, while there's still time!"

The idea was repugnant to her, yet his intensity was moving. She hesitated, searching his face to see if she could find someone she knew there.

He drew her closer, his right hand on her left arm. He slipped his other arm around her, pulled her to him and whispered into her ear. Slowly she relaxed against him. He undid the buttons of her blouse and pulled it open. She wore no brassiere. He put his hand over her breast.

Clunk and screech at the door! Erica started but he held her so she couldn't pull away; after the first instant she remained still. Ted looked toward the door and turned just enough that Hartz could see his hand on her breast.

"*Enschuldigung*," Hartz said. "I thought it best to check." He closed the door again and this time Ted heard the key turn in the lock, and then the light went out.

He released Erica and sat up. "Now."

"What can we do?"

"I don't know. More than we could do with them watching us."

He got his feet under him and stood up, holding the wall for support. Suddenly the room seemed to tip, the floor to press up under his feet. His pulse sledgehammered in his head and he blacked out for a few seconds. But he managed to remain standing.

"Are you all right?"

"Good enough. I may need a little help."

She put her arm around him and he leaned against her shoulder. For someone so soft, she was reassuringly solid.

"Let's go up," he said.

Hugging the wall, sliding their feet forward on each tread until their toes touched the next riser, with agonizing slowness they climbed the stone stairs that led up to the second story. The tower must have been the oldest part of the castle; the living quarters, where they had entered, had been added later. Renovations were in reverse: The tower was empty, unused. Its second floor seemed to be like the first—a great square chamber. They were in total darkness.

Ted was on the verge of nausea. "I don't think I can leave the wall, Erica. You'll have to go out into the room and try to find something."

"What?"

"Anything. A place to hide. A weapon."

She took her arm from around his back and was lost to him.

"Erica!"

"*Ja?*"

She had moved away only a few feet but in that instant when she ceased to touch him, it was as though she had gone from his life completely. He was desolate until she spoke—a voice from the spirit world but still with him.

"Which way are you going?"

"To my right."

"Count your steps. Count out loud so I can hear you."

"*Einz, zwei, drei, vier* . . ." The sound of whispered numbers receded as she drifted across the room from him. ". . . *sechts, seben, acht* . . ." She moved slowly, fearful of bumping into something, hoping desperately she *would* bump something, anything, that they could use.

Ted fantasized an opening onto a second stairway. Didn't castles always have them? Secret passages behind the walls, cobwebbed stairs winding down to a hidden door, a section of stonework that would grind open at the touch and release the prisoner to freedom.

". . . *neun-und-dreisig, viersig* . . ." Growing louder, coming back, but not directly toward him; moving toward the wall but ahead of him. Disembodied.

He was all too corporeal, all the torments of his body as solid as the rough wall that he pressed his hand against. That body didn't want to move, but her voice drew it.

". . . *sechts-und-viersig*, ooh!" She had struck the wall. "Ted, where are you?"

"Here."

"I did not think I was ahead so far."

"Not too far."

"I found nothing."

"Go across again. Keep moving back and forth and ahead. If we don't find anything before we reach the other end, we'll go up to the next floor."

"How long do we have?"

"I don't know. I can't keep track of time."

"This is so slow."

"I don't know what else to do."

"*Ja.* I go. Talk to me so I do not go the wrong way."

"They're working on this tower, repairing it. Maybe they left some lumber or stones around. We might barricade the stairway." The image flashed into his mind of one slender woman and a falling-down-dizzy man trying to wrestle great blocks of stone through total darkness to a place they couldn't see. Insane. "Maybe there will be some tools, something to fight with. Erica?"

"*Ja?*"

"Keep counting."

"*Vierzehn, fünfzehn, sechtszehn.* . . ."

"I'll move along the wall here and you come back toward me. Be careful. Just slide your feet along."

"I do so. Now again is the wall."

It seemed a contradiction: The room was large enough—it took so long to cross, their whispers back and forth were so faint—that there was no sense of being boxed in. It was more like an endless void. But then there were walls. It was like the idea of the universe having limits.

"Come back again. Come back to me. This way."

The "shsss-shsss" of her sliding steps approached and suddenly—fingertips stretched out ahead—she touched him; and then their arms were around each other, holding tight. Her cheek pressed hard against his, her hair was across his face. They felt each other's breathing, each other's heartbeats. Each felt the immeasurable joy of another person, warm and alive and real in all that black emptiness.

Neither knew how long they stood that way. Probably it was no more than a few seconds.

"We'll have to go up."

"*Ja.*"

They had searched from the stairway at one side of the room to that on the opposite wall. As before, they felt their way up. As before, Erica started slowly working her way across the chamber.

There were tiny slits in the walls, high up in dark recesses. They tantalized with glimpses of sky and occasionally Ted or Erica could see a star. But no light could push down to them. They trudged through thick blackness like deep-sea divers. Erica made excursions across the room on a lifeline of whispers while Ted kept them anchored to the wall. They found no treasure.

"Nothing."

"There should be room for you to cross once more to the other side and back. Try again."

She went off slowly and carefully, one sliding footstep every two or three seconds. How many footsteps had been wasted on the floor below? How many more would they have until the hour Hartz had given them was shuffled away? Ted tried not to think about it.

"When we're out of this, Erica, we're going to go up into one of the high meadows and just sit in the sun all day. We're going to sink down into the grass and flowers and smell the earth and feel the hot sun and make love and drink wine." He was talking to keep in contact with her and to distract their thoughts from the sound of the last seconds of their lives sliding away. But then the vision became real! He could see them sitting under a tree at the side of a pasture, looking out over the whole valley. He heard the buzzing of bees. He imagined butterflies. "Butterflies. If your hands are salty and you reach out and you're very still, they'll land in your palm."

He heard Erica reach the far wall and start back toward him.

"Where shall we go? Where's the best place? Up above on this side or across on the valley? If we're on the north side, we'll have the sun on us all—"

There was a loud crack and she screamed. He pushed away from the wall. His head reeled but he forced himself to bear on the point in the blackness where he thought she was.

"Erica!"

"*Lieber Gott!*"

"What is it?"

"*Der Boden!* The floor! It breaks!"

"Are you all right?"

"*Ja.* I have to the side fallen."

"Where are you? I'll come and—"

"*Nein!* Do not come! I do not know how big is the breaking place!"

"Are you all right?"

"*Ja.* I will come back. I must feel where the floor is safe."

He heard her brushing back and forth.

"Did it break through?"

"No. Thank God. Only beginning, when I step. *Ach*!"

"What?"

"Here also is weak. I can push with the hand. *Und hier*!" Suddenly her whisper rose in pitch. He could sense fear constricting her throat. "Ted, where are you? I cannot find anyplace—I can not see anything!"

"Here. I'm right here. Take it easy. You must have gotten turned around."

He imagined her wandering in the terrible isolation of that void, only the boards under her feet giving any surety, and then those boards falling away. He imagined her now, on her knees, trying to keep to the little piece of floor that held her weight, disoriented, fighting against a growing belief that nothing anywhere was solid. Nothing could be certain anymore: Any move—one step, an inch, a half-inch, even one deep breath—could send her tumbling down into chaos. He had felt that way himself; sometimes he had dreamed it. He knew the horror.

Could he reach her? His head had steadied. "Erica, stay still. I'll come to you."

"No! You must not! I will . . ." She moved. There was a sharp crack. "*Ach*! I cannot find . . . where I was before is now breaking too!"

"Don't move!" They were both on the edge of an abyss—of panic.

"Erica, it will be all right. Do you hear me? Face toward my voice."

"*Ja*. I hear. I turn now."

"Move toward your left. You've been over that part before. Go to your left."

"I hear. Moment. *Ja*. Here is okay." Her tone was clipped; she was in control again.

"That's the way. You should be clear by now."

"*Ja*. Now I get up."

He heard her rise and start toward him. He guided her. "Here. This way."

She reached the wall, came along toward him and he took hold of her arms and held her.

"Thank you. It is now okay." He pulled her to him but she resisted. "We must hurry."

"Are you sure you're—"

"*Ja*. It was bad for one moment only. Because of so dark."

She took his hand. Hers was firm. His shook.

"You must not think more," she told him. "When the bad moment is finished, you must not think more. Come. We go up."

They went up to the fourth floor—and there they found freedom. It was all around them: sky; mountains; the whole valley; lights in the village; the bright, just-past-full moon filled the sky with light. All they had to do to reach that freedom was to fly.

They were standing on a platform. It was made of wood, and roofed, but sections were open above chest height on all sides between the turrets placed at the four corners for shooting arrows or pouring down hot oil.

Ted's plan had been to go upstairs and find some way out, a place to hide or something to fight with.

They looked down.

"*Nein*."

They looked up.

"Could we get up on the roof?"

Erica took hold of a post. "Help me." Ted didn't understand at first; then he didn't believe. She intended to climb up onto the railing. "Come!"

He was too amazed to protest. He boosted her up. Standing on the rail, holding the post with only one hand, she leaned out over the sheer drop and tried to look up past the overhanging roof.

How can she do that?

She swung back. "I don't think so. The outhanging is too far."

Ted helped her down. They stared at each other for a moment.

"So."

He waved his hand helplessly and looked across the valley. There were no clouds although there was a haziness to the north and west. Those few lights in the village were isolated: they could give no glow to a sky so full of moonlight.

Concentrate! We can't climb down. We can't climb up. Shout? Nobody anywhere near. Signal? Fire?

"Erica, do you have any matches?"

"No." She was walking along the rail, looking down the wall below.

Why did I give up smoking?

"If we could start a fire. . . ."

"I have no fire."

We can't signal. We can't escape. We'll have to fight. How? Ted walked back to the head of the stairway.

Suddenly, "Ted, come!" Erica was leaning over the rail near one of the turrets. She pointed. "Look!"

A thick line ran down the side of the tower near one corner. A cable. Ted peered at it and could see that it was clamped or pinned to the stone at intervals and that there was some slight slack between those points. He looked up and down its length. The cable ran up and disappeared over the roof. He identified it. "Lightning rod."

"What?"

"Lightning rod. *Blitzen.*"

"*Ja. Blitzableiter.*"

"So what?"

"We can climb down."

He stared at her blankly.

"The stones, they are not smooth. One can put one's feet . . . hold the lightning—"

Preposterous. Ted could only shake his head. "You're crazy. We can't—"

"*Ja! Ich habe ofters* . . . I have such a cliff climbed many times."

"You!"

She was exasperated. "*Ja*. On my holiday. I told you, I go to the mountains."

"I didn't know . . . climbing. You're a climber? But this isn't . . . you don't have equipment. We don't have ropes or—"

"*Ja*. It is not the same. It has much danger. Here is not so safe either, *ja*?"

He stared at her in wonder. Her logic was unassailable. A million-to-one chance is better than none at all. That was why he had tricked Hartz and gotten them up here in the first place. But . . . to talk about climbing down a vertical wall! He had a sudden image of Erica carrying him draped over her back as she descended the side of the tower like Errol Flynn carrying one of his heroines. "I can't."

She stared into his eyes, defying him not to.

"I can't. I haven't the skill. And I'm afraid. I can't do it."

She looked out across the valley. At night, with the highway almost invisible, it must have looked the same to the guards in that tower eight hundred years ago.

"I'm sorry, Erica."

"*Ja*."

They stared at each other. *How can I ask her to try, to take that chance? How can I ask her to stay, to give up the chance?* Ted couldn't say anything. Erica made the decision,

"Give me your shoes, Ted."

"What?"

"Shoes! Boots!"

She had dressed for their dinner in low-heeled, sling-backed pumps. He looked at them and at her, understanding. Then he took off his boots. They had stiff, nonslip soles. Erica sat against the rail and laced them on. They would be big for her, but they would help. After that she stood, pulled up the hem of her skirt and tucked it into her waistband, giving her legs more freedom. Even in that perilous moment, he admired her legs. And now he knew why they were so strong and well-shaped. She turned to the rail. He touched her arm and she came to him. They pressed together, mouth to mouth, loin to loin, their arms encircling as though they would force their two bodies into one.

At last they pushed apart and she smiled. "Later we will finish that, *ja*?"

Ted helped her up onto the rail again. Holding the post with her left hand, she swung out and around until she could take hold of the cable with her right. She pulled at it, testing it. She brought up her right knee, planted the sole of her boot flat against the side of the tower, let go of the post and swung away from him. She grabbed with her left hand as her weight took her past the cable. She brought up her left foot beside her right, hung in a "U" out from the wall, swinging from side to side for a moment. Then she began walking slowly down the tower in that position, monkeylike, her hands and feet moving together. When she reached the first pin holding the cable to the wall she carefully adjusted her feet, then hung out from her left arm as she moved her right hand below. Then she transferred her left hand. Keeping her hands in place, she walked her feet down, feeling for a toehold. She found a gap between stones, put her weight on it, rested, her full length flattened against the tower's face.

Ted couldn't believe it. He wouldn't have thought anyone could do that, much less. . . . He tried not to be a male chauvinist; he knew women climbed mountains, he'd read of them. But Erica! He was in awe.

She had gone down a little more than one body length in her first move. Now she started again, more or less upright, holding herself close to the wall, extending one leg and then the other to find toeholds. When she found none, she would brace her feet flat against the wall, lean out and walk down it. She would descend about the distance of her own height, rest for half a minute, then move again.

Ted's initial incredulity faded as he realized that she *was* doing it. Then he began to think about *what* she was doing. *That is a lightning-rod cable. It is not meant to bear weight. The stone is old, weathered. What if she tires? It's so far down.*

Suddenly she slipped. Ted heard a stone falling, probably a chip broken from a corner she had tried to stand on. She dropped to arm's length and he heard her grunt with pain; his own arms ached at the sockets as he imagined the strain on hers. He expected to hear the pull of her weight pop pins from the wall one by one, but the cable held. Only her right foot had slipped. The blocks of stone were crudely dressed, the mortar between them weathered away in many places. Her left toe seemed still to be jammed into a joint, and she had kept some of her weight distributed between the cable and her handhold. She felt with her right foot, found another indentation, tested, then stood on it.

Although Ted was leaning over the rail to watch her, he found his knees bending. Instinctively he was trying to hunker down, to get as close as possible to solid floor. His hands shook as they clutched the rail. His stomach knotted with the feeling of dropping in a fast elevator. Had he been able to consider objectively, he might have thought the tower not really so high after all—not high like the kind of cliff face rising hundreds of feet that Erica must scale for sport. But now as he looked down along the dark stone, the tower seemed vastly high; her figure tiny; her face, and legs, white and fragile in the moonlight.

Then something happened at the periphery of his vision. At first he couldn't take his eyes from Erica to see what it was, but its happening bothered him. He looked up and saw nothing. *What was it?* He looked out across the peaceful, dark valley. So quiet, so calm, so oblivious to the ordeal Erica was experiencing and to their danger. What—in that dark tranquillity—what could it have been that troubled him?

Dark valley. Too dark: The lights in the village had gone out. Ted stood unmoving for half a minute as the implication of that sank in to his consciousness.

Then he heard a shout. Muffled as it was by distance, he could sense its urgency. Moments later there were further sounds. From outside the castle came the boom of a heavy door thrown back, the crunch of feet on gravel in the courtyard—all from the opposite side of the tower. Ted tore himself from the railing and ran across the platform.

Schimmel emerged from the car, turned on a flashlight, quickly went around and opened the lid of the trunk. A light went on. Ted saw him lean in, straighten, then turn. He had a sub-machine gun in his hands. Quickly, but not running, he reentered the castle.

Ted ran back to watch Erica again. She was still resting, standing vertically on an inch-wide ledge thirty feet above the ground.

There was a burst from the machine gun down below in the tower. It was not as loud as Ted had expected. Not as loud as he had hoped. It might have been loud enough to attract attention during the day when people were around, but not now, especially not through the stone walls and the sound-absorbing forest. Erica heard the noise and started moving down again.

There was a second burst, still muffled but loud to Ted's ears. He was sure that Schimmel would never have stepped through the gap on the ridge and been taken by surprise. Obviously the man was coming up each flight of stairs firing, then pausing and methodically sweeping each room. Hartz would be behind with the flashlight. Shoot first, see what you've hit afterward.

The third burst came, louder, closer: They were coming up to the third floor now. Erica was fifteen feet above the ground—still too high to risk dropping onto the rocky, sloping bank below. There was a sustained burst—it swept the room. Then silence as they checked around with the light. Next they would cross the room and start up to the platform.

Ted ran over to the stairway. "Hartz! I give up! Don't shoot!"

There was only silence below him. Then a foot scraped. Two steps.

Another scraping, this one on the other side, down the wall. *Can I delay them until she reaches the bottom?*

"I surrender. Don't shoot! I'll come to the head of the stairs with my hands up. You can see me. Don't shoot!" He recognized that they might have given up all subtlety and just shoot him outright, but he walked over to the stairs anyway.

He heard the sounds of whispering, stone dust crunching underfoot, cautious steps approaching.

What can I do? Can I get them to the place where the floor's breaking? Maybe if I go down to them—they're probably near the bottom of the stairs—they may move to the side as I come down.

"I'm coming."

He held his hands above his head. He could see nothing in the black rectangle below. For a moment he lost the nerve to walk down into it.

Silence. He shifted his weight forward. Suddenly—he almost jumped, it was so close— "Don't move! Schimmel will cut you in half if you even blink!"

"I know. No trick, Hartz. I haven't got one." *At least not the one I hoped for.*

Light flashed into his eyes and he did blink, and terror went through him. They searchlighted him up and down.

"Step back slowly."

He did so. Schimmel rose up out of the stairway as though Ted were hauling him at the end of a rope. He held the machine gun to his shoulder, aiming it at the center of Ted's torso. Hartz was right behind him, step by step, with his pistol. Schimmel's stare never left Ted; Hartz looked everywhere except at him. They were like one creature with two heads.

"Where is she?"

Within a split second Ted thought about and rejected the idea of a flip answer. "She's gone."

"Where?"

"Down."

Hartz stepped quickly to the wall and looked down. It was the wrong side. He moved around the platform, reaching the other side just in time to see Erica running for the woods twenty yards from the tower. He fired, shouting something to Schimmel. Schimmel took a step toward the railing, turned back and put the gun down. Before Ted could lower his hands, Schimmel had grabbed him, half-dragged, half-carried him to the parapet, lifted him bodily and held him by one arm and his belt, balanced on his back, halfway over the rail.

Terror paralyzed Ted; his body went rigid, yet it seemed as empty of strength as the pale moonlit void that—so disoriented was he—he felt he would fall upward into. Not knowing what he did, he swung his free arm but could find nothing solid to cling to.

Schimmel shouted something in German. He shouted twice and only the second time did the words penetrate Ted's panic. He couldn't understand more than "come back . . . drop him," but he comprehended the meaning, the purpose. That comprehension brought back some rationality. Everything inside of him screamed, "Don't come back, don't come back!" He started to shout it aloud, "Don't come—"

Schimmel swung him, released the grip on his arm and—holding only his belt—let him start to fall headfirst. Ted clutched Schimmel's arm and was pulled partway back up.

Ted had not thought before shouting. He had only known that Erica must not come back. If she came back, Hartz and Schimmel would kill them both. If she escaped, they might both be safe. They might not kill him; they had no protection in that; it was better for them *not* to kill him. And whether or not they did, she would still be free. Ted did not rationalize all that. He knew only that she must not return. Then Schimmel showed him that he must not try to tell her . . . *She MUST know. She WILL understand.*

He was hanging upside down, his hands locked around Schimmel's wrist, knowing in some corner of his mind that should Schimmel release him, the grip would break; yet he hung on in desperation. His head strained upward as he tried to see Schimmel's face, to read there what Schimmel saw, to see the fury when Erica didn't return, to see the decision made to pull him up or drop him. He had no sense of how long he hung there: two seconds? two minutes? It was an eternity, out of time.

Suddenly, without change in his expression, still looking toward the woods, Schimmel hauled Ted up and let him slide back so that he was almost sitting on the rail. Ted twisted to look behind him.

Erica stood at the edge of the woods, half-hidden behind a tree, watching.

Slowly Schimmel thrust Ted outward. Ted tried to grab the rail but could only lock his lower legs behind it as he was forced down head-first again. As though he were being pushed below water, horror rose up to engulf him.

Then all at once Schimmel swung him up over the rail and set him on the floor. *I knew it was only a bluff! Now I just have to—*

Ted looked down. Erica was walking back to the castle.

SATURDAY, JULY 16 09:00 HOURS—
OBER-FLATTACH

Emil Glaessel lit another cigarette, which seemed to annoy the man from Vienna: He waved his left hand in vague irritation as he continued to read. *Good*. Glaessel was more than annoyed himself with these big-shots who come into the provinces and interrupt everything you are doing and make you do it all differently and then don't like any of it . . . unless what you were doing proves to have been the right thing after all, in which case they take credit for it.

Glaessel exhaled a blue cloud as thick as his resentment and stared out the window. He could see into the street below. A line of small children, blue or red packs on their backs, was being led off for a day in the mountains. He had promised his own children an outing. It was a fine morning for it—bright and sunny, the finest Saturday in a month, one he would have had off but for whatever maniac it was who had killed the little barmaid.

Glaessel had privately accepted the maniac theory. He

191

and his men would check everything, of course: the possibility of some feud involving the girl's family or the café owner, a crime of passion—preposterous, except that anything seemed possible with children these days. But the only theory that really made sense was that the crime did not make sense and that it had been committed by a madman who undoubtedly had left town—although he might yet be here because he was mad.

"An American. She was serving an American?"

"Yes, Herr Tolz." Lieutenant Steiner stood at virtual attention by the end of the table where Tolz sat. Glaessel took another drag on his cigarette, the bite on his tongue somehow a satisfying substitute for the scorn he wanted to show Steiner. *Yes, Herr Tolz. May I kiss your ass, Herr Tolz?*

Steiner came around. "Permit me, Herr Tolz." He leaned forward, fingered through the pages of the report Tolz was holding. "Here is his interrogation."

"Thank you."

"Thank you, sir." Steiner stepped back smartly.

"Theodore Barstow." Johann was leaning over Tolz's shoulder, scanning the report with him. He shrugged.

". . . from Salzburg . . ." Tolz read Ted's answers aloud, ". . . this morning—no, just after noon."

Johann calculated. "He would have to have left there . . . on the express, at about ten-thirty, ten-forty-five."

Tolz turned to look up at Johann, then back at Lieutenant Steiner. "Would you describe this man?"

As Steiner did so, Tolz stared off into space with the expression Johann always thought of as "about to kiss a frog."

"Johann. . . ."

"Sir?"

"Could it be possible that we have underrated Rinehardt Erbacher?"

"How?"

"We assumed he made a mistake at the station yesterday, that he turned in the wrong direction when he went away from the American, Hollings. What if there were two Americans? What if—the Americans call it a 'sleeper.' "

"A decoy?"

"No. Hollings would be the decoy. Some other person who sleeps out of sight until the last moment."

"And we never suspected. We let him go."

"Inspector Glaessel."

"Yes?" This Tolz's ID carried no indication of rank. Okay then, he would get no "sir" from Emil Glaessel.

"We must find this man, this Barstow. You have only two men?"

"Yes. *Only* two." Naturally there were no detectives in a country village. Glaessel and his assistants had come up from Spittal. "And they're tied up running—"

"Inspector Glaessel." Tolz raised his right hand, managing to keep the forefinger from lifting in admonishment. "It is essential that we find this man. I don't mean to interrupt your investigation, but finding this Barstow will lead you to your killer—or killers. I have no doubt that *he* was the intended target of this shooting."

Glaessel smoldered through his nostrils. It was insufferable. This pomposity arrives, reads two pages of a preliminary report and believes he has solved the crime. "And just what makes you think so?"

Tolz did not respond for several seconds, during which time Johann's face registered first shock and then the probability that he would cross the room to administer chastisement himself. "I have intelligence," Tolz said levelly. He let it sink in before elaborating. "Special knowledge." He turned back to glance over the report once more.

"Well, I'm glad to know it. It's a lot easier to solve a

crime when you have 'special knowledge' about it. Where does your special knowledge suggest I start looking for Barstow?''

Tolz did not look up. ''You have his hotel. If he is not there, please try to find out where he has gone. It is important that we locate him before he gets there and leaves again. Since he came by train, he will not have an automobile unless he rents one. Therefore he will travel locally by taxi, bus or on foot.'' Tolz turned to face Glaessel. ''Those possibilities should be enough to get you started.''

''We'll try.'' Glaessel pushed away from the wall with his shoulder and started to cross the room toward the door.

''Inspector Glaessel?''

''Yes?''

''Do you like provincial police work?''

''Yes.''

''Good.''

Although it was mid-morning, the haystacks had the look of afternoon. The hillside was so steep that sun at almost any angle cast long shadows. Tolz looked past them to the wooded slopes southward across the valley and then up to the peaks. Directly opposite, a ridge of points led back and up to the jagged summits of the range. They seemed to tear the tender sky. Tolz did not like mountains. Mountains revealed nature's essential character—hard, cruel, totally uncaring for man and his destiny. Tolz had been made sufficiently aware of that character through all the years of his work and his life.

Johann and the police driver brought the farmer up from the meadow. He nodded to Tolz and offered ''*Grüsse Gott*'' with deference but reserve, then stood still, his right hand resting on his scythe as though prepared to swear by it. He was short—typical of people of the area—and untypically thin. He had the stolidness Tolz associated with such peasants, but his eyes were wary and calculating, as though suspecting this official from Vienna might visit celebrity or calamity on him, either without comprehensible reason.

"Herr Katernig?"

"Yo."

"You have a daughter, Ilse?"

"Yo. What's she done?"

"She is not accused of a crime, Herr Katernig. We believe she may have some information that would help us in our investigation."

"Yo?"

"Yes." Tolz paused but Katernig simply stared back at him, offering neither information nor curiosity. Although the man's land might be worth millions, Tolz realized he had little else and gave nothing away. "Do you know where Ilse is?"

"No." Katernig's eyes shifted past him.

"When did you last see her?"

"I don't know. Three years, four years."

"She left home?"

"Yo."

"Where did she go?"

"I don't know." He looked at Tolz again. "I heard she works in Bad Gastein."

"Yes. We have been there. Did she go to Bad Gastein when she left home?"

"I don't know where she went. I told you."

"You haven't heard from her since?"

"No. Never a word." Katernig gave that information freely, looking directly into Tolz's eyes with pain in his own. That, at least, was something he had enough of to share. "Not even a word on my birthday."

"You live by yourself?"

"Yo. The girl's mother died when she was six. I'm all alone."

Tolz nodded slightly. "I also live alone."

Katernig returned the nod, acknowledging their bond of suffering. "It's terrible to be alone. It's not right for a man to have to be alone."

"And she's never called you, or written, or sent word at all?"

"Never."

Tolz shook his head in apparent dismay and commiseration. Then, "So. We will have to inquire elsewhere. Did she have close friends that you know of?"

"No." Again Katernig looked away as he answered. "Maybe some girls in the village, from school. Not up here." He indicated with his chin the entire shoulder of the mountainside. The nearest neighbor seemed to be across an erosion gully, more than a kilometer away by the road that ran around it.

"According to her employment records at Bad Gastein, Ilse is seventeen now. She would have been—you say— thirteen or fourteen when she left you. That seems young to leave home."

"She was old enough."

"Old enough for what?"

Katernig opened his mouth, closed it and then answered: "To get herself into trouble."

"What kind of trouble?"

"The kind a girl gets herself into."

"Was she pregnant? Did she have a boyfriend?"

"How do I know? I couldn't watch her every minute. I have this whole farm to take care of all by myself. She went down to the village. How could I watch her every minute?"

"Then how do you know she was getting into trouble?"

"I didn't say she was. I said she was old enough for it.

You just had to look at her—at the clothes she wore, the way she let her boobies show through her blouse. Doesn't surprise me at all she's in trouble with the police now." Katernig paused, cleared his throat, shifted his hand down onto the neck of the scythe handle and looked again up the hillside.

Tolz seemed about to ask something more but paused and nodded. "So. Thank you, Herr Katernig. You have been helpful. We will detain you no longer from your work."

"We must keep Glaessel and his men searching for the American. There will be no point to finding the girl if he or Brunner and Janovich get to the pictures first. We should be able to have help down from Salzburg within another hour."

Tolz and Johann sat in the rear of the police car. Johann caught glimpses of the view ahead through the front window. The entire valley lay before them, little clusters of villages strung at almost regular intervals along the twin ribbons of highway and river.

"The village police can continue to check hotels for Brunner and Janovich," Tolz went on.

"Perhaps roadblocks?"

"We will consider it. I will remain at the police station. I will ask the lieutenant to accompany you, and you begin on the girl. She must have had some friend she stayed with, at least at first, when she left him."

Johann nodded, then turned and looked out the back window at the old farmhouse now high on the shoulder behind them. "The filthy bastard."

SUNDAY, JULY 17 04:20 HOURS— *OBER-FLATTACH*

Trust not and you will not be betrayed. Ted was not surprised that Erica had come back. He hadn't had time really to think about it, but if he had, he would have expected it. It seemed sometimes that everyone he had ever really needed had betrayed him—including himself. *Like my being taken in by Hartz. If we can't remember how to prevent ourselves from being hurt, how can we expect others not to hurt us? I shouldn't call it betrayal. Erica meant to save me.*

"How could I let him drop you?"

"He wouldn't have."

"I thought he would."

"It was a chance we had to take. He's going to kill me—both of us—now anyway."

"But it would have been *I* that killed you."

Ted didn't reply. *It happens even when we want to help. The only hope lies in never trusting, never becoming involved.*

"How could I live the rest of my life thinking always that I killed you? How could I live knowing you thought . . . you died thinking I killed you?" She stared at him in agony, as though the lines across her forehead were a head strap twisting tight. Her fingers were linked like chains, and her hands struggled against them.

Her anguish cut through his self-pity. He touched her cheek and smiled at her. "Thank you, Erica. Thank you for wanting to save me. It was very brave of you to come back." He put his hand over hers and squeezed.

"You *are* a charming couple."

Neither of them responded. They sat together on one of the black-leather couches. Hartz sat on the other one, across from them, holding his pistol.

"And an amazing couple. Fraulein, that was spectacular! Speaking from a disinterested point of view, Barstow, it's too bad Fraulein Stendler couldn't have saved you a second time. Give a nice symmetry to the whole adventure."

Ted asked what he meant and Hartz told him of how Brunner and Janovich had stalked him at the concert. The story was interesting, but Ted was beyond surprise. Only one question occurred to him: "How do you know? You didn't get to the village until Saturday morning." Hartz only grinned and Ted thought it out for himself. "You had someone else here already. He must have followed me from Salzburg."

Schimmel came back into the room. "*Nicht gehört.*"

Hartz nodded.

Ted inferred that Schimmel had been on the telephone to that "someone else," who had heard nothing of the gunfire.

Hartz took a deep breath and sighed. He smiled at Ted and Erica benevolently. "Well, I guess we can go now."

"All right, Hartz," Ted said. "You win. I'll give you the coordinates." Even without hope, Ted might have been glad to say it just to see Hartz's expression. His expressions. Initial shock gave him the look of a poached egg. Then one side of his mouth tried to turn down in negation and disbelief but the other side wanted to rise to welcome possibility. The likelihood that Ted was tricking him sharpened his stare, while triumph raised his brow. After twisting for a moment, Hartz landed on his feet.

"You don't have the coordinates. You are Barstow, and you are trying to trick us again."

"I am Barstow, and I don't have the coordinates, and I am trying to trick you again. So you'd better shoot me so I can't give you the coordinates I don't have." Ted grinned at him. There were no dimples, but it was a reasonable imitation.

Hartz showed that he could take it as well as give it out. He laughed. Then he studied Ted for a moment, then grinned back. "You *are* a deep one. You must be, because on the face of it, that was stupid. We have already established how we can get information from you."

"No need. The coordinates are forty-three degrees north, twenty-seven degrees west. Or twelve meters right, seventeen up." Hartz looked blank, then annoyed. Ted went on. "If you don't like those, I can give you some others. They might sound better to you but they won't necessarily be more accurate." He paused. "Yes, I am deceiving you. I'm not going to give you the coordinates, I'm going to sell them. The price is our freedom. Now *you* come up with a way of guaranteeing it."

Schimmel exploded. Ted couldn't follow the curses in German. Before he could half-turn, Schimmel came from behind and slapped the back of his head with an open palm. It was worse than when he hit the stone floor because he didn't pass out. It was as though his head had been used to strike a great bronze bell. Lights flashed before his eyes and he was thrown forward. Schimmel came around to the front of the couch. Through a red haze

Ted could make out his legs like posts. He expected Schimmel to batter him; he cowered and tried to lift his arms to cover his head. Erica sprang up swinging at Schimmel. He shot one palm toward her that threw her bouncing down on the couch. He did not hit Ted.

When Ted's head cleared enough for him to see, he peered up at Schimmel, whose face was as impassive as ever. "No more," Schimmel said. "We will no more having. Understanding?" He turned and spoke to Hartz in rapid German. Erica drew in her breath and cried, "*Nein*!"

Hartz's face stiffened. He looked at Ted for a moment, then shook his head. "Schimmel doesn't enjoy these games as we do, Barstow. He puts the matter bluntly: We give you nothing; you give us the coordinates. We send someone to check them. If they do not check out, we do something nasty to the woman—I won't even mention what he suggested, but it was sexual and it would torture her body, mind and spirit simultaneously. We keep doing it until you give us coordinates that are correct."

Ted looked back at the man with hatred. Hartz couldn't take that. He shifted uneasily and put his head on one side. "Come on, Barstow. It's been a long night. We're all ragged. But we can deal with this on a higher plane, okay?" He tried to smile.

Ted regarded him steadily for as long as he could, stalling for time to think. Hartz did look tired; he was puffy under the eyes and his tan was like makeup on a wax dummy. Ted didn't want to imagine how he himself looked. Only Schimmel looked the same.

Ted sighed, turned away and stared at the floor. His shoulders slumped. Finally, in a small voice, he said, "Okay. The coordinates are eight centimeters north and fourteen centimeters west."

Schimmel shouted, "*Centimeters*?" Hartz just closed his eyes; the wax seemed to melt.

"Those are the coordinates but they're not what you expected, are they?"

"No. They are not what we expect."

"That's the point."

Hartz opened his eyes. Schimmel stepped back—to be out of Ted's reach—and squatted so he could look directly into his face.

Ted smiled scornfully. "What did you expect they'd be, degrees?"

"We are sure they are in degrees."

"They can be. Maybe they were. What do you do when you're given coordinates in degrees and you want to find the location?"

Schimmel spoke levelly and Hartz translated. "No games."

"You look up the point on a map. I have given you a point on a map. Eight centimeters north, fourteen west."

"Of what?"

"I don't know."

Schimmel stood abruptly, contemplating violence again.

"It's true," Ted said. "It's on paper. It was a safety: Neither the coordinates nor the paper are any good alone."

"Why not?"

"Erbacher gave me the paper—"

"He did not!"

"He didn't? Were you there on the bench with us? Who was there who can swear Erbacher didn't leave a little piece of tissue paper folded up behind him; didn't pass it to me behind his satchel?"

"He wouldn't have been so stupid as to put the coordinates down on paper."

"The coordinates weren't on the paper. He told them to me. What's on the paper is a base point—just some key marks and a point. The point isn't anything obvious, like a peak, that I could remember. It's just a point made with a ball-point pen. I put the paper over a map and marked the point through to the map. I didn't mark out the coordinates or figure where they lie. I didn't plan to do that until I got closer just in case something like this happened. I can't tell you where the location you want is. It's a point on a map to be found from another basepoint."

"What map?"

"Obviously the Kreuzeck Gruppe hiking map." Ted hoped his answer would be "obvious." Hartz had tried his reaction over and over to the name "Kreuzeck."

"Where is the map?"

"In my backpack. Up on the approach to Rotzahn. I hid it yesterday when Brunner and Janovich were chasing me."

They didn't believe him. They knew they shouldn't believe him. Their expressions were those of old confidence men approached by a kid with a gold brick for sale. They could hardly believe he was so foolish as to try to trick them. They stared into Ted's eyes, waiting for any flicker, any nervous twitch, by which he'd release the tension of lying. But Ted had detached. He had slipped out through the back door into the cold outside, where he spent most of his life, and they couldn't see him there. They knew he was lying. But they couldn't not believe him either.

Putzi brought bread rolls and two litre-cans of milk. For that Ted was glad to meet him. He was interested also to see the man who had followed him from Salzburg and through the crowd at the band concert and had never been noticed himself. Putzi was a small man, nearly sixty, with one of those faces in which—without strong bones to hold it in place through the years—the skin has pulled down thin over forehead and nose and begun to fold and sag around a narrow jaw. In a pink-and-white checkered shirt, black-corduroy hiking knickers and a Tyrolean hat, he was unmistakably a bookkeeper from Hamburg on a two-week holiday. Someone must have slipped the revolver into the pocket of his jacket as a practical joke.

They had breakfast in Putzi's rented car, a faded-green, eight-to-ten-year-old Mercedes: six to the mile on any moderately crowded highway. With Ted's help, they were thinking of everything. They were parked beside the bank, close to where Janovich had waited the day before—to all appearances just a group of friends having a snack before hiking.

No one else was out for hiking. It was Sunday morning, early. And not a good day. Local people know the signs: Yesterday had been too good, today would not be good at all; gray sky, temperature dropping.

Ted had insisted on warm clothes for Erica. "She's your pressure on me. I'd just as soon you shot me now, I'm only going on a chance for her sake. She has to go too, and she has to be dressed for it." The wife of the dentist who owned the castle had unknowingly obliged. In one of the bedrooms they had found a pair of slacks and a sweater, even boots more nearly fitting than Ted's. The fad spread and both Schimmel and Hartz wore aprés-dentistry fashions. For a change, Schimmel was the better-dressed. Evidently the dentist was short and thick-waisted; his bulky charcoal-wool sweater distributed well over Schimmel's shoulders. Hartz looked slightly ludicrous in a fleece-lined windbreaker too big and too small for him at the same time. He buttoned and unbuttoned the cuffs, rolled and unrolled them; tried the front zipped up, half-open, loose—not all at once, but fussing with it every few minutes to try to find a way of making it look good.

The bread was still warm from the oven, delicious even without butter and jam. The milk was fresh and cold. Ted felt better after eating. He knew it was merely a physiological lift; if you eat and raise your blood sugar, you feel better. He had absolutely no other reason for feeling better.

What next? How far can I play it? How long will they accept not finding the map?

Ted thought of the story: A cruel king orders a wise man killed. "Spare me for a year, Your Highness, and I'll teach your horse to talk." His friend asks, "Why say that?" The wise man replies, "A year is a long time: The horse may die, the king may die, I myself may die of natural causes. Or—who knows?—the horse may learn to talk." Ted had always liked that story.

They drove up to the head of the valley and parked some distance from the barns and cabin.

"Of course the old woman's all right," Hartz said. "We told her we were waiting for friends. We had some *schnapps* with her. Several glasses. She got sleepy. I couldn't have hurt her, dear old soul: She reminded me of Granny. Now what do you think of us?"

"Less and less."

They went directly into the woods to avoid the cabin and then made their way over to the trail. Looking up, Ted had seen clouds behind the toothed ridge. There was no wind but the air seemed colder. Although he had no hope, the possibility of a plan began to form in his mind.

He was put first, then Erica, followed by Schimmel, pretending the sub-machine gun was a salami wrapped in a towel, then Hartz, then Putzi.

"Where is it?"

"Way up. Beyond the idiot's hut. Remember, I still thought I was going to find help when I got to that hut. I didn't get rid of the pack until farther up, when I knew I'd have to fight."

They came out of the woods onto the knob and went up the rise toward the hut.

"*Schnell, schnell.*"

"I'm going as fast as I can!" Ted wasn't, but he saw no reason to hurry.

"*Schnell*!" Schimmel jabbed Erica in the back with the barrel of the gun. She gasped with pain and shock. Ted spun to his left, took a step back down the hill and, using the momentum of that step, he swung a roundhouse right to the side of Schimmel's head. Whether staggered or simply in reaction, Schimmel jumped away. The gun came up and he pawed at the towel.

"Anton!" Hartz shouted. "*Nein*!"

Schimmel's jaw muscles were rigid. Ted bit his lip. The forces they tried to beam from their eyes would have clanged together exactly halfway between them. But they had no forces, and Ted had no gun. That truth got through to him. He stepped back.

"Hartz, we have a delicate balance here," he said. "It's in your favor, but not by much. I expect you to kill me. I go on because—moment by moment—it seems better. Kill me now, you lose your last chance at those coordinates. But if you hurt her, if you push me too far, I'll make you kill me."

Hartz regarded him, then spoke to Schimmel. His tone was calm and reasonable, one of persuasion. That began to darken in the lines of a picture Ted had been forming.

"All right, Barstow, let's go on. At a delicately balanced rate of speed, right?"

He's no fool. I've got to keep that in the picture too.

They started up again and passed the hut, now apparently empty, and moved toward the viewpoint rise. Ted knew he would have to do something soon. There was no hope of repeating the trick on the ridge, and they knew he hadn't gone past the ridge.

They went over a slight hillock. They looked toward the rise. By now the bank of clouds had built on the western side, risen and spilled over the ridge. Mist began two hundred yards ahead, and heavy fog just beyond. The clouds had poured down the grassy side of the ridge toward the little valley.

"We're almost there," Ted said.

Schimmel kept his eyes on Ted and Erica steadily as he unwound the towel from the gun. With his dark hair, and bulky, dark sweater, he loomed against the milky whiteness behind him like a mountain ogre. Hartz stood just to one side. In the dampness, the meticulous waves of hair at his temples were sagging. Only two paces away, Putzi seemed to be behind a gauze. Tendrils of mist groped down from the clouds just above their heads as though trying to find some grip on the earth. The lower air was still warm enough to make them draw back, coil around the humans and then drift away.

The group stood on a nearly level shoulder, one of a series of levels between rises that formed one wall of the valley and stepped ultimately up to the peak. Each rise was greater than the one below, each level had steeper sides. Where they stood, the side toward the valley began dropping at an angle of about forty degrees, becoming less severe as it went down.

That's the way to go, Ted calculated. Above, in the fog, there was only the saw-toothed ridge, followed by the peak and then another ridge curving around to form the head wall of the valley. Seen together in a single sweep, the two ridges made the west and south sides of half a bowl. The only escape route possible was into the bottom of that bowl, then down again to the valley and back through it.

However, they couldn't try that route unless Ted could persuade Schimmel not to shoot them.

He took Erica's hand and said to the others again, "I didn't intend for them to see the backpack. That was the whole point."

Schimmel dropped the towel. He held the gun in a ready position, not aimed directly at them but pointed only an inch past Ted's elbow. His eyes had locked on target and were waiting only for Ted to move or to add one more lie and overbalance the pile.

Hartz didn't believe Ted either. "So you threw it away."

"You're not being chased. You've got all the time you need to think about it. Okay, even with that advantage, you tell me something better I should have done."

Moments passed and Schimmel didn't shoot, so Ted went on. "I took it by the straps, swung it back and heaved it out as far as I could. I can't point to where it hit. It probably rolled some. I figured I'd have to look later, but I knew I'd find it again."

Ted imagined Schimmel was trying to decide whether he really wanted to expend the energy necessary to play out this part of the charade. The story, like the assurances of a man sitting on an anthill that he was perfectly comfortable, was becoming increasingly improbable. But Schimmel's choices were to either parade back and forth on the mountainside in the fog like a fool or to shoot and possibly walk away like an even greater fool from the map that might be only sixty feet away. He decided to be a hopeful fool.

"From here? You did from here throwing?"

Ted judged carefully—Schimmel, not the location. "Yes. Somewhere between there and . . . there." His boundaries were about thirty feet apart; not intolerably vague but sufficiently broad to widen the area of search.

Schimmel actually allowed a flicker of expression to cross his face: a tired, cynical resignation. Then he jerked his head toward the slope. Still holding Erica's hand, Ted started downhill.

The possibilities arising from that move became evident to everyone at once: Ted and Erica were out ahead, facing down a hill so steep they could hardly keep from running, and heading into a dense fog.

"*Halt!*"

They reorganized—Schimmel first, then Ted, Erica, Hartz and Putzi—and started down again. Hartz slipped. His shoes were a fashionable over-the-ankle mock riding-boot style with smooth leather soles. The hill was steep, the grass slick. One foot went out from under him. He found himself sitting on the other foot. In that split second Ted thought to throw himself downhill against Schimmel. Fortunately, his reactions were too slow. Even before he might have moved, Schimmel had turned and braced himself, the gun up and ready: sheer instinct, triggered by Hartz's grunt as he went down. Ted froze, but Schimmel recognized what might have been.

They reorganized—Hartz first, then Ted, Erica, Schimmel and Putzi. Hartz half-slipped again, righted himself and continued down sideways, placing his feet carefully, slowly. The others had to wait for him. Schimmel was impatient.

They reorganized—Putzi first, then Ted, Erica and Schimmel, with Hartz trailing behind. After they had descended about thirty feet, Putzi turned, questioning.

Ted shrugged. "Could be. Here or a little farther down. I'd start looking here."

Schimmel gestured to the right. Putzi started across the slope, the rest in file behind him. Visibility at ground level was less than eight feet to either side. They would have to traverse the hillside slowly, looking from side to side, then descend fifteen feet and sweep back again. Given the odds of a reasonably good throw and of the pack having rolled a bit, they might have to drop down and make the sweep five, even six, times.

They were not efficient as they were—all together, one behind another. A searching party should be spread out, side to side. And neither Erica nor Ted could be expected to report the pack if they saw it; Hartz was still having trouble with his footing; Schimmel had to give half of his attention to guarding. The absurdity of the procession became apparent as they reached the limit of the first traverse. Schimmel called for Putzi to lead down and around. As they all followed in train, Erica giggled. "We should have a band: bum-bum-bum-boom!"

That she should retain a sense of humor despite what they had been through and what they faced. . . . A wave of bright heat made something in Ted's chest suddenly swell and he touched her arm.

Schimmel hadn't understood. "*Was?*"

"*Wir sölten die Kappelle haben.*"

Schimmel was not amused. "*Halt!*"

He gave quick orders in German. Ted and Erica were to stay where they were; Hartz was to guard them. Schimmel and Putzi, side by side, would sweep the hill. They moved away and disappeared, fading from sight by gray degrees, yet so quickly, completely and silently it seemed they had never been at all. The ridge above had never been; there was no mountain, no valley; above, below, place, time were meaningless. In the instant Schimmel and Putzi vanished, Hartz, Erica and Ted felt they had been together eternally in that one-place no-place: three people standing alone beyond the universe.

Hartz connected back to reality. He drew his pistol. "Lead is a great remedy for that fading-away feeling." He tried to burn off the mist and chill with a grin.

Ted and Erica were half-turned from him. Without looking around, Ted squatted on his heels. "You'd better sit down, Hartz. You'll probably slip again and blast your toe off."

Erica knelt beside him. After a moment of indecision, Hartz let himself down onto the grass.

Despite—or perhaps because of—the grayness, the col-

ors of the flowers seemed especially intense. Ted and
Erica stared at them. "*Schön, ja?*" Erica cupped a blue-
bell in her hand.

How can she do that? Erica didn't seem to Ted to be
like himself, trying to take life by bits since chunks were
too heavy, and all of it together crushing. He had the sense
that she believed each moment by moment led to a happy
ending. But how could she—*now*—pause at this moment
to admire a flower? She was actually smiling, her face
bright with delight.

"Beautiful," he said. But he concentrated on the *next*
moment, looking over his shoulder at Hartz, who sat with
his knees drawn up, his hand with the pistol in it resting on
them. "You're going to get your ass wet, Colonel."

Hartz regarded Ted for several seconds, and then pushed
himself up onto his heels.

Ted nodded. "Good. It's hard enough to have respect
for somebody who wears fruit boots and keeps falling
down the mountain, but nobody can respect a colonel with
a wet ass." Ted studied Hartz sardonically. "But of course
you aren't a colonel, are you?"

Hartz was nonplussed, as though after catching him with
his hand in the silverware drawer, Ted had torn away his
false beard, pulled the pillow from under the red jacket
and only then begun to suspect that Hartz wasn't the true
Santa Claus.

"I mean in anybody's army, Hartz. You got the intro-
ductions reversed. Schimmel's the colonel and you're the
flunky. Isn't that right?"

"Schimmel and I are partners."

Erica looked back and forth between them.

"Sure. Like an organ-grinder and his monkey. Only this
time it's a gorilla holding the chain and you rattle the cup
and do the tricks."

Erica giggled.

Hartz's eyes narrowed, his mouth turned down. "That's not how it is."

"It sure looks that way. You kept me so shaken I didn't see it at first, but I should have. Every decision that had to be made, Schimmel made it. He nearly shot me before; you had to talk him out of it. But when he wanted you to stay here with us, he just ordered you to do it. He just detailed you to the job that takes the least talent. He's the boss. You're the front man. You've got the pretty face, the wavy hair, the gorgeous smile—I'll give you that, your smile is gorgeous."

Erica huffed. "Plastic. My dentist has one on the shelf in his office."

"Well, you can't win them all, Hartz. I fell for the smile. But it's all out front. You're like one of those pretty dummies they prop up in front of TV cameras and play news through. Schimmel winds you up and you dance."

The skin over the bridge of Hartz's nose drew tight, his nostrils widened. Then he caught himself. His lips didn't want to smile but he willed them into line. "You're clever, Barstow. But I know the relationship between Schimmel and myself. You're not going to split us to your advantage. You're not going to get out of this that way."

"I don't flatter myself. That wasn't the point."

"What is your point?"

"Just a little personal satisfaction at the end of the road. There isn't anything you can do to me beyond what you're already planning to do, so I might as well have the satisfaction of letting you know how I feel about you."

Hartz shrugged. "If it makes you feel better. . . ."

"It does."

With a shock—it was like suddenly meeting Martians—they saw Schimmel and Putzi half-solidify out of the white nothingness fifteen feet down the hill. The pair passed slowly and in silence without seeming to notice them, as though they were all figments of unrelated dreams. They must have seen them, though, and used them as a marker. They turned downhill and faded away again, going back the other way.

Now. I've got to do it now. "You really are ridiculous, Hartz. You say you like to think you're a professional." Ted snorted. "You're a laugh a minute. I met you only about fifteen hours ago and I've already tricked you half a dozen times. You don't know right now—this minute— whether I'm tricking you again: whether I'm tricking you into believing I have the coordinates or whether I'm tricking you into believing I don't." Ted leaned toward Hartz confidingly. "Well, I'll tell you. I *am* tricking you." He looked directly into his eyes and laughed. "That's the truth, Hartz, and I don't mind telling you because I know you haven't got the brains to figure out how."

Hartz's eyes narrowed again but he tried to keep it light. "Scores on both sides. I tricked you too."

"That's what hurts me the most, Hartz—that I let myself be taken in by you even for a little while. I try to excuse myself by saying I was tired, but even tired, I should have seen. . . . You're such an *obvious* phony. To be taken in for one minute by an aging beachboy! Somebody as easy to see through as a 'sincere' cigarette ad. I deserve what I'm getting, Hartz, but I don't deserve it from you."

"Ted, he is not worth being angry." Erica picked up the play as though they had planned their lines beforehand.

"That's exactly why I'm angry! Schimmel, at least, is authentic. He's smart, tough, keeps to his cover. You expect to lose to a man like Schimmel. When Schimmel comes back, I'm going to go for him so at least I'll be shot in the front by a *man*. This stuffed-shirt phony. . . . Look at him! Take away his tailor-made jacket, he's a clown."

The pouches under Hartz's eyes sagged and Ted could see a vein in his temple throbbing.

Erica kept it going. "*Ja*. So you should laugh. He does look so silly." She began giggling again. "Look at his hair over his ears. He is like a wet chicken."

"He's a chicken, all right. Shoot you in the back, but he hasn't got the guts to—"

Hartz broke. He lashed out to whip Ted across the face with the pistol barrel. Fast. He would have hit if Ted hadn't been trying to provoke him to do it.

Ted rolled off his heels, throwing himself backward downhill, simultaneously reaching forward and grabbing Hartz's wrist and hand, deflecting the gun and pulling him after. Hartz was yanked up onto his toes and over. He started to fall on Ted, who was making a simple backward somersault. Ted's legs came up naturally, his knees against his chest, the soles of his feet facing up. As though they were trained acrobats, their movements conjoined. Hartz's abdomen came down onto Ted's feet; they were one body rolling up onto Ted's shoulders. He drove his legs up and beyond his head, flinging Hartz downhill and bringing himself through the circle and onto his knees facing uphill.

Erica was already on her feet.

"Run!" Ted shouted. "Run!" He was running himself even before rising—pumping his legs to keep them under him—not so much running as falling from one step to the next. He sprinted uphill for a few yards and then cut to the side and down.

Hartz had clutched the trigger, firing one shot as he was thrown. Now his gun cracked several more times. Erica fell . . . and Ted had time to know she was dead.

His insides withered and shrank, leaving only anger to flare through the emptiness. He was as good as dead himself—and he didn't care. His legs drove on mechanically and she rolled head over heels three times down the slope.

She came to her feet and was running again without an instant's hesitation. Ted screamed, "Erica!" He bounded— *flew* out, touched earth and bounded again to come up beside her; they grasped hands and ran together straight down into the cloud . . . and out of it.

Tentacles writhed toward their heads, but they were too deep to be touched. Like a living thing, the cloud hunched over the mountain, groping but unable to clutch into the layer of warmer air below. Now Ted could see clear to the bottom of the great bowl. Under an eerie light filtering from above the cloud mass, the grass glowed as though from within. Normally when Ted saw that glow, he went home, imagining he might meet among the crags hairy, huge-handed creatures with twisted horns. Now, though, he had less fanciful monsters to avoid.

The cloud-covered ridge was directly behind them, rising to their right to Rotzahn's peak. He and Erica could turn and climb and be hidden but they would have to climb ever-steeper, ever-more-dangerous slopes—inching their way up a wall they could not surmount. If they were seen, even glimpsed, through the drifting fingers of fog, their pursuers could back them up against the sky.

Or they could retrace their steps to the left and up into the cloud cover so Hartz and the others couldn't see them unless they were close. Or, finally, they could go down, keeping their lead but remaining visible. The bowl was high pasture. Perhaps a mile away from where they stood it ended abruptly in another drop down to the valley. That slope would be forested. If they could reach it, they had a good chance of escape. After only a moment's pause, they started down.

They slowed their pace, compromising between fear of

capture and fear of falling. As they descended, the pitch would flatten and they could go faster.

A call came from the left, moving behind them and then to the right; it was far away, yet all around them. Another came from a different direction, yet again from everywhere. The echo of the third shout also rounded and rolled from the mountain walls. The weight of the great clouds pressed down and absorbed the sound. The muted calls were more terrifying than harrying by dogs might have been. That, at least, would have focused their fear. Echoes made the danger seem to be everywhere. A glance back over their shoulders could fix their pursuers at definite points, but the quality of sound was dreamlike, unreal, irrationally menacing.

And Ted and Erica felt so small. If the bowl were an amphitheater, an arena for combat, the fighters should have been giants. The walls should have resounded with crashes of stone hammers; the trees below should have writhed from roars and bellowings; the mountain itself should have shaken under pounding feet. But they were tiny, only to be noticed as they ran—a dot of yellow, a dot of blue.

Hartz was a rock-tan speck above, and moving toward their right. Putzi was not as fast, but he was closing the way behind and to their left. And far down the mountainside, Schimmel loped like a black bear. Their calls to one another carried, yet seemed only to intensify the silence: Their voices were so thin and puny, so incapable of filling the vast expanse.

Ted calculated as he ran. *Can they ever catch us in so great a space? Yes.* The place was a bowl. The only way to go was down and into it. Their pursuers were spread out, hundreds of yards from each other, but convergence was inevitable . . . unless he and Erica could reach the woods first.

Schimmel was fast, and quick-thinking as well. Unlike the others, he had not set his line toward his quarry but ran on a vector toward where they must go. He would reach the edge of the pasture before they did. No matter how they swerved, Schimmel would cut them off. Even though they were half a mile apart, he would be at the bottom first; the others would drive them to him.

If it weren't for the guns! I could take Putzi easily, probably take Hartz too. But Ted knew that each of them carried around himself a black-magic circle he dared not enter. He and Erica ran faster now, but he had no hope left, not unless they could fly, sink into the earth or vanish.

They sank into the earth and vanished. What had seemed a smooth bowl was actually ribbed with gullies made by the snow and ice that ran off the slopes above. Hardly noticeable from higher up, the gully they came to suddenly— up a slight rise and down a grassy bank—was at least twelve feet deep.

"'*Eine hutte!*"

There—sheltering against the bank, down below the crest and out of the worst of the wind—was a small hut. It was only twenty feet square, stone-walled and with a slate-covered roof. A refuge for herdsmen or hikers.

"We can here hide."

"No. It's a trap. We'll be cornered." Being in the open and able to run might be only an illusory freedom but Ted preferred it to waiting passively to be found. "We might get past them if we go uphill. They expect us to go down. If we keep to the bottom here, then go up, they may run by us and we can climb back above them."

Their thighs stiffened and ached as they were made to work uphill again. Ted and Erica scrambled up the gully for the distance of a hundred yards.

"I'll take a look." Ted turned up the bank, keeping low, then dropped to his knees and finally lay prone. Crawling the last few yards, he peered through the grass.

Putzi was directly in front of him. He was about fifty yards away, descending almost parallel with the gully. He would pass them. His line of approach would not intersect the gully until he was well below them. Ted's pulse rate went up. *It's going to work*! Their positions would be reversed and he and Erica could move up in any direction they chose. They might not be seen, and even if they were. . . .

He took a deep breath. The air so close to the earth was wet, rich and green-smelling, subtle and layered with many scents—a nectared sweetness, pungent humus and tangy bitter dandelion. He laid his cheek on the grass and felt the sweet coolness of mercy. He closed his eyes and breathed in again, and suddenly that breath froze and the ground turned cold and clammy.

Where is Hartz?

Peeking through the grass, Ted looked farther up the hill to his left. Then farther. Then along his left shoulder and up the gully bank.

Maybe he's already passed us. Maybe he's fallen and broken his leg. His chin in the grass, Ted swept his gaze back and forth from shoulder to shoulder.

Nowhere. If he's not around, that's good news. I should be feeling better and better. But he felt worse and worse. He took a chance on raising his head. Then he raised himself on his elbows. He was aware that a faraway ringing hum inside his ears was swelling to a roar. The skin on the back of his neck prickled. Still prone, he turned on his right elbow to look back down at Erica. Instead, he saw Hartz.

The man was standing on the other side of the gully, two hundred yards away, just standing there quietly looking at him. He had watched him crawl up the slope like an Indian, hiding behind blades of grass and taking such care not to be seen.

Ted was too far away to see Hartz in detail. He could only imagine that he grinned. But he could see a large gesture, as when Hartz brought up the pistol at arm's length, clasping it with both hands. He moved deliberately, and Ted might have jumped or rolled down the bank . . . but he couldn't move. He stared at where he thought Hartz's eyes must be, until the raised gun blocked them. Then he stared at the gun.

The sound of the actual shot was no more than a distant snap, but against the sounding board of the mountain wall it would be heard throughout the bowl. It was the sound Hartz pointed, of course. He had little chance of hitting his target at that range with a handgun. The sound was slower than the bullet, but more deadly in this case.

Putzi had passed on by, but not far enough. As Ted turned to look in that direction, Putzi was already moving back uphill. Ted pushed to his feet, and ran down to Erica.

"Hartz." He pointed. "He's seen us."

Hartz had stepped over to the edge of the bank, from where he could look directly at them. He waved. Then he waved across to Putzi, pointing out their position.

The way off that mountainside was down. Ted and Erica turned to their appointed direction. They trotted, no longer running away and in no real hurry to get to where they were going either. Hartz simply walked. He saw no need to exert himself.

When Ted and Erica came to the hut again, they went inside. That at least preserved the illusion of choice.

The walls were of heavy fieldstone, at least eighteen inches thick. Ted put his hand against the wall just inside the door. It was rough, hard, very well-built. Good wall, he thought. He knew that they couldn't shoot through that wall. Nor through the stone floor. If they wanted to shoot through the roof, they would have to climb up, lift off the heavy rocks that held down the slate, lift the slates that were over an inch thick and two or three feet square and then shoot through the wood-slab ceiling. Ted didn't think either Hartz or Schimmel would go to that trouble. If they wanted to stay outside and shoot, they would simply shoot through the window.

Someone must have been proud of that window. Most such huts didn't have one. The stonework around it would have to be planned. The window would have to be framed. Glass would have to be carried carefully halfway up the mountain. Most builders of huts wouldn't bother. But the builder of this one had cared. It was only a little window, no more than a foot square, but it would allow a person inside to enjoy natural light, to check the progress of the storm from which he huddled, to see the ray of sunlight that meant he had survived. It would allow them to spray bullets over most of the room.

The only places Schimmel wouldn't be able to hit were the window wall itself and the corners next to it. Unless he leaned in. That would be difficult because the window was so small. Ted imagined how it could be done. He saw Schimmel pushing his gun through, his arms in up to the elbows, pointing the gun down and then sweeping it back and forth across the wall. *If we're directly below the window and escape the first spraying, when he pushes in with the gun, I could reach up and grab. . . .* Ted didn't like it. But it was what he'd try if he couldn't think of anything else.

The door was unbelievable: It was unbelievable that such a door would hang on a refuge hut high in the mountains. It was old and weathered, grain-raised, ridged and rotting at the bottom; but under its surface grayness there was the rich red-brown glow of fine walnut. It was carved in panels—Austrian Flamboyant Baroque. *What is it doing here? What are we doing here?*

Ted swung the two-inch-thick door closed and slid home the broad bar designed to hold it against battering winds.

Two: hide under the window, grab the gun. One. . . .

Erica had come in and looked around as Ted had. Then she toured the room, starting with the wall on the right. She seemed not to stand and consider possibilities. The tour was short, the only points of interest she found being two ancient cans of beans and a small pile of firewood.

"Ted! Look!" From behind the firewood Erica brought up an ax. It was ancient-looking, with a fan-shaped blade, rusted and nicked. "Look!"

Oh, yeah, look at that. They have two pistols and a sub-machine gun, but we have an antique ax. A deep funk as heavy as the clouds outside seemed to be settling over him.

Erica stared at him in growing anger. Suddenly she jabbed the ax against his side. "It is *something!*"

It is *something.* He took the ax from her. "Okay. I'll stand behind the door and when they come through. . . ." He regarded the door. *How are they going to get through?*

The door was massive and the bar across it was something like two-by-six, hardwood, thrust into a slot in the stone wall. Ted's heart began to thump again with hope.

"You think the door they cannot break?"

"Maybe not. Not the bar anyway. But the bottom's rotting. If we could block it. . . ."

"The firewood?"

"No, not unless we could wedge it."

"A stone!" Erica bent over and began examining the stones in the floor. Unlike those in the walls, they were not mortared; they were simply heavy, flat rocks fitted together with earth packed between them. "Here."

She had found a large stone, irregular but nearly two feet across in each direction. Frost had lifted one edge.

"With *der Axt*."

Suddenly there was a shout outside—Putzi to Hartz. Then a reply. Their voices were close.

Frantically Erica and Ted scratched and pried at the edge of the stone, raised it slightly and jammed the end of a pointed stick into the crack to help lever it with the ax. The edge of the stone rose. Ted levered again. The stone lifted a bit more . . . but it seemed to rise so slowly! Against the constant pressure of panic, Ted governed his movements. Erica moved with him, setting out wooden wedges, lifting with quick deliberation like an operating-room nurse.

Hartz called again from the uphill side of the hut; Putzi answered from just below. Ted and Erica managed to get one corner of the stone well up and held in place with pieces of firewood. He straddled the upraised edge and strained upward. Erica dropped down beside him and pushed. The rock lifted.

Gasping, they raised it up onto one edge. Now vertical, it could be moved more easily. They rocked it out of its depression, walked it end by end over to the door and dropped it leaning against the bottom. They were shaking from exertion.

Voices came from outside, close. The room darkened as someone looked in the window. They jumped, flattening themselves against the window wall.

"*Ich kann Niemand sehen.*"

"*Sie sind da drinnen.*"

The figure moved on and the room lightened again. They heard further conversation, all of it in matter-of-fact tones. The speakers were at ease, totally confident the chase was over. Erica and Ted stood pressed against the wall, her hand clutched in his, their hearts racing. Hartz said something and Putzi laughed and said something back; then they both laughed. The voices moved around to the front of the hut.

Wham! A kick at the door reverberated around the walls.

"*Ja. Ganz fest.*"

They moved away. Ted caught, "Wait for Schimmel." Schimmel would be having a long walk uphill.

Ted did not think they could break in the door, neither by kicking it nor with their shoulders. Now if they had a battering ram . . . but there were no trees or timber around. Could they weaken the door by shooting, by riddling it, then break in? He supposed he would find out. *In the meantime, we're safe.*

The room darkened again.

Safe as fish in a barrel.

SUNDAY, JULY 17 11:45 HOURS—
OBER-FLATTACH

There was no chimney in the hut. Smoke from a fire inside would pour out and up all around from under the roof. The walls had been built first, then beams had been put across; they projected beyond the walls, with rafters going up to the ridge. The finished roof extended well beyond the sides of the hut, leaving an open space between it and the walls.

Ted and Erica lay head to head, jammed into that space over the window. Every so often a gust of air blew up under the roof, chilling their backs, and there would be a faint clicking sound on the slate above them.

Hartz and Putzi had gone around to the side of the hut opposite the window for shelter. Ted and Erica could hear the murmur of their voices. All waited for Schimmel.

"I'm sorry, Erica. I'm sorry I got you into this mess. I'm sorry I haven't been able to get you out of it."

"All is true, as you have told me? All is from mistaken identity?"

"It's true. All of this . . . the little girl, Maria . . . Because an old man in Salzburg thought I was someone else. It's insane."

"So. So, it is not your fault."

"But it's all because of me, and I'm sorry."

"I am sorry too. But it is not because you did something bad."

"You're right. I know you're right, but I can't help thinking. . . ."

"*Ja.* I know. Always you think. I like you for thinking, Ted. You are interesting because you think. But sometimes you think too much."

Ted thought about that.

The wind gusted strongly and they shivered. Outside, someone said something Ted believed the equivalent of "goddam son of a bitch."

"Yet you are thinking."

"Yes."

Erica assumed he was still thinking about their predicament and his responsibility. "This is not because of you. And you have done all anyone could do. Each moment. More. Few people could be so calm, make such tricks."

"I know. I keep going over everything. Except for trusting Hartz, which was reasonable, I can't think of a single choice that might have made a difference except. . . ."

"What?"

"No. Nothing. It wouldn't have mattered anyway."

They were silent for a while. Then Erica spoke again, quietly. "You think I should not have come back to the castle."

Ted tried to imagine what that clicking was on the roof.

Her voice was so low he could hardly hear it. "That would have made a difference, *ja*?"

He had to answer her and it didn't seem like a time for lying. "I think you should not have come back. It was a gamble either way, but the chances would have been better. . . ." The wind blew again, but suddenly he felt colder inside than out. "Erica. . . ."

She was silent. He twisted around so he could look at her. Tears ran across her face.

"Erica, I'm sorry. I know what you meant by coming back. I appreciate it. I just think it wasn't the best thing, the best plan. Going on, getting the police. . . ."

"*Ja*. I understand."

Ted began to think he would like to unbar the door and go out to them. "Erica, it doesn't matter whether you did the smartest thing. I still feel the same about you. I still care about you." He reached over and put his hand on her hair. "I've never met another woman like you. Throughout all of this . . . Erica, I admire you more than any other person I know."

"Admire. *Ja*. Thank you."

"What's wrong?"

"Admire is not loving."

"You can't love someone you've known for only two days."

"Why not? Is it a rule?"

There was a shout from outside.

"Erica, I think you care too much about being loved."

Another shout.

"Maybe. We may not either have our problems much longer."

Schimmel had arrived. There was a conversation, some of it angry, although Ted could understand only a few words. Then by a sudden darkening in the hut he could tell that someone was at the window again. Its size and location allowed anyone standing outside to see only the opposite wall and about one-third of each of the side walls. Looking in would not allow him to see Ted and Erica.

Ted began to shiver. Not from fear, but because the

draft up under the eaves was continuous. Schimmel spoke, almost directly beneath him, and Ted caught "damned rain!" Now he understood the clicking on the roof; it had started to rain.

There was another kick at the door. And another. Then half a dozen more, and hammering. A pause, a word, a loud bang. Schimmel was showing the others how the job should be done. Bang again. Whatever effect the exercise may have had on Schimmel's foot or on his standing as the strong man of the gang, it had none on the door. *Good door. They can wear their feet down to their knees on that door.*

There were more shouts and curses. They moved all around the hut, looking for a way in that they knew wasn't there; it was the kind of futile motion people go through to avoid admitting there's nothing to be done. The sound of rain on the roof had increased in tempo to a steady rush, and rivulets of water began to splash and pour from the eaves to the ground.

The men outside ran to the door again. There were heavy thumps as two shoulders were thrown against it simultaneously. The door rattled, gave a fraction of an inch but held.

The message of that rain sound came through to Ted: Their positions were reversed now. He and Erica were secure; those outside were in peril. Over six thousand feet above sea level, it was cold—probably not down to freezing yet but not many degrees above it. There was a rising wind. People caught in storms like this in the mountains, even in the summertime, frequently died from exposure. That's why the hut was there—this hut they couldn't get into.

Then the windowpane was smashed. Hartz called in. His voice was calm at first, firm but easy. "Open the door, Barstow."

He expects me to obey!

Hartz always expected people to obey; he started with that. Charm first, then coercion if necessary. After all, he and the others were in control. They had guns. They held life and death in the crooks of their fingers.

"Barstow?" Could it be that he hadn't been heard? Could it be that he had been misunderstood? Those were the only possible explanations for Barstow's inaction. Hartz stood like a Victorian father, razor strop in hand: It was inconceivable that he could be disobeyed. He began to be angry. He shouted. "Open that goddam door or Schimmel will blast this room from end to end!" Pause. "We know you're in there. Even if you're in the corner, we'll reach you!" Pause. Finally all control gave way. He screamed at them, "Open that door!"

Ted pictured him, his hair plastered down the sides of his face, rain dropping off his ears and nose, wetness soaking through the shoulders of his borrowed jacket. The fleece lining would do him some good, even when wet, but his trousers and shoes would be sopping by now, wicking off his body heat into the wind. And Putzi in his sunny-day shirt and cotton trousers; his jacket was meant for no more than the temporary chill of a cloud crossing the sun.

Hartz shrieked, "Barstow!"

Ted jumped and almost fell; Erica started too as the sub-machine gun roared under them. The first burst was aimed over the area Schimmel could see from outside; then he pushed his arms through the window—as Ted had supposed he would—and swept the barrel from side to side, firing continuously, knocking out chips from the wall, throwing bullets across the room.

The firing made Ted feel better even though the noise and violence of it shocked him like a blow to the stomach. Shooting was irrational. They may have thought the threat of shooting might make him unlock the door . . . but how could he do that if he were dead? Not only was the storm weakening the outsiders' physical stamina, it was battering their ability to think.

Schimmel scattered many bullets, then stopped and drew back. Ted had almost swung down with the ax he had brought up with him and now held against himself. He thought better of it in time. Even if he were to hit the gun or Schimmel's hands, it would reveal his position and allow them to find a way to shoot up into the crack between the wall and the roof.

There was no thunder. The storm was not a sudden shower on a humid summer day, the kind that drenches and cools, after which the clouds pass and the air turns hot and sticky again. The rain had started slowly and built gradually. The clouds holding it were the Himalayas piled on top of the Alps. It would take all day and all night to drain them. Hartz, Schimmel and Putzi had to find shelter. They conferred, shouting at each other over the howl of the wind. Someone should lean through the window and look around. Since Putzi was the smallest, he was elected. He objected loudly but was overruled.

His arm came through the opening. Looking down, Ted could see only his hand. Of course the little man could not get his shoulder and head in after it. He tried again—with his arm out, his head in. The window was set squarely in the middle of the thick wall. He couldn't get in far enough to see more than two-thirds along the side walls.

Now the pitch of the wind rose to a rage, driving fiercely against the hut. Outside, the men shouted to each other, trying to match their squeaks against the roar of the storm.

They ran back to the door. There was more kicking, still ineffective. Then a command. A burst from the machine gun chewed into the door—not wild shots but grouped just above center. After a moment of silence, there was a hammering on the weakened spot, then another burst.

Carefully and quietly, holding a cross beam, Ted pulled himself away from the wall and dropped the eight feet to the floor. Erica stared, shaking her head "no," but Ted motioned her to come down. Keeping against the wall, they moved up beside the door.

There was pounding again, and splintering—a small hole appeared. Now those outside could look in. They shouted in bewilderment. They couldn't see anyone inside from the door either. Someone ran back to the window. Ted and Erica flattened against the window wall.

"No, I can't see them!"

"Come back!"

Another long burst from the machine gun sent splinters flying. Slugs dropped to the floor inside, then carried through to chip the back wall.

Could they sliver the entire door? Would it disintegrate shred by shred until they could walk right through it?

Not yet. Again there was a pause. Someone was pounding on the door, hammering with a pistol butt. Wood splintered around the peephole. Then the pounding stopped and fingers pulled at the shreds of wood. Someone was shouting, *"Schnell, schnell, schnell."* The fingers tried to hurry but they were stiff and cold, fumbling. *"Schnell, schnell, schnell!"*

The three men huddled against the wall by the door; the wind would knock down anyone who tried to stand alone.

There were several holes now. Fingers pushed through them, wriggling. Thin, white from the cold, wet, they seemed not like things that had a human being attached to the other end. Ted and Erica watched in horrified fascination. The fingers moved as though each were a separate sensory organ, waving, testing the air for scent, feeling for warmth.

"Wieder!" Again. The fingers withdrew.

Schimmel held the machine gun close. Bullets ripped through the splintered door. Then the hand came in again—the hand, the forearm—groping through and down, reaching for the bar. The bar was too low, the arm pulled back. More pounding, more breaking. The hole was enlarged. "*Schnell, schnell!*" It was Hartz shouting. The arm came back in again, up to the elbow this time, swinging, pawing. It touched the bar, closed over it—a hand stretching out of a soaked black-corduroy jacket, pulling against a pink-checkered shirt. The angle was awkward; the fingers slipped.

"Hurry, hurry!"

"I'm trying! I can't . . . !"

"Reach farther!"

"I'm trying!"

"Hurry!"

Putzi worked at the bar. It moved half an inch.

Ted stepped from the wall and set his feet apart. He swung the ax with all his strength. It bit through and into the bar. There was a scream of agony; the arm was snatched back; the hand dropped to the floor inside. Erica gasped, threw her hands over her eyes and turned away.

The machine gun roared. Bullets slammed into the door furiously, up and down, from side to side . . . all wasted because their targets were flat against the wall again. Schimmel ran around to the window, thrust the the machine gun through, spraying continuously toward the door. Then he stretched in, trying to reach the corner but holding back just enough to avoid Putzi's fate. The fiery blast of the gun, its surge and power, may have released his rage, but it accomplished nothing else.

Suddenly there was silence—no, only by contrast. The wind and rain roared, Putzi still screamed, but the gun was empty. At the start there had been one clip in it, and a spare in each trouser pocket. Now all were used up. Even

Schimmel had lost his control, not so much from fear of the storm as infection from its fury.

Erica and Ted huddled together, pressed into the corner. They couldn't be seen or shot at from either the door or the window, not unless Hartz or Schimmel were inclined to reach in.

Putzi's screams subsided to moans, seemed to come from farther away and then were lost. There were no other human sounds.

It was only noon. Ted and Erica waited breathlessly for a while, then let out their breath but stood tensed against the wall. Finally they were calm enough to be tired, to sink down and sit in the corner, trying not to stare at the brown stain on the door or Putzi's hand on the floor.

SUNDAY, JULY 17 12:00 HOURS— *OBER-FLATTACH*

Lieutenant Steiner was disappointed. Not only in the lack of any results, but in the process. Herr Tolz and Herr Zimmerman were counterspies of some kind. They looked as counterspies would look—absolutely ordinary, the acme of professional sophistication. But behind the bland exteriors, Steiner knew, were minds that hummed and clicked. Ten minutes at headquarters, two pages of preliminary report— the case had been solved. Steiner was confident that his own mind was like that too—in potential. All he needed was training, to learn the methods, the tricks. An assignment to work directly with Zimmerman was an opportunity undreamed of.

But instead of leaping from summits of surmise to a peak of revelation, they had spent all Saturday afternoon and evening slogging around visiting the school principal, a former employer who had once given Ilse a room in the village, a handful of classmates—one by one. Slow. Tedious. He could have done it by himself; or he would have sent an officer to do it, it was so routine. And they had learned nothing.

"I don't think she had any friends. She kind of kept to herself."

"Stuck up. Always seemed to think she was better than everybody else—just because she was pretty and she . . . developed . . . earlier than the rest of us. And the truth is, she was just a peasant from up on the mountain."

"Shy. If you got to know her, I think she would have been very nice."

"Left her father? I never heard she left her father. She always went back up the mountain on her holidays."

Several of them agreed that Maria Rauschenbach had been closer to Ilse than anyone—if anyone had been close. Maria Rauschenbach had married a tourist from Cologne. It took until Sunday morning to enlist the help of German authorities, find her and determine that she thought Ilse had had some bad feeling for her father but (Maria thought) still stayed with him when she wasn't in the village.

After they heard that, they went back over everything and Steiner himself made the jump that—as he thought about it afterward—might take him to Vienna. Johann was reviewing matters while Tolz nodded as each point was reiterated. Tolz's nodding was like rocking—it seemed more an occupation than a reaction.

"No one knows much about her. No one knows anyone she might have stayed with after she left her father. In fact, no one knew she had left him."

"Perhaps she did not." Tolz held himself still. "Perhaps Herr Katernig was deceiving us. Perhaps she is still there."

"Do you think so?"

"No." Tolz shrugged and Johann shrugged back. "So, yet we must ask where she stayed."

"With Frau Rogel," Steiner said as though he had

known it all along. "Forgive me, Herr Tolz, but . . . if I may . . . it occurs to me that if—during the time she worked in the village—people still thought she sometimes went back up the mountain to stay, then she must have done so. With someone who would keep her secret— Clearly it was of great importance to her to keep it secret. Frau Rogel is a widow. She lives alone. She is a neighbor of Katernig's."

Instantly Johann was on his feet. Tolz, slower, was pushing himself up by the arms of the chair. Only Steiner remained motionless. "But we cannot go there now. The road will be a river until after the storm."

Tolz held his half-standing position, considering whether to contradict the young officer or nature. But he had learned the folly of the latter. He sank back, pursed his lips and nodded.

Johann was not as easily defeated by reality. "Does the woman have a telephone? We could call to see if the girl is there."

That was stupid. Johann was not to be allowed to be stupid unintentionally. "If she were there, do you think she would remain if she knew we suspected it?" Tolz held Johann's eye for an awful moment, then nodded to show it was past. "How long will this storm last, Lieutenant?"

"For at least twelve hours, Herr Tolz; perhaps longer."

"Then let us have a good luncheon and some sleep. Lieutenant, please make arrangements so that we can go up as soon as possible."

Tolz again began to raise himself. Suddenly there was a knock at the door but before permission to enter could be given, a young policeman burst in.

"They have found the American!"

"Where?"

"I don't know, Herr Tolz. Inspector Glaessel is on the radio. Please, if you will come, sir?"

Tolz moved with a speed unexpected by either Steiner or the young officer.

"Tolz here."

"Glaessel. We've traced him."

"Where are you?"

"Up at the end of the valley above Ragaschlucht. Barstow was here yesterday."

"Yesterday? Where is he now?"

There was an instant's pause before Glaessel answered. "If I knew where he is now, I wouldn't be telling you where he was yesterday."

Tolz paused also. Then, keeping his voice neutral, he asked, "What have you discovered, Inspector?"

"We finally found the driver of the bus he took. He went to Lienz last night for a wedding today." Glaessel was pleased with his work and he wanted Tolz to know it. "We talked to the woman who's caretaker at the *schlucht*; she has identified Barstow. Now we're at an *alm* up at the end of the valley. Barstow was here just twenty-four hours ago." Tolz could hear another voice, high-pitched and chattering; then Glaessel left the mike, calling out. When he returned, he said, "Old woman here. Says she thought Barstow was crazy. Kept shouting something about death at her, and bad men. There must have been a convention: Two men did come after Barstow—told her they were his keepers—and then two others later."

"Get descriptions."

"I thought of that. You want them now?"

"Please, Inspector."

The old woman saw few people closely; those she did, she remembered. From Glaessel's report, Tolz recognized Brunner and Janovich. He did not know the others but assumed they were Tobler's associates.

"Their car is still there—the first pair's car. Gray Opel."

"She hasn't seen them again?"

"Hasn't seen any of them. She went to sleep. When she woke up, the second pair was gone. Their car too. Dark red car, very expensive-looking. She doesn't recognize makes. There's another car here now: a Mercedes 280 sedan, green. Parked half a kilometer away. Could be hikers. We're checking it."

"Good. Did the woman see which way Barstow went?"

"Yes. He took the trail up toward Rotzahn. The first pair went after him."

"And none of them seen since. Inspector, we must send someone up the trail."

"Not now. Nobody's going up there today."

Putzi was lost almost at once. With his right wrist clutched under his left arm and spurting blood, his eyes wide with horror more than with pain, screaming continuously, he staggered off and was lost in the driving rain. Hartz kept up with Schimmel for a minute or two, then fell behind. Schimmel didn't care. Hartz would make it or he wouldn't; it was each for himself.

Schimmel ran, crouched, when he could—taking a half-dozen steps in the lulls when the wind pushed merely with the force of a heavy man running behind him. When it struck with its own strength, it blew him over like a blade of grass. He crawled on hands and knees, running on them if he could, squirming forward when knocked flat. He never stopped; he knew he would die if he did. Hartz stopped from time to time, although not by decision. He crawled until he fell flat, started up again when he could.

They followed the gully down. Without that guide they would have wandered and each soon perished. When Schimmel reached the trees, he knew he would survive. His hands, feet and face were cold past pain and into numbness. The muscles in his shoulders and thighs felt as though they were pushing chunks of stone. But the thick wool of his sweater trapped enough heat to keep him going, and then the forest shielded him from the worst of the wind.

Hartz felt better in the forest too. He reached it long after Schimmel did. He felt *much* better, not cold at all. His fear dissolved. He was tired, more tired than he had ever been, but as soon as he rested—only for a few moments until his strength returned—he would proceed to safety. A feeling of satisfaction and well-being seemed to flow through him.

Schimmel was well on his way by then. He went on slipping, falling and crawling, pulling himself up against a tree, lurching from one trunk to another. He staggered from the last tree, not realizing it was the last, and felt again the full lash of the storm. He reeled, toppled over and then crawled until he saw an indistinct gray shape ahead.

Inside the barn, he burrowed down and lay gasping until his shivering warmed the cocoon of sweater and hay. Then he drifted into an exhausted sleep for three hours. When he awoke, realized the storm continued, he went back to sleep.

Again he awoke, startled. What had he heard? Something. Then he comprehended the sound—quiet. The wind had stopped. Heavy rain beat on the roof above, but there was no more wind. Schimmel dug himself out, and looked through the doorway. It was night. He could get away even if someone were watching—not that he had reason to suspect that anyone would be. Half-crouched, he trotted carefully down the road toward the place where they had left the Mercedes. The key was with Putzi, but only a few moments would be necessary to hot-wire it.

Emil Glaessel lit his last cigarette. His children had given him the lighter for his birthday. It produced an immense flame and his colleagues joked about how he was the only policeman who carried a flamethrower. Light from that flame diffused by mist on the windows made the entire car glow like a beacon.

Schimmel saw the light flash. He dropped down beside the Mercedes. Then he began crawling toward what he recognized must be another car. He swung away, passed it, came closer and crawled up along its side from the rear. Raising his eyes slowly to the level of the rear-seat window, he could see—by cigarette glow—one person inside.

Glaessel had delayed having that cigarette for over an hour. Finally he decided it was more logical to suffer later when he had none than now, when he had one but wouldn't smoke it. He was going to suffer in either case. Although the storm was lessening—the rain simply poured straight down instead of smashing against the car windows with the force of a high-pressure hose—it would not exhaust itself for several more hours. He looked at his watch. Just after nine. Pitch black outside. There should have been twilight at that hour. He rubbed a patch clear on the windshield. If he turned the headlights on, he could probably see the road for a few meters ahead, enough to let him drive slowly up to the old woman's cabin. The temptation was strong.

While it had seemed sensible to put one man in the cabin and the other in the car down the road—with the Opel and the Mercedes in between and escape from the mountainside boxed off—the storm quickly proved the idea ridiculous. Neither of the men could see anything a meter away, even when it was light; they couldn't get past the static on the radio intercom to each other or to headquarters if anything had been seen. So they had sat by all day, wasting time. At least Otto was inside, by a fire, probably enjoying some stew—Glaessel tried not to think about it. Instead, he cursed himself again for the misguided noblesse oblige that had led him to take the car position himself. Every so often he had started the engine and let it idle long enough to heat the interior again. Since the wind died, he hadn't needed to do it.

Now he took a deep drag on his cigarette and settled back into the corner against the door. Suddenly the door flew open. His arms flailing to seize the wheel, trying to catch himself, smoke in his lungs choking him, he began to fall out.

Schimmel opened the trunk of the Mercedes, took out his valise and returned to Glaessel's black Audi. Inside, contorting himself, he stripped and dressed in clean clothes. Then he drove down to the highway, heading toward the village, until he reached the telephone booth on the out-skirts of town.

Folded in Rudi Bischl's wallet had been a piece of notepaper—there for some time by the look of its creases and smudges—on which were written several phone numbers. Some of them had names beside them, some did not. All of them, naturally, had the four digits of the individual subscriber's number. Three had exchange pre-fixes as well: information necessary when a city has more than one exchange. But the remaining four numbers had no prefix—not a necessity if the prefix for the small town where the subscriber lives is known. It took Schimmel a while, training his eye to look through the area directory for the Ober-Flattach prefix first and then to the number. But he finally found a name—Rogel—matched to a num-ber on Rudi's list.

"Oh! Can I help you, sir?" The young gas-station attendant had paled with shock when Schimmel appeared out of the rain at the glass door of the office. The boy dropped his feet from the desk, hastily trying to stuff the girlie magazine in the chair behind him as he got to his feet. Who would have expected a customer? There had been none for hours, and Schimmel had pulled in from behind and stopped a distance away from the pumps.

"Yeah. I'm looking for Rogel. Wilhelmina Rogel."

"Frau Rogel?"

"Frau Rogel, yeah." Schimmel barely nodded, as though no assent should have been required.

"She lives up above Uberbrüke. Here, sir." The boy pointed to an area map framed on the wall. "Go to the Uberbrüke turnoff, go through—past the Gemsbock—and the road up is just beyond."

Schimmel stared at the map, fixing it in his mind. "Thank you."

"But you can't get up there now, sir."

Schimmel aimed his eyes and dared the boy to oppose him.

"The storm. Water comes down the road—it's just a dirt road, you know."

"How long?"

"Well, the storm's slacking off. . . . Four, five hours. Maybe three, four o'clock."

Schimmel glared at the window, at the storm; but it could not be daunted. Four or five hours. Then, if he found the girl, he would need more time to get to the pictures. It would be morning. There would be light.

The police knew something—they had been waiting there in the storm for him; he had to assume it. He would have to run, have to hide until he knew for certain. Maybe he would never get back to Salzburg, in which case he would lose all his connections there. Everything would be lost, nothing gained except the paltry one million from Bischl. But if he took the chance and won. . . .

He turned back. He noticed several vending machines and got change from the boy, bought three Cokes, a dozen packages of cookies, some candy bars and a cup of brown water fraudulently advertised as coffee. At least it was boiling hot, still hot five minutes later when he pulled into a side road to wait. He drank, ate and dozed until moonlight through parting clouds awoke him.

SUNDAY, JULY 17 17:00 HOURS—
OBER-FLATTACH

"And so, for what has been all this?"

"I don't know." Ted had finished telling Erica the whole story—the incidents he had been aware of, the parts pieced together afterward—and it ended only with a shake of the head. "I don't know.

"What can it be, these coordinates? Did he say nothing more?"

"Hartz told you more than he ever told me. He assumed I knew. The coordinates mark a place. There's something there they all want."

"He said not money. A secret? A military secret? Perhaps it is plans for war!"

"Could be, I guess. It doesn't really matter."

Erica's jaw dropped in amazement. "Does not matter! All of this does not matter to you?"

"Of course it . . . people trying to kill me matters. Getting out of this alive matters—a lot. That's what *really* matters. To *me*. I don't care what it is that matters to them."

245

"It must have meaning!"

"Why? What else does?"

That stopped her. For several minutes they sat and listened to the storm. They didn't have to wonder whether they should stay inside the hut or whether the others might be outside lying in wait. The storm was danger enough. Before the end of the first hour it had become obvious that their enemies could not possibly be lurking outside. Wind stronger than any man could stand against screamed down the mountainside, hurling rain and sometimes sleet before it like volleys of spears. It clubbed at the walls and roof of the hut, grabbed through the broken window and door and from under the eaves. Even inside they might have been in danger had they not found matches stored in a little glass jar behind the beans. Ted shaved slivers of wood for tinder and built a small fire; now they were sitting behind it in a corner, burning a stick at a time.

"Nothing for you has meaning?" When Erica spoke again, it was with a tone somewhere between the incredulous outrage of his Sunday-school teacher on hearing he didn't believe in God anymore and the terrified suspicion of a playmate confronted with the deeper heresy about the Tooth Fairy.

"Lots of things have meaning, Erica. They mean what they mean because . . . not because of anything inherent to them, but because of how we feel about them. You can either make something important for yourself or you can feel nothing about it. I find it better not to look for meanings."

That seemed a moral offense to her. "How do you live?"

"In reduced circumstances."

"What?"

"I live as best I can. In as much comfort as I can manage. Even with some pleasure from time to time.

Without expecting anything more. Not even expecting that.''

She shivered. Ted put another piece of branch on the embers. The flame licked up and the wood crackled. The act kept the illusion that the cold was only outside, not between them.

After some time Erica looked at him. "I do not understand you.'' She put her hand on his arm. "You are like two people. You speak like a person who. . . . I see a poor dog that has many times been beaten, always hiding. But with Hartz and Schimmel—and the others you tell me about—you are never giving up, always again trying.''

"I guess sometimes I forget what I know.''

"You should more often forget. I believe living can be good, *froliche* . . . joyous. One must bring together the good things, not think always of the bad.''

"It must be nice to believe that.''

The storm raged through the afternoon and evening and into the night. They talked about whatever came into their heads.

". . . it's an old Colonial house—from before our Revolution. I got the place because I promised the man who owned it . . .'' Ted told Erica about the house, the woods and the brook, and how he held the old farm like a fortress against the barbarians suburbanizing all around him. And she told him about her family. He was astounded. "*Nine* brothers? All those people in one house at once!''

"*Ja*. We were Catholic. But I was the last.''

"The only girl.''

"Sometimes that was very nice.''

"I'll bet they spoiled you rotten.''

"*Ja*. But sometimes to be so special is hard. And for us the war did not end—only slowly. I was born after, but life was difficult still for many years. I remember cold like this, but more. I remember eating soup with gloves on our hands.''

She shivered again and Ted put his arm around her for warmth. They talked about their childhood, about his dog, her cats. He told Erica about college, about working in New York and not liking it, about not learning to play his flute well enough, about his record collection. And she told him about finding it easy to learn what foreigners were saying, about the joy speaking with them gave her, about her fear of snakes, about refusing to hang baubles from her earlobes, and about reading and memorizing poetry. She recited some of her favorite verses.

They talked and then dozed from time to time, and laughed at first when their stomachs growled. Hunger came and went in cycles, sharper with each return; each time it came, they reevaluated the likelihood of getting food poisoning from those beans. Then they dozed again.

Light awoke Ted. He must not have been sleeping soundly because he had no difficulty in emerging. He knew instantly where he was and what had happened. It might have been better had he floated slowly toward the light, not sure of when he broke the surface into fog, uncertain of whether the shapes surging around him were mouths and coils or merely shadows in the current. He could have breathed again and told himself they were shadows. Instead, he remembered instantly, and instantly was afraid.

He lay still for a moment, his senses alert. He had heard a noise outside—a sort of snap? Like a dog, his ears twitched toward the sound. He waited, not breathing. It came again, softer this time. A twig breaking? But they weren't in the woods, there weren't any twigs. He had to breathe, but did so shallowly. A pebble dropping? Again. Something creeping toward the hut?

Nightmare and reality became one and he felt himself whirlpooled down into blackness. *Not again! Not coming back for us again!* If he could have moved at all, he might have run out of the hut, hoping to be shot and killed quickly and been done with it.

The noise again! Suddenly he knew—it was water dripping from the roof. Nothing but water dripping. It was all right.

He lay still for several minutes, enjoying the sound. He let it wash the tension out of him.

He tried to move his arm without disturbing Erica, but she awoke. She began to snuggle against his side, then started fully awake, remembering.

"*Ist Morgen*?"

Ted looked at his watch. "One A.M." He tried to get up and gasped. Cuts burned, abrasions smarted, bruises stabbed, and every muscle, tendon and sinew ached. Wincing and grunting, he managed to get himself up and hobble over to the window.

The world was gone. Dense cloud had descended, enveloping everything. He couldn't even see the ground. Only occasional splashes from the roof recalled the rain. But the fog was thinner above. Brightness from the just-past-full moon was diffused through it.

He went to the door, stopping for a moment and staring at the hand lying there before kicking it into a corner. Then he strained at the stone.

"Wait. I help." Erica took hold beside him. They tipped up the stone, walked it away and dropped it over.

Ted looked out through the hole in the door. There was nothing to see—he could have been staring at a white wall. As he unbarred the door, he had a momentary misgiving; what might be waiting out there? Did they want to leave their security? But he knew, rationally, there could be no danger. Irrationally, he picked up the ax.

They stepped out into solid cloud. They could see earth for only a few feet before them. After the stuffy smokiness inside, the cold, moist air was sweet. They breathed deeply and, holding hands, started down the mountainside.

Despite the wildly remote possibility that their pursuers might still be waiting for them, it seemed best to follow the gully. It would lead to the edge of the bowl and prevent them from wandering off to one side. They needed such a guide. The cloud was like a spell dulling the senses of travelers through that land. All was quiet. There were no scents or tastes in the air. Surfaces were wet and smooth. There was nothing to be seen but the gray-white fog. Any landmark—a humpbacked stone, a gnarled shrub— that loomed suddenly was lost as quickly. By keeping to the gully, they held their way against enchantment and walking was easy; in ten minutes they reached the end of the pasture.

Ted had anticipated having to climb down through the forest over uneven ground, foot by foot; but almost at once they came on cow paths that traversed the hillside, criss-crossing each other and making a reasonably direct way. Ted went first, holding Erica's hand and helping her down the steepest places—an unconscious reversion by both of them to custom.

The brightness remained almost constant. Ted pictured the cloud lying over the mountain slope and following its contours. Tree trunks in the mist made a constantly changing abstract of vertical shapes in black and shades of gray. Trees slightly farther off resembled strokes of charcoal on gray paper, and thirty feet away the trunks had almost to be known by a sense other than sight.

Pine needles were thick under foot. There was no wind. When beads of water strung on lower branches fell, they made no splash. And Ted and Erica kept silent between them, stepping with care. It didn't seem that anyone could be lying in ambush, but Ted was uneasy and would be until they sat across the desk from the police captain.

They were about halfway down when suddenly Erica's hand tightened, gripping his with a tension that caught his breath and froze him. He lifted his head slowly, then turned gradually to look along her line of sight. He saw nothing to fear at first but then made out a faint shape just to the right of the direction in which they were heading. It was irregular, rounded, low against a trunk. It could be a bush, but they had seen no other bushes. Or a rock—there were rocks, but none that large. Or it could be a person.

They stood as unmoving as the trees for over a minute, knowing that if they could not see the shape clearly, it could not see them any better. Ted stared, trying to resolve the form into something recognizable. *Maybe it* is *a rock. But it doesn't look like a rock.*

They couldn't stand there forever. Slowly Ted leaned close to Erica and whispered, "Get behind a tree." He squeezed her hand and released it. Then they sprang, each behind a large trunk.

No shot, no shout, no sound of movement.

Carefully Ted sank to his knees, using the ax handle as a prop. He lowered himself as close to the ground as possible and moved his head by quarter inches until he could see with one eye past the trunk. The shape had not moved.

It has to be a rock. But I don't think it is. He waited for nearly two minutes. The shape didn't move.

It must be a rock. Want to bet your life on it?

He stood up, sprinted downhill and caught himself up against another tree. There was no sound. He peered around. The shape still had not moved. Holding the ax ready to swing, he edged out from cover and moved cautiously down the hill. With every step he felt increasingly ridiculous over his timidity and elaborate caution. It had to be a rock.

But it wasn't.

Hartz sat slumped against the tree like a drunken swineherd. The cordovan boots were clumped with mud. One bare calf stuck straight out below a twisted, baggy trouser leg. The trousers were soaked and mud-stained. Mud smeared his cheeks and nose; it was caked under his fingernails. The borrowed jacket was bunched around his waist, making a paunch. His head was thrown back and to one side, his mouth open, his jaw slack.

Ted was sorry Hartz had died that way. It would have been painless, at the end at least—a fuzzy-mindedness, an overpowering sleepiness. As deaths came, it was probably a good one. But Ted was sorry Hartz had died looking like that.

MONDAY, JULY 18 03:45 HOURS—
OBER-FLATTACH

Light from the desk lamp was yellow, as substantial as Tolz sitting in the chair behind it. Ted and Erica faced him, still wrapped in blankets they no longer needed. Lamplight on their faces seemed the touch of living warmth, drawing them back from the moonlight that reached through the window out of the chill night and lay on their shoulders.

Tolz had sat erect through the interview, his forearms on the desk before him, lamplight glinting on the rims of his glasses, sometimes even making his eyes seem to flash as he asked questions. He held the position through a pause, then sat back in the swivel chair. "Preposterous," he said.

"It's true." Ted spoke firmly, looking directly at him.

"It *is*, everything!" Erica echoed.

Tolz raised his hand from the desk. "It may *be* true. When the report that we have requested from the FBI arrives, I have no doubt it will confirm the identity you give us, Mr. Barstow. It is that fact that makes everything you have said preposterous. But . . . if I told you that a

253

shy young man studying musicology should—overnight—become a policeman to escape military service, should use his position to betray his government, and from that experience would spend his life in counterespionage, you might call that preposterous too." He shrugged. "I have developed some ability to judge people and their stories. I believe you. I believe your story, in part perhaps because it is so unbelievable." He nodded abruptly. "So. You must be exhausted. I will have you escorted to your lodgings. Please, though, do not leave until—"

Erica's patience reached its end. "*Nur eine moment, Herr Tolz!*" She switched to English for Ted's benefit. "What is the meaning of these Kreuzeck coordinates?"

Tolz regarded her for a moment. "I do not know."

"I believe you do know."

Tolz let out a tiny sigh, as though confronted by a child who doesn't understand the need for social fictions. "No, Fraulein."

She wouldn't play the game. "You know."

He raised a hand to protest and she exploded at him. "You do know! I know that you know! It is wrong to lie! It is *wrong*! You are of the police, from the government. It is not right that *you* should lie! Are you just like those others?"

She threw out a blast of righteous anger that seemed to burn through Tolz's clothes, leaving him mortifiedly pink. "*Ja.*" He seemed to be saying it to himself. Then he looked at Erica: "I apologize. Fraulein." He met her eyes. "I do know, but I cannot tell you."

"Why not!"

"Because you have no need to know. This is a matter of great importance. Most important is it that few people should of it have knowledge. I am sorry."

"This is not right! We were almost killed. All we have suffered—for what?" Erica reached forward and slapped the desk in front of Tolz. The blow may have hurt her hand but it was outrage that brought tears to her eyes. "It is not right!"

"Tell her, Tolz!" Ted didn't care himself. Although he was curious, he didn't really care. But Erica did. Seeing the hurt to her spirit made him angry too. "If you want to keep your secret. . . . You haven't got the chance of a pig in a Chinese kitchen unless you tell her!"

Tolz looked at Ted for an instant blankly, then blandly. In that slight shift from one nonexpression to another, Ted caught the faint hum of precision machinery. He knew he should be careful but he went on. "You aren't the only person involved in keeping this secret. We don't know what it means, but our part would be damned interesting in its own right to some people."

"As a story. Perhaps as a film. But it has no reality."

"There are people who make a business of investigating stories like ours. You know I'm connected with the publishing business. I have friends who are journalists. Investigative reporters." Ted tried to make it sound like the Inquisition. He didn't really know an investigative reporter but he went on as though he had direct connection with the Recording Angel. "I know some who have made headline exposés starting with fewer facts than I can give."

"Mr. Barstow, it would be unwise to threaten a government official who is carrying out an investigation." Tolz's voice was as soft as one piece of greased steel against another.

"Don't you threaten me! I have already been threatened. People a lot scarier than you have been threatening me—trying to kill me—and they're all dead! And *I* am *here*!"

A slight tension around the mouth and eyes was the only indication that Tolz was running in high gear too. Ted didn't care. It wasn't that he had lost his head in anger or that he didn't take Tolz seriously. But he felt capable of dealing with Tolz or anyone else. It was a new kind of feeling; perhaps it clouded his judgment but he had confidence in it. On the basis of that confidence, he eased back. "Look, let's not either of us make threats. Just let me suggest that the best way of enlisting our cooperation—now, and when I'm back in my own country—is to convince us of how important all this is by telling us *what* it is."

Erica had wiped away her tears. She stared first at Tolz, then at Ted. The moment went on longer than Ted had expected. There seemed to have been plenty of time for all the possibilities to have been run and all the cards sorted before Tolz spoke. Finally the corners of his mouth twitched in what might have been a smile.

"Very well, Mr. Barstow. If I tell you what I know, perhaps it makes only a small difference." He cleared his throat and decided how to tell what he would tell. "We have six days ago received information. . . ," he began. He told it all in generalities, without identifying any of the principals and saying only that the affair involved blackmail.

Erica was outraged. "But we had not the information, and yet they would kill us!"

"They believed we had no evidence to arrest them unless you identified them."

She was impatient for the finish. "But you have it now, the information?"

"No, Fraulein."

"So what will you do?"

"We have traced one of the original parties. My assistant has gone for her now."

They were silent for a moment. Tolz made a noise with his tongue and raised his eyebrows at Ted. "Are you now satisfied? May we expect your cooperation?"

"Erica?"

"But yet we know nothing. Who is this important official?

What may happen if the blackmail is successful? Gives it war, or does he only lose his position? Perhaps that is good.''

"These things I do not know, Fraulein. That is the truth.''

"Erica . . . we know enough. Not the details, but enough to understand why. The rest doesn't matter.''

"It does! It should. Maria is dead. All those men are dead. We almost . . . even if they were bad men, there should . . . what people die for should have meaning.''

"It should, Erica, but we just have to accept—''

"I do not accept!'' She whirled on Ted. "Why?''

"*Why* doesn't matter. Suppose we found out . . . suppose we had found that there is something hidden worth . . . a thousand dollars.''

"A thousand dollars?''

"A thousand schillings, fifty groschen. Nothing at all. So what would we think? All that danger, all those lives, for zilch. It wasn't worth the effort to save ourselves.''

"It is not so.''

"You're right. So suppose it's something worth five million dollars. What do we think then? Does it have more meaning? Suppose it was fifty million. Suppose nations could fall. Does that make it okay that Maria was killed?''

Erica was stunned by Ted's vehemence. But her wanting to make it all *meaningful*—to explain, to justify—made him angry. Tolz observed and understood. He might have shared Ted's anger; he would have shared it ten years earlier. Now his exasperation with idealists filled him only with weariness. He would have cut her off, had her taken home, ended this unpleasant waste of time, except for surprise at hearing Ted speak in terms of reality and wondering whether he could make himself believed.

Ted rushed on. "I'll tell you what the coordinates mean. The coordinates mean that life can get you for nothing at all. For greed and blackmail and corruption. They mean you can be shot in the head by a bullet meant for someone else—someone else who wasn't even the right person himself. That's what they mean—that there isn't any meaning. The secret hidden at that place is that there isn't any secret. No ultimate purpose that makes everything worthwhile. No golden key that lets you into a world where nothing bad happens anymore!''

Erica stared at Ted, shocked and appalled, then looked away. Tolz watched both of them. It had been put well, he thought. Of course the woman had not been convinced— such people never were. Ted's anger and Erica's refusal to accept the truth combined to fan some heat in the embers of Tolz's own emotions, but he damped it.

''So,'' he said, ''I have given you such facts as there are, hoping to satisfy your curiosity. What meaning they have, if any, you must decide for yourselves. But I trust you will do so privately. This affair should be ended quickly, as soon as my assistant returns. Go and rest now. I trust that by the time you awake again, this adventure will be no more than a bad dream to you.''

''Ilse?''

Moonlight through the tiny window at the end of the hall reflecting from the polished wooden floor made Frau Rogel's nightgown seem to glow. She appeared to float, a spirit come in the reaches of the night with tidings of doom. She tapped and called with that voice which means to awaken without disturbing.

Ilse was already awake. At the first knock on the door below, she had started. She lay paralyzed, her stomach tight, until the second knock broke the shock. Then she was out of bed and dressing before Frau Rogel was downstairs to call through the front door, ''Who is it?''

Frau Rogel lit no light. She knew her way around her

house in the dark, and with the moonlight shining in, it was not dark anyway. She did not open her door after nightfall either.

Ilse heard the question, not the muffled answer. But she knew; she didn't know exactly, but exactly didn't matter. Anyone who had come had come for her.

Someone coming for her was the second possibility for which she had been preparing since Wednesday night, when Rudi had called and then hadn't called again. The first possibility was that Rudi had taken the money and abandoned her: Betrayal was always her expectation. She had denied the thought as quickly as it came, each time it came. Not Rudi. Not dear, gentle Rudi. Not *him* too. But as Thursday passed, hour by tedious hour, she knew he had not simply been delayed. Someone had captured him—just as he feared, just as he had warned her. She had insisted—for the sake of the chance, for the wonderful future in which they could buy a shop outright. That would make it possible for her to work with him so that he could do his own work—artwork that he would sell, that would bring recognition, commissions, travel. . . .

No more.

On Thursday she had wept and then no more. She had weeded Frau Rogel's garden. On Friday she had washed all of Frau Rogel's spotless windows, and planned. Planning took all day because there was so little she had to plan with. She could not return to Bad Gastein, so she had no job. She had virtually no money. On the other hand, she realized that having nothing is like having infinite wealth in one way—all things are equally possible. Ilse considered what she might do, and where she might do it. Among the possibilities, of course, was selling her sex, which she made herself consider coldly and rank among the others. The only option that did not occur to her was suicide.

She did, however, recognize death as a threat. If Rudi had been captured, they would come for her. She was hidden, but she never believed herself secure. She spent all day Saturday up on the hillside above Frau Rogel's little house, where she could be signaled if—miraculously—Rudi called, and from where she could watch for strangers approaching. It was the last day she would give to hope. She watched the road, she watched the shadows of clouds pass over the mountains opposite. She watched the farmer to whom Frau Rogel sold her hay working in the field below the house. She knew her father would be working in his field too, around the shoulder of the hillside. Long ago she had made herself able to recognize her father's existence without any feelings whatsoever.

But Sunday, before she could leave, the storm struck.

"Ilse?" Frau Rogel tapped and called again.

"Yes, Frau Rogel."

"Someone is here, asking for you."

"Yes, Frau Rogel. Please tell them I will come at once, as soon as I am dressed." As she spoke, she was pulling on the gray-wool cardigan sweater Frau Rogel had knitted for her last Christmas.

"Should I ask them to come in?"

"No. I will be down directly."

Ilse took a pair of heavy wool socks from the drawer and picked up her boots. Frightened as she was, she did not panic. She had put on her black skirt and dark-blue pullover. Not that she had many clothes to choose from, but she had at once selected those most suitable for escape at night. Her money—what there was of it—and papers were in the leather pouch that normally held change under her apron when she worked at the hotel.

She pushed open the window beside her bed. Frau Rogel's house was built into the hillside. It was two full stories high in front but the windows behind were only five feet above the ground. Ilse straddled the sill, then pushed off and dropped.

From the crouch in which she landed she immediately sprang forward up the hill. She clutched the boots under her arm; she would not take time to lace them on until she was far above. Her shadow, long from the low moon to her left, detached from that of the house, its black feet, her white ones, dashed together and apart up the steep slope.

As she went, another shape detached itself from the shadows of the house—angular and jagged, scuttling over the uneven ground. Thrusting, churning, racing after her.

The chase was silent over heavy grass at first. Then sounds could be heard—breath sucked through clenched teeth, gasping. Over her own she heard his. She forced herself not to look back and tried to muffle a moan in her throat.

She heard him gaining. Her small legs moved even faster but his strong ones covered more space with each bound. She did turn, finally, even as she ran, and hurled one boot back at him. It struck his chest and bounced away without effect. He leaped at her then, grabbed her sweater and jerked—spinning her about. As she wheeled, she knocked his arm away, tried to keep her stride. But he was too close, too strong. This time he clutched her upper arm. Again she whirled, threw the other boot and slapped at him; but he caught that arm too, used her struggling to throw her off balance and fell on top of her, holding her writhing body with his weight until he could gasp out: "Stop! You are under arrest. Security . . . Security Bureau!"

"National Security Bureau," Ted confirmed.

"And he had some sort of identification?"

"A card in a wallet. I didn't see it clearly. Schimmel still had the machine gun on me, so I was too scared to look anyway. What's happening?"

"What usually happens, Mr. Barstow. Things have gone wrong." Partly it was from frustration, partly from a feeling that Barstow was a kindred soul: Tolz was uncustomarily explanatory. He had been called to the communications room before he could have someone escort Ted and Erica back to their rooms. They were still in the captain's office when he made his way back, leaving the captain to arrange roadblocks.

"My assistant called in. The person he went to find—it is a young woman—has been taken. Someone arrived just before he did, claiming to be from a National Security Bureau."

"But Hartz is dead!"

"His partner, this Schimmel, we must suppose."

"But he must be dead too. He couldn't . . . that storm. . . ."

"Evidently he did."

"Who is the girl? What will happen to her?" Erica felt the point of the story differently.

"It doesn't . . ." Tolz reflected. Everyone would know about Ilse now anyway. "Ilse Katernig. Do you know her?"

"No. Her father—he is a farmer, *ja*?"

"Yes. And what will happen, we do not know. Probably she will tell Schimmel where the . . . material . . . is located."

"What are you going to do?" Ted still was fixed on practicality.

"We'll put up roadblocks, watch the terminals—railways, buses, so forth. We have the description you have given us. We will ask you both to be available for possible identification."

"You think you'll get him?"

"Probably. But there are walking paths in every direction all through the mountains. It would be better if we could find the location first.''

"You must find *her*!''

"Yes, Fraulein, of course. To find her, we must find him, or this place.''

"You don't have any clues?''

"Oh, certainly, Mr. Barstow. More than a clue. Erbacher was told that the location is marked by a blue cross somewhere along a certain road leading from the village. Saturday afternoon, as soon as we knew *what* village, my men began searching every meter of that road: no blue cross. Perhaps she was deceiving him. Or perhaps it has been washed away.''

"But is it here—I mean at this village? Couldn't she have used some other village she could get to easily?''

"That seems not to be the case, Janovich and Brunner came here.''

Ted and Tolz stared into space, considering logical classes of hiding places. Erica tried to think of where she herself would be likely to hide something.

"I don't believe it would be buried along the road.'' Ted offered. He had a sudden vision of Hartz and Schimmel seeking the treasure. Hartz with sextant and rolls of maps under his arm, shooting the sun; Putzi carrying a surveyor's tripod; Schimmel with pick and shovel. Dirt flying. "Not there?'' Taking another reading, moving four feet away. "Try again.'' Schimmel in a hole up to his waist. "Still nothing? Well, it's sure to be right here somewhere.'' Digging up a whole mountainside. Ludicrous. "I mean, how would this Ilse know the exact coordinates down to the foot? If it were a place, something that stands out on a map. . . .''

"She did not give coordinates. I have told you.''

"But I told you, that's what Hartz asked for.''

"He did not know. Only Erbacher—and we who listened—heard Ilse speak."

"Then where did Hartz get the idea . . . ?"

Tolz began rocking very slightly. "Indeed," he said. *From Rudi Bischl*, he thought; and then he thought about that.

"Hartz must not have known, Ted," Erica put in. "I would myself say a place: the Posacher farm, at the apple tree, for instance."

"But if it's someplace along a road, coordinates would give the general location, and then specific directions—a mark—would. . . ."

Tolz spoke as much to himself as to the others. "She did not give coordinates. But her partner must have thought she would."

"That is like a man to think. But it is so much easier—"

"It's easy enough to find coordinates on a map, Erica. You look for the nearest place where the latitude and longitude lines cross and you scale off—"

"*Ja!*" Tolz sprang up from the swivel chair as though its spring had catapulted him, sending him across the room like a projectile. On the wall opposite the desk there were several framed maps: Austria, Kärnten, the Spittal Gemeindeschaft, the Kreuzeck Gruppe, the village district. The captain liked to know where things were. Tolz swept from one to another, halted, struck one with a stubby forefinger. "*Ja! Vielleicht so!*"

"*Was?*" Erica leaned around in her chair to see. Ted jumped up and went to stand by Tolz. Tolz's hand was on the Kreuzeck map. Near where his forefinger pushed against it there was a faint blue cross—the intersection of reference lines. It lay just alongside the yellow line that indicated a road. As Ted looked closer, he could see a tiny black dot showing some structure located just beyond the cross.

"Yeah!"

Tolz smacked the map and grinned at Ted for an instant of shared triumph. Then he turned and headed for the door.

"We go also!"

"No, Fraulein. This becomes serious. There is no place—"

"But we have the right!"

Tolz did not intend to stand for an argument. He simply turned again and started from the room, heading down the vaulted corridor. "You have no right. I will have someone take you—"

Erica rushed after him. Ted followed her.

"After all we have suffered, we do!"

"Come on, Tolz." Ted was more infected by the excitement of the hunt than by any sense of principle, but suddenly he wanted to be there too, to know if and how it was all ended.

"No! Absurd. This is no business for amateurs." Tolz reached the stairway and started down.

"We have almost died because of—"

"We may be amateurs, but you wouldn't know where the place is except for us. Maybe we can help you."

"*Vielen danke.* I think we may cope."

"We *do* have a right!"

"*Nein*! No one has rights." Tolz paused at the door and turned to look directly into Erica's eyes. "Life gives us no 'rights.' You live in a dream, Fraulein."

Erica returned his stare, then shook her head in denial of his words.

Ted tried to be more practical. "Okay, but maybe we *can* help. What if it's not where we think? Maybe we can think of something else— Come on! We want to know. Be human."

Later Tolz was fairly sure he had not been persuaded by

the practical argument, and he was certain that the ridiculous appeal to principle could not have moved him. It was, he decided, fatigue, causing him to lose control over his anger and to act perversely. He felt fey. *Yes. Let them come. Let us all drive out to the country and pass around the dirty pictures. Perhaps that will satisfy the Fraulein's insistence upon a happy ending.*

MONDAY, JULY 18 03:45 HOURS—
OBER-FLATTACH

Schimmel waited until the police car, whose lights he had seen approaching, went around the upper turn. Then he coasted down out of the hayfield. He turned back onto the dirt road, still drifting with lights off. He rolled slowly around the lower bend and farther yet until he was sure that no one above would see or hear him. He jump-started the engine but continued to drive by moonlight alone.

"Where are the photographs?"

Ilse stared ahead without answering. She sat leaning against the right door, as far away as she could from Schimmel. Partly it was from aversion, partly from necessity: Her wrists were cuffed together, the chain between them run through the handgrip on the door.

Schimmel tried to think of the sort of thing Hartz would have said. Hartz's ability to get things from people quickly, with little effort, had been of great use. It would be missed. "You're in a lot of trouble, you know. If you're smart, you'll make it easy on yourself."

Ilse continued to ignore him. Her silence began to irritate him, and instantly he felt the thrill in his chest that he loved. Ted Barstow had been wrong in believing Schimmel felt nothing. What he did feel—a euphoria more exciting than that from any known drug—was the thrill of power: power not only over other people, but—perhaps even more strongly—over himself. Seldom could anything anger, grieve, depress or frighten him. Whenever any circumstance threatened to arouse such emotions, his will pounced, wrestled them down and smothered them under the triumph he felt at the victory. His will had been defeated during those moments at the hut in the storm. It redeemed itself by standing against guilt at the failure. Now it had to keep him calm, calculating, in the face of provocations of anger, of lust (the girl was beautiful and totally vulnerable) and of danger.

He tried to persuade her once more as the car came down the last grade into the crossroad of Uberbrücke hamlet. "You know what's good for you, you'll tell me. If I put in my report you cooperated, maybe they won't charge you with anything. We don't really care about you, it's the big fish we're after."

Isle looked at him for the first time since he had put her in the car. "What charge do you make?"

"Blackmail."

"I blackmail no one."

Schimmel let it rest until he was past the Gemsbock *gästhaus*. Then he pulled to the side of the road leading out to the highway. He checked his mirror. The moon had set behind one range of peaks; the sky over the opposite range was light. He had little time . . . just enough to pause for the necessary moment. He turned toward her, putting his right elbow on the back of the seat. "Don't play games with me. We know all about the pictures. You sold them. You could go to prison ten years for that."

Ilse looked directly at him, meeting his eyes, holding her own steady. When she turned her head forward again, it was clearly in dismissal. "You are not a policeman."

Schimmel seized Ilse's hair. She gasped, then suppressed a protest between clenched teeth. She grimaced and tears welled up in her eyes as Schimmel rolled her head, brought it up against the window post and made her face him.

"It makes no difference who I am. I want those pictures."

"Where is Rudi?"

"He took the money and ran."

"No he didn't. Did you kill him?"

"I'm going to kill *you* if you don't give me those pictures."

"If you kill me, you'll *never* get them."

With the speed of a striking snake, Schimmel grabbed with his left hand, clutching the bottom of her skirt, pushing it up her thighs. His hand forced its way between her legs, his fingers digging. "The *way* I kill you, I get them!"

She tried to stare back at him but couldn't control her tears against the pain. "They are in the village church. I will show you."

Schimmel relaxed the pressure for a moment, then yanked her hair again, jerking her chin up. His other hand dug and pinched. "No lies!"

Ilse could no longer hold back the scream. "I tell! I tell!"

He found a map in the glove compartment and she showed him the place. He started the car again and was approaching the highway intersection when—blue light flashing—a police car came hurtling around the bend a kilometer away. He slammed into reverse, shot his car backward, screeched around one hundred and eighty degrees and began to bolt forward when—in the mirror—he saw the police car flash by and continue along the highway.

He halted, trying to imagine what was happening. Suddenly—feeling like a fool but angrily crushing the feeling—he reached forward and turned on the radio. It hissed and crackled, shouted at him, ordering highways blocked, describing him, identifying the car he drove.

Schimmel paused while his thoughts raced. He became aware that Ilse was watching him. Was she smiling? Laughing at him? He flicked his arm toward her and struck her across the mouth with the back of his hand.

A flash caught his eye. Looking up, he saw light moving down the mountainside toward him. It must be the police car from which he had hidden earlier. It was still high up. He had a few minutes in which to think.

He was about to be boxed in. Unless he tried to run a roadblock. . . . No, it would be better on foot—there were trails and paths in every direction. He would have to give it all up, cut his losses and run. His will clamped down on anger and dismay.

No! They were now blocking only the highways. Searching inward would come later. He could take some mountain road and drive up as far as possible before having to go on foot. And if he was going to do that, the road that led past the photographs went in a direction as good as any.

But the car. . . .

He drove back to the Gemsbock parking area. One of the four cars there was a Saab and Schimmel chose it at once. It took him three minutes to start it and to get Ilse transferred. He was aware continually of the lights swinging back and forth around successive hairpins and coming down toward him, but he worked without haste. It did not worry him that the police car came around the last bend into the hamlet as he was crossing the highway and dropping down the incline beyond toward the river. He drove at moderate speed. Since the police did not know where

the pictures were, they would have no reason to look for
him on that back road unless a speeding car called attention
to itself. He reached the river road and turned right.

The sharp sides of peaks gleamed yellow-white against
the green sky but the valley was shadowed. Everything
there seemed heavy yet, in sleep, exhausted by yesterday's
storm—even the gray police car by the roadside was as
dull and still as the haystacks in the meadow beyond. It
stood, idling, on the river road, just beyond where the lane
from Uberbrüke joined. The two black cars coming from
behind slowed, the leader pausing beside the gray car.
Tolz spoke briefly across to Johann and Steiner. Then his
car pulled away and Steiner and Johann fell in at the end
of the procession.

The paved road passed a farm and a *gästhaus*, turned to
dirt and began climbing with increasing steepness. Around
the next shoulder it switched back, returned to a point
almost above the farm and then turned back again. Along
that particular stretch, for the most part the road was only
a shelf—a bank on one side, a sharp drop on the other. But
at one point an outcropping jutted forward on the downhill
side. When the road was cut—by hand, long ago—it was
understood without thought by the deeply religious country
people that the spur was meant for erecting a shrine.

Schimmel stopped beside it. He looked at Ilse to check
the location, to assure her of the consequences should she
be lying. This time she avoided his eyes. Staring ahead,
she nodded once. Schimmel stepped out.

He hadn't much time, he estimated. The sky was filling
with light. He went to the door of the shrine and tried to
open it. It was locked. He stepped back, smashed his foot
against it. The wood around the latch broke at once. He
stepped in, reaching up to feel the expected gap between
ridgepole and ceiling. There was none. He stood for a

moment to overmaster his fury and then went back for Ilse.

It was then that he heard the cars. He paused, looking over the spur beside the shrine. He could see part of the roof of each of the cars as they passed below—two black, one gray—with the blue lights on top.

In three bounds he was back to the Saab. Its motor was still running. He released the emergency brake, punched into gear and jammed the accelerator to the floor. The wheels spun, dirt and gravel were thrown back and the car slued off. He kept it floored all the way through the kilometer to the next bend, tapped the brakes, started his skid, powered again to come around to the next, higher, leg of the road.

Tolz's driver came to a stop beside the shrine. Tolz, Ted and Erica got out of the car. The two following cars stopped behind. Within one step Tolz perceived the door standing open and the broken section by the latch. He turned, saw and smelled the rubber fumes, the dust. Then they all heard the whine of the car coming toward them on the stretch of roadway farther up the hill.

"*Er fliet! Schnell, schnell!*" Tolz shouted, pointing up the slope. The driver of the second car responded instantly and Lieutenant Steiner only a second later. Both cars shot back gravel and smoke as they sped off in pursuit. Tolz's driver and the other man were barely out of their car. They stood there, hesitant, but Tolz gestured furiously, waving them on.

Tolz, Ted and Erica watched the three cars skid around the distant bend, then followed the sound as it came back. Tolz broke away first.

"So," he said, only half-aloud, and turned to the shrine.

"You think they'll catch him?"

"Of course. In the meantime . . ." He moved again.

Erica took a step to follow him, but Tolz wheeled back at the door and held up his palm. "*Nein*! No. Absolutely. If I find the photographs, I will tell you." The hand swiveled, became a pointing finger that jabbed every other word. "But you are not to come in. You are not to try to see them." He stepped into the shrine and swung the door closed behind him.

Ted and Erica looked after him for a moment. Then Erica turned back to the slope. "Do you think they will find her?"

"Sure. Why not?"

"Perhaps he has killed her."

"I don't think so." But he did. "Once he had the location, what would she matter to him?"

"Why would he want to kill us?"

"Well, we could have identified. . . . Now it doesn't matter anymore. She'll be all right." He tried to sound convincing.

"*Ja*. We must hope." Erica turned away from the sound of the cars above to look at the view over the valley. Sunlight now struck halfway down the mountain slopes. Soon it would reach the shrine, although the valley would have another half an hour of twilight. All was peaceful, the sounds of racing engines somehow accepted into the mountains' vastness, no more disturbing than the hum of bees finding flowers at the roadside. Villages and hamlets nestled on the valley floor and seemed protected. With the storm gone, man and nature lay together like lovers sleeping after a quarrel. Ted put his arm around Erica's shoulders. He hoped the gesture would reassure her.

The tiny shrine was plain, empty except for crucifix and altar. It was only about two and a half meters wide by three meters long, Tolz estimated. Enough for a family of hikers to kneel together. Whitewashed stucco walls had seasoned to a creamy gray. The wood of altar and ceiling was dark with age. Only the faded painting on the Christ and the bits of stained glass in the small side windows relieved the monochromatic severity. There seemed to be no odd corners, no unders or in-back-of's.

Tolz looked carefully around the room, scanning the walls section by section, running his fingers around crucifix and altar. He went to his knees and looked under. Rising again, he stepped back to the door. The ridgepole was half a meter over his head. He reached up, felt along its top. The joint between beam and roofing planks was tight where he first touched it. He slid his fingers back and forth, found a space into which he could get a fingernail. He took another step and continued running his hand along. Over the altar, warping and shrinkage were just enough to allow an envelope to be slipped in.

His fingertips felt in a corner and he knew at once. He pulled out the envelope, took out the photographs and spread them on the altar. Then he heard the voices.

Ted had heard the crunch. He turned and dropped his arm from Erica in shock and horror.

"Schimmel!"

Schimmel was not obsessed with the photos. He had not abandoned his car and come back for them. He had abandoned it in calculated flight. The road went nowhere but up. They would inevitably catch him if he followed it. The only way they might not expect him to go was back down. He had skidded to a stop, shifted to neutral, held the brake while opening his door, then jumped. The car began to roll backward. Ilse screamed.

Schimmel bounded over the side of the road and continued jumping down the steep slope until he was among the trees. When he reached the lower stretch of road, he was nearly opposite the shrine again.

He had not come back for the photographs, but luck—or fate—or his will—had brought him to them. As he stepped out of the woods and dropped the three meters to the road below, he felt triumph as though he were flying. He was ready to believe it was will, that he had power even over destiny.

He had drawn Glaessel's gun before leaping from the bank, so when Ted turned, he saw Schimmel still crouched from landing but with his arms extended, pointing the weapon.

Erica turned too and half-gasped, half-shrieked with surprise.

Shock had made Ted call out Schimmel's name. After that it left him speechless.

Schimmel came up from his crouch and jerked his pistol to direct Ted and Erica toward the shrine. They hesitated, then moved sideways, afraid to turn their back on him. It took until the third step for Ted's wits to return.

"Schimmel, what are you doing here? How did you get away? Look, they're all after you. You'd better run. Leave us alone, we can't hurt you. If you shoot us, they'll know you were here anyway. They'll hear you, you'd better. . . ."

Schimmel jerked the gun again, making it clear he wanted them inside the shrine. The girl hadn't been lying. The pictures must be there—the presence of these people proved it. Somewhere else along the beam. . . .

Ted reached the door. He pushed it inward, then stepped sideways so as to leave room for Erica. He pulled her behind him so she could enter first.

Schimmel came up quickly so there could be no chance of their slamming the door in his face. He stood in the doorway, filling it with a threat that drove Ted and Erica back against the altar. He stepped in. Still holding the pistol in his right hand, he reached up and felt along the ridgepole with his left. He took another step forward, came upon the beginning of the space. He actually smiled. He took the next step.

Erica was backed against the altar, almost bent over it as Ted's body pressed against hers, instinctively trying to keep distance between himself and the pointing pistol.

Behind Schimmel the door began to move. It swung slowly, touched him gently—not a touch so strong to cause him to begin squeezing the trigger as fast as he could at the targets in front of him to render them harmless even as he wheeled to hit whatever was behind. The door just brushed him, as though swinging of its own weight. It was sufficient to make him pivot an eighth of a turn, swinging his pistol automatically with his body. And then—all at once—there was an explosion and he jerked upward puppetlike, as though strings had pulled his head toward the ceiling above the altar. His eyes opened wide. He lifted onto his toes, toppled and fell like a tree.

Erica screamed, twisted away from behind and staggered across the room until she struck the side wall. She threw her arms against it, buried her face and sobbed hysterically.

As soon as Ted registered fully that Schimmel was dead, he went to her, and took her shoulders. He was shaking as much as she was.

Tolz regarded Schimmel's body for a moment, then put his pistol back into its holster under his arm. He took out a handkerchief and wiped his hands. Then, noting Erica's distraught condition, he took out the other handkerchief—the folded, clean one he always carried as an extra for emergencies. He extended it, rapping against Ted's shoulder for attention. Ted took it and pressed it into Erica's hand.

Tolz always found such displays of emotion distasteful and difficult. There really was nothing to be done about them, at least nothing he could do. The sound of an approaching car provided him with a distraction. He stepped over Schimmel's feet and went to the door.

The car skidded to a stop. Johann and Steiner sprang out.

"Got away!" Johann called as he came around to Tolz.

"We'll get him." Steiner assured him. "Abandoned the car. Left the girl. Let her roll back toward us. She reached the brake with her foot—cuffed to the door! He must have gone up on foot, but we'll get him yet."

Tolz held up his hand. "He is here." And then began to explain.

Inside, Erica brought herself under control. She wiped her eyes with Tolz's handkerchief, and turned around. She saw Schimmel's body and jerked her glance away—up and to the side, to the altar. The sun now shone through the little window, dappling the altar and the wall behind it. Erica moved toward it.

Ted realized what she was doing. "No, Erica! We're not supposed. . . ."

Erica looked down at the spread-out photographs. They were on black and white film but the light falling on them from the stained-glass window colored the figures with appropriate luridness as they contorted themselves to illustrate a catalog of lust. The man in them was plump and balding but neither fat nor old. With clothes on, he might have looked as distinguished as any "highly placed official" should look. Official pictures would present him as "mature." The girl was not mature, except—in the one picture that revealed her full face—around the eyes. Her hair was young—light, fine, worn long and straight as young girls wear it. Her baby-doll mouth would always seem young. Her eyes, though, already had that droop of the aged who are wise enough to shield their sight from the evil they have seen so long so clearly.

Erica turned away. Tears ran down her face again but

she did not sob. She went out of the shrine and Ted followed her.

Her emergence made Tolz aware, suddenly. He was appalled with himself. "Fraulein, I have told you. . . ." But Erica walked away, making a vague gesture that might have meant either that she hadn't looked or that it was not important if she had. Tolz watched her for a further moment, then went in quickly and retrieved the photographs.

Two paces brought Erica beside the car. With a shock she realized that someone sat in the rear—the girl in the pictures. Erica stared at her. Ilse tried to ignore her at first, but then she raised her eyes. Erica blinked her tears away and managed to smile at the girl. Ilse tried, for an instant, to return the smile. Then she looked forward again. Erica turned to see what she focused on.

Tolz was handing the photographs to Johann. Johann looked at them intently. He whistled softly at the identity of the man, although an observer might not have realized that. That identity was the only real interest Tolz took in the pictures, but young Johann could not help noticing the girl as well, and the things she was doing. Nor—though usually a decent and considerate man—could he quite prevent himself from looking up from the pictures to Ilse.

Erica saw the look and saw Ilse shift the focus of her eyes off into space. Ilse continued to look ahead and her chin was up. But tears had come into her eyes.

Erica turned back and walked along the car, slowly, toward the men. Johann and Tolz stood directly in front of the car, Ted back a step toward the shrine, Steiner beyond Tolz, in the road. Erica turned as though going toward Ted but continued around Johann. He had returned the photos to the envelope, which he was extending to Tolz.

Erica grabbed. She snatched the envelope from Johann's hand and backed away, trying to tear it in half. The pictures were too thick. "No!" she shouted. "It is not right! Let her go—"

"Fraulein!"

"Erica!"

"—let it be ended!"

Johann caught her by a shoulder. Ted leaped and smashed against him. Erica broke free, whirled and began to run down the road. Johann tried to throw Ted off and to pursue her, but Ted clutched him in a bear hug. It took Johann only a moment to break the grip and knock Ted back, but by then Erica was a dozen meters away.

Before she had covered half that distance, Steiner had brushed back his holster flap and seized his pistol. He drew, one hand flinging up above his head, the other coming to meet it as it dropped again. His action was trained, without thought: Fire once over the head for warning, then to hit.

"*Halt, Fraulein, halt!*" Tolz shouted. The pistol cracked beside him.

Steiner controlled the recoil, letting it raise his hands so they could drop onto target again.

"Steiner, *nein!*" Tolz threw himself sideways.

Steiner's grip was contracting as the pistol lowered. It was too late to stop its action. The trigger slipped its catch, the firing pin struck. But Tolz knocked the aim away. The shot went into the woods.

Thirty meters down the road, Erica managed to get the photos out of the envelope. Holding them against herself, she separated them so she could tear them one at a time. She tore each in quarters and flung out her arm to scatter the pieces as she ran. Some fell to the road behind her, some into puddles left from the storm; some blew into the wild flowers along the edge of the road. A few were caught by a waft of air and they flashed and sparkled in the sunlight as they were borne out over the mountainside.

MONDAY, JULY 18 16:30 HOURS—
OBER-FLATTACH

Steiner stood erect, hands clasped behind his back, in the posture he felt best personified the law's awful majesty. He was confident the effect was achieved even though Ilse did not look at him. She stared only at the wall of the windowless room where they had left her for the two hours since Tolz had finished his questioning.

"You have committed a most serious crime, Fraulein. It is true that you did not yourself approach the man in question, demanding money; it is also true that the photographs no longer exist. These are mere technicalities. But that you intended, and did set in motion, a crime of blackmail is established." Steiner paused, letting silence convey a sense of impending retribution heavier than any sentence in words. "However . . ." His tone did not change: Justice could be merciful without losing strength. ". . . Herr Tolz has recommended that, as this is the first offense of any kind on your part, and as we have received favorable opinions of your character previous to this incident . . ." And as the matter ought to be kept secret, although Steiner did not give that reason. ". . . you are free to go."

Ilse looked at him for the first time; but beyond surprise, she showed no more emotion than she had when Tolz had interrogated her.

He had inquired at the end as though it were only one more from his list of questions. "Where will you go after all this is over? What will you do?"

"I will live. I will try to find work."

"Doing what?"

"Serving drinks. That's all I know."

Johann had broken in. "Your school principal said you were good at mathematics. Couldn't you find something . . . office work perhaps?"

"That requires training."

"Couldn't you obtain some training?"

"That requires money."

"You can earn money, Fraulein," Tolz had said.

"Yes. A little. After a time, perhaps enough."

Ilse's look at him had been direct, undismayed, but as though weighing a burden she knew she must carry. She looked at Steiner in the same way. "Thank you. Now?"

Steiner nodded. Ilse put her hands on the arms of the chair to rise. He stopped her. "But . . ." He hesitated, seeking the words. The next part was not according to regulations. "Herr Tolz. . . . Among the effects of the person known as Schimmel was found . . . since there is not to be a prosecution, it is not needed as evidence and it would not seem to belong to anyone . . ." Steiner realized his posture had slipped. He straightened. "This must have been taken from your friend, Rudolph Bischl. Herr Tolz instructs me to give it to you." He brought the envelope from behind and extended it. When Ilse did not take it, he placed it in her lap. She looked down and he straightened again, cleared his throat and decided there was nothing more to say.

Five minutes later, when he put his ear to the door, he could still hear her sobbing; but after ten minutes she was gone.

Erica and Ted spent the evening together. It was Monday night, exactly one week from the day Rudi Bischl had first contacted August Tobler.

They went out to dinner. Everyone stared at them and whispered, and they talked about the weather. When they went back to her apartment, they seemed unable to talk about anything. They didn't want to go over the past—that would bring back not only the pain and fear, but their disagreement. They couldn't talk about the future. There was too much to be said and they couldn't say any of it. Ted couldn't say it. *What can I say? Come away to America with me? Marry me?* He didn't intend to marry anyone ever again, much less a girl he had known only three days—even if she could climb down a castle wall!

They made love, unsatisfactorily, and pretended to sleep. Morning came at last.

"Will you write to me?"

"*Ja*. It will be good for me to practice my English." Silence. "Do you like some more coffee?"

"No, thank you." He pushed bread crumbs into a little pile, working carefully from all around toward the center. "My vacation . . . I went to Tyrol and Salzburg first, but next year I can spend all of it here."

"That would be very nice."

They said good-bye standing on her balcony. She had to go to work. She didn't see him off at the station.

Tolz and Johann did see him off. Johann helped him with his bags, although there were only two small ones.

Tolz advised him when the train would leave, and when it would arrive, and how long the journey would take. Both thanked him and complimented him, and wished him good luck, and stayed until the train left so they could wave to him.

"A nice young man," Tolz said as they turned away.

"Yes. Amazing. Think what he'd be like if he had training."

They walked back toward the car. "Too bad about the photographs," Johann said. He had avoided speaking of their loss, and Tolz had not referred to it as they had pieced together and summarized all the parts of the affair. Johann knew responsibility for the failure was his, even though Herr Tolz had erred in allowing the woman to see the photos in the first place. After having had a good night's sleep, perhaps now it was time to learn with what seriousness his incompetency would be viewed.

"Yes. Well, not *too* bad, Johann."

Redemption was offered. Johann breathed deeply. He could speak of the fall-back without appearing to excuse himself. "No. We do still know who he is. What do you think the government will do?"

"I don't know. Earn his gratitude for not exposing him; his government's for doing it discreetly to them. Perhaps we'll sell him some of our light tanks—whatever they think most useful. It doesn't matter."

Ted was elated to be at home again. He bought a large order of groceries and didn't go out of the house for nearly three weeks. Drafts of articles arrived in the mail and he edited them and sent them back. Every day was calm and quiet, just as he liked it. By immersing himself in the familiar and the routine, he was gradually able to suppress the fears that had swept over him after the fact. He told himself that his yearning for Erica would fade as well.

It did not. His loneliness now was loss, not merely lack of something he'd never had. He fought it for another three weeks, until the maples and yellow birches flamed against the bright autumn skies. He knew she would have delighted in them and he ached to show them to her, to share them with her.

He made himself go over it again: his belief that life is capricious and probably malevolent versus her wanting to embrace it like a lover; his chronic sense of betrayal versus her inate openness and trust. They were fundamentally incompatible. It had happened to him before, with Janice. Erica wasn't like Janice, but the principles. . . .

It could never work. It's hopeless. Like being tied to a chair in the bottom of a castle tower? Like—

There's no future. You can't expect to build a life together on a fantastic three-day adventure.

Don't expect anything. Try it for a year. Who knows? The horse may talk.

He went in and started to write all those things to her—worked until nearly midnight revising, trying to get it all down correctly. Then he stopped, calculated the time difference, and called and simply said it.

And so they were married, and have lived in reasonable contentment since then.

BESTSELLING BOOKS FROM TOR

MORE BESTSELLERS FROM TOR